# "So, you're not going back to San Francisco?"

Shea pushed his mug away before answering Tate. "If that's not a problem for either of you. I know you'd probably like to sell the winery, but I imagine a property of this size would take some time, and I have no place else to be right now. So I can hang around after you guys are gone, tidy up a little and show any prospective buyers the place. What do you think?"

"Sounds all right to me." Mike rested an arm on the back of the booth. "If you don't mind company. I need a change, too, and I was about to offer to stay behind and see to things."

Shea seemed at once pleased and horrified. "The two of us together? We'd kill each other before Tate got to Portland Airport."

"I'm not going to Portland Airport," Tate said. "I was planning to stay, too."

Mike looked at Shea, then at Tate. "You mean, we're *all* staying?"

## ABOUT THE AUTHOR

Muriel Jensen *loves* wine. But she limits herself to one glass at a time because it brings out her tendency to sing...in French. Living at a winery would be her ultimate fantasy, but since she doesn't, Muriel decided to do the next best thing and set a series of stories at one.

Muriel is the award-winning author of more than forty novels—most of them written for the Harlequin Superromance and American Romance lines. If you'd like to write Muriel, her address is P.O. Box 1168, Astoria, Oregon, 97103.

## Books by Muriel Jensen

### HARLEQUIN SUPERROMANCE

468—BRIDGE TO YESTERDAY
512—IN GOOD TIME
589—CANDY KISSES
683—HUSBAND IN A HURRY
751—THE FRAUDULENT FIANCÉE
764—THE LITTLE MATCHMAKER

Don't miss any of our special offers. Write to us at the following address for information on our newest releases.

Harlequin Reader Service
U.S.: 3010 Walden Ave., P.O. Box 1325, Buffalo, NY 14269
Canadian: P.O. Box 609, Fort Erie, Ont. L2A 5X3

# FIRST BORN SON
## Muriel Jensen

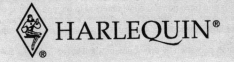

HARLEQUIN®

TORONTO • NEW YORK • LONDON
AMSTERDAM • PARIS • SYDNEY • HAMBURG
STOCKHOLM • ATHENS • TOKYO • MILAN • MADRID
PRAGUE • WARSAW • BUDAPEST • AUCKLAND

ISBN 0-373-70825-4

FIRST BORN SON

This edition published by arrangement with Harlequin Books S.A.

® and TM are trademarks of the publisher. Trademarks indicated with ® are registered in the United States Patent and Trademark Office, the Canadian Trade Marks Office and in other countries.

**Printed in U.S.A.**

To Tom Potter, architect and friend, and Ron Reinebach, lawyer and friend, who answered countless questions with patience and ready wit.

And to Dennis Allen, Yamhill County health officer and complete stranger, who also cheerfully answered all my questions.

Thank you for fortifying my opinion that a woman's daily life is filled with heroes.

# *PROLOGUE*

"GOOD MORNING. Delancey, Markham and Free-ee." Tate Delancey stood against the back wall of his office, sorting through bluelines as his secretary answered his phone. She gave the last name of the partnership a melodic two syllables. Then she giggled.

"Well, we'd love to handle your divorce, ma'am, but we're architects, not attorneys." Cece caught Tate's eye and giggled again.

"No, that's all right.... Of course.... Thank you. Goodbye."

With the Bergman Building bluelines in hand, Tate went back to his desk, thinking wryly that he probably *could* handle someone's divorce. His own had been friendly, but so painstakingly detailed that he felt as though he now knew common law better than he knew the building code.

Cece leaned over his desk to replace the receiver, then handed him the mail and overnight faxes.

"I swear," she said, going to the coffeepot on his credenza to pour two cups. "String three names together and everyone assumes you're a lawyers' office. The lady apologized. Said architects and attorneys are side by side in her *Boston's Best Business*

*Guide.''* Cece handed him a steaming cup and took a moment to sip from her own.

Tate got a whiff of something cinnamony and concentrated on not betraying disapproval. Cece Phips was only twenty and filled with an energy and enthusiasm that outdistanced her secretarial skills. But she'd tried harder in the four months she'd been there than anyone else on the firm's clerical staff, and she had an optimism he found contagious. Which was good. He was producing very little on his own lately.

Intrepidly, he sipped his coffee.

"Cinnamon hazelnut praline," she reported.

Trying new coffee flavors every week was an attempt on her part to perk up—he forgave himself the pun—his life.

"What do you think?"

He nodded, managing to mask a grimace. It was better than last week's vanilla white-chocolate macadamia, but he still longed for good old Colombia Supremo.

"Good," he said, unwilling to criticize her efforts. "Good. Are Bill and Gina in?"

"Mr. Markham is on his way, but Ms. Free will be home with their baby today. He's teething. She said she faxed you the Carver Theater specs."

Tate had gone to M.I.T. with Bill Markham and Gina Free, and the three of them had reconnected ten years ago at a party, shared a bottle of Perrier-Jouët and decided to form a partnership. Since then, they'd designed the Back Bay Library, the exclusive Dorchester Apartments, Revere College and scores of other projects over which they'd slaved, sweated, laughed and cried, building a solid working relationship along the way.

Bill's and Gina's decision to form a personal partnership had happened just three years ago. Jacob Tate Markham's appearance had followed shortly thereafter and was now testing their abilities to juggle work and home lives, while also bringing them great joy.

No one knew better than Tate how difficult juggling could be. He'd been married to Sandy for fifteen years, and in that time he'd had to juggle his career as well as hers as a decorator and the many activities of their two daughters.

He'd found most of that a pleasure. But Sandy's father was a United States Senator, and Sandy thrived on the parties and receptions, the socializing and the gossip. Unfortunately, they bored Tate to distraction.

Sandy maintained during the countless arguments they'd had that she drew 90 percent of her client base from those affairs. An inability to resolve the issue had been one of the biggest reasons they'd finally divorced a year ago.

"So, how're you doing, Boss?"

Cece stood in front of his desk, frowning in maternal concern. Considering she was half his age, that always amused him. Which was another good thing, because she'd asked the same question every morning since Sandy and her new husband had moved with Tate's daughters to Paris a month ago.

He gave her the same reply. "I'm doing fine, Cece. I'll be...fine."

She balanced her cup in her free hand and shook

her head at him. "It's okay to admit that you're lonely, Mr. Delancey. I mean, I know you have to present this in-charge, everything-under-control image to our clients and maybe even to the rest of the staff, but you can be honest with me. I'm a psych major, remember? I know *all* about feelings of abandonment and rejection."

He put the mail aside and thumbed through the faxes, looking for something he could claim required his immediate attention so that he could send her back to her desk.

"I wasn't abandoned or rejected," he said, trying to sound distracted so she'd leave on her own. "Sandy had to follow her husband to his new appointment at the embassy in Paris, and my daughters had to go with their mother."

"But secretly," Cece said, sitting on the edge of the client's chair, "you wish they'd asked to stay with you, don't you?"

He looked up at her, his patience fraying. "That's none of your business, Cece," he said firmly, bracing himself to withstand her hurt feelings.

She simply looked more sympathetic, instead. "I know. But someone has to care about you. You don't return any of the calls of the women trying to date you. You work sixteen hours a day, then you go home to that condo on the bay with only yourself for company. It has to stop. Please." She reached over the desk to place her hand on his.

*Oh, God,* he thought. Not only was he being hit on by a child, but he was liable to end up before a judge for sexual harassment if anyone walked by his open office door and saw it!

He tried desperately to think of some way to fend her off that wouldn't destroy her and ruin their working relationship. "Cece, I—"

"Mr. Delancey," she interrupted, leaning earnestly toward him, "Let me introduce you to my mother."

His pride caved in right on top of his patience. Her mother?

Fortunately, he was saved from reacting when Lita from the bagel shop on the first floor got off the elevator with a tray of her wares. Cece excused herself to join the crowd converging across the office.

Tate swore to himself and took a long pull on the cutesy coffee. The really pathetic thing about all this, he realized, staring at the pile of faxes, was that she was right.

While his brain knew better, his heart did feel somewhat rejected by the cheer and excitement Susan and Sarah displayed when he'd waved them off at the airport. They'd hugged him and told him how much they'd miss him, but he could see in their faces that the move was a big adventure.

He wanted them to be happy, he told himself. He just wished they could have been happy with him instead of with Dudley Bartholomew Binghamton of the Charleston Binghamtons, in whom his ex-wife found everything she'd considered missing in Tate. But at thirteen and fourteen, the girls needed their mother.

By the nature of Binghamton's work with the diplomatic corps, Binghamton was required to attend every social event within a hundred-mile radius of

Washington, D.C., and he knew everyone and everything within that space.

Tate found him enormously annoying yet somehow likable. "Don't worry about your girls," Dudley had said with a casually fraternal pat on Tate's back just before boarding the plane. "I'll take good care of them. I think they're wonderful, too."

It was impossible to hate a man like that.

Tate rubbed his brow and sighed. He'd talked to the girls by phone once a week since they'd left, and they e-mailed regularly. They had settled in and were enjoying their new experiences.

He was the one who had to find a new direction, some other target for all this energy, all this...love that now had nowhere to go. And until he could figure out how to do that, he had a business to run.

He pushed the coffee aside, pulled the faxes toward him and sorted through the advertisements and solicitations, looking for Gina's specs.

Then he spotted the fax from French River, Oregon, and sat forward, setting the others aside. His uncle Jack had lived in French River until he'd gone out one day on some undisclosed mission and never returned. Had they found him at last?

Tate read the fax. It was from Lloyd Reynolds, attorney-at-law.

Dear Mr. Delancey:
This is to inform you that the court has declared your uncle, John Harvey Delancey, presumed deceased as of this date, January 19, 1999, seven years from the day he was reported missing.

As executor of his will, it is my duty to advise you and your brothers, Michael Anthony Delancey and Shea Xavier Delancey, that you share jointly in the inheritance of the vineyards once known as the Valley Winery on one hundred acres near the town of French River in the Willamette Valley.

There are more details that I would prefer to discuss with the three of you in person. Since you are scattered from Boston to San Francisco, I would appreciate it if we could meet here at your earliest convenience.

I can be reached at…

Phone, fax and e-mail numbers followed, along with his French River address.

Tate reread the letter, stared at it, then read it again.

He felt new disappointment that Jack hadn't been found, but the man had always been an eccentric, and the family had long ago accepted that he either left of his own accord—a threat he'd made occasionally when life was difficult—or he'd met with some kind of accident and, if that was true, he was now in better company than they could offer.

Once Tate accepted that again, he came to another fascinating realization. He owned a winery. He couldn't quite believe it. He and Mike and Shea had spent a whole summer there when Tate had been about twelve, and they'd loved it. They'd visited their father's brother sporadically after that until adult responsibilities began to consume their time, but Tate had always thought of the winery with great fondness.

He could close his eyes now and see rolling hills covered with vines, and the wonderful old buildings that were part of what Jack had called "the compound."

Excitement surged through his veins. *He owned a winery!*

Cece returned and placed a paper plate on his desk. She pointed to the bagel it held.

"Garlic and Gorgonzola. Good for your system. About my mother..."

He pointed her to her desk. "Would you get my brother on the phone, please?"

She studied him worriedly. "Is everything all right?"

He nodded, wondering if garlic and Gorgonzola combined with cinnamon hazelnut praline coffee could have a toxic effect on the system. "Yes. Everything's great."

She backed several steps toward the door. "Okay," she said doubtfully. "But I didn't know you had a brother."

"I have two," he said. "Check the Rolodex under Delancey. Michael and Shea."

"Which one do you want first?"

"Whichever one you can get."

She stopped on the threshold and asked hopefully, "Shall I call my mother while I'm at it?"

He smiled apologetically. "No, thanks."

She sighed and turned toward her desk. "Bummer," he heard her mumble.

# *CHAPTER ONE*

TATE SEARCHED for Mike as the stream of passengers came off the flight from Dallas. It had been just a few months since they'd seen each other, but Tate had the most unsettling feeling he wouldn't recognize him.

Mike's voice had been cheerful enough when Tate called him two days before to discuss meeting in Oregon, but then Mike's success had always depended upon his ability to talk a good line.

There he was, though, tall and looking fit as he strode across the waiting area in jeans and a leather jacket, a blue vinyl athletic bag slung over his shoulder.

Tate wound his way through the throng and went to meet him.

Mike's step was brisk, his smile in place, but Tate saw the wounded look in his eye before he even reached him. He felt his brother's pain as if it were his own. They'd forged a relationship over childhoods spent vying for top spot in their sibling hierarchy. Mike, though three years younger, had constantly challenged Tate and Tate had never given an inch.

The battle continued to this day, though in subtler ways, but now Tate was able to empathize with Mike that only an accident of birth prevented him from ever being the eldest.

Tate opened his arms instinctively as he reached Mike, then wondered if he was doing the right thing. Mike had been rejecting offers of comfort since he was four and had fallen backward off the front porch.

The question was answered an instant later when Mike wrapped his arms around Tate and held him for one protracted moment. Then he stepped back and grinned.

"A winery, for God's sake. I don't even like the stuff. Why couldn't Jack have been in the brewery business?"

"Your bad luck, I guess. Did you stow any baggage?"

"No." Mike indicated his bag. "This is it."

"All right." Tate pointed to the signs that led them to the exit. "I rented a car when I came in this morning and my bag's already in it. About the winery. Look at it this way. There'll never be a bottle of beer worth thousands of dollars, but old wine can be worth that much. Wine's really a better investment."

Mike stepped behind him as they reached the escalator going down to the terminal. "Always thinking like a businessman. But Jack's been gone for seven years. The place must be in complete disrepair."

"Might be." Tate turned on the descending stair to look up at him.

"But I went back with Dad when Jack first turned up missing, and he did have a wine maker who intended to stay on as caretaker until Jack returned, or his disappearance was somehow resolved.''

"Yeah, but that was seven years ago. Don't you think he would have become discouraged by the lack of a paycheck? Watch where you're going, or you're going to end up on your keister. Not that I wouldn't enjoy that.''

Tate turned to step off the escalator, then waited for Mike. "I'm warning you not to start with me," he said, relieved to see that despite the grim look in his eyes, Mike still seemed to have a combative spirit. "I could still lay you out in a matter of seconds.''

They strode across the terminal toward the doors, Tate with his hands in the pockets of his cashmere overcoat, Mike turning up his jacket collar at the sight of rain beyond the windows.

Mike made a scornful sound as he held the door open for his brother. "Yeah, right. You've been sitting behind a desk for twenty years, while I've been chasing down bad guys.''

Tate repeated the sound as he stepped outside. "On a motorcycle and in a patrol car. Like that builds muscle and stamina. I have a Nautilus machine at home.''

Mike followed him out and stopped beside him under the protective overhang. Rain fell in sheets. "I play basketball every day.'' Then he added mercilessly, "And I'm three years younger. We're getting to the age where that's starting to count, you know. You're thirty-nine, Tate. That's really up there.''

"All right.'' Tate took Mike's bag. "I'll race you

to the car. I'll even carry your stuff. We'll see which one of us is 'really up there.'"

Mike rubbed his hands together. "Do you think you could give me a fighting chance by telling me what you're driving and where you parked it?"

"Too much trouble," Tate joked. "You'll be following me there anyway."

"Aren't we witty in our maturity."

"Silver Camry wagon," Tate said, "third level. It has a roof rack. And no fair using elevators. You have to run the ramps."

Mike frowned. "I didn't think they *made* a Camry wagon."

"They did ten years ago."

"You rented us a ten-year-old car?"

"At the last minute, it was the best I could do. You want to race me to it, or you want to walk fifty miles to French River?"

Mike's reply was a quick look left, then right, then a burst of speed across the street to the parking structure. Tate pursued him with a laughing curse and a determination to beat him.

He ran for all he was worth. By the time he reached the second level he'd gained speed and realized this energy wasn't all attributable to his need to stay ahead of his younger brother. He also felt a strange freedom. For the first time in more than twenty years he wasn't confined to a schedule.

And no one was dependent on his presence. Bill and Gina had the office under control; his daughters were in Paris. He was a free agent, and while there were definitely aspects of that situation he didn't like, he had to accept it. The best thing he could do for himself was enjoy the other parts of the situation that were fresh and new.

He spotted the Camry as he topped the third-level ramp and ran for it, privately exulting that Mike was nowhere in sight. He dropped Mike's bag on the concrete floor.

"Yes!" he shouted, raising both arms in the air, certain Mike was right behind him. "I'm still number one!"

"You might want to count again," Mike suggested lazily, sticking his head out the driver's side window. "And get in before you embarrass me further."

Tate leaned against the car to catch his breath. "How come I didn't see you in front of me?"

"Because I am the wind," Mike replied.

"You got that right. A big wind."

"Hey, mister!" A little boy of seven or eight in baggy jeans and a red-and-blue parka came running toward the car. He held a pen out in front of him. "You dropped this in the elevator. Mom said I should give it back to you 'cause it looks expensive." He pointed to a plump woman with a baby in her arms, waiting beside a green van.

Mike gave Tate a brief, guilty glance, then smiled reluctantly at the boy as he accepted the pen. "Thanks, dude."

"You're welcome." The boy ran off.

"Cheater," Tate accused as he stowed the bag in the back. Then he climbed into the passenger seat and buckled his belt. "And you a cop. I'm mortified."

Mike held a hand out for the key. "I could mortify you even more and tell you I no longer *am* a cop."

Tate dug into his pocket and put the key with its paper tab in the palm of Mike's hand. The process gave him a minute to try to assess whether or not Mike was serious. "I thought you were tested, declared sane—though I did question that myself—and sent back to work."

Mike inserted the key in the ignition and nodded. "I was." He backed out of the space and followed the painted arrows down to the first level.

Tate waited for him to explain, knowing that prodding for answers would be futile.

When they reached the bottom, Mike turned left onto the road that wound around the parking structure, then stretched out like a long ribbon toward the airport exit.

"It happened again," Mike said, adjusting the rearview mirror, "my second week back on the job."

"Another hostage situation?"

"Yeah. In a bank this time."

Tate bit back more questions, mostly because he didn't know what to ask that wouldn't be insensitive and stupid. In his heart, he was praying the situation hadn't ended as badly as the one that had resulted in his being forced to take two months off and have sessions with a police department psychiatrist.

It had been a domestic dispute, an abused wife trying to leave with her two children. The neighbor had called police when she'd heard screams, and their arrival had precipitated a standoff with the husband, to which Mike had been called.

He'd talked to the man for hours, Mike's boss had

told Tate, but in the end everyone in the house had died at the hands of the father, who'd then killed himself.

The psychiatrist had insisted there was no one to blame, that the situation had been lost before Mike had even arrived. It was one of those inconceivably tragic events over which Mike had had no control.

The thought that his brother might have had to relive that experience left Tate speechless.

Mike slowed as they approached the exit. "Which way am I going, anyway?" He glanced at Tate. "I'm sure you bought a map and looked it over while you were waiting for me so that we wouldn't waste any time. Am I right?"

"Good thing one of us is prepared, isn't it? We want to pick up I-5 south, then 99W. Then it's a straight shot to French River."

Mike eased out of the airport and into the traffic headed for the freeway. "I seem to remember a long road off the highway into the hills."

"That's right."

"When are we due at the attorney's?"

"Ten a.m. tomorrow."

"I hope Shea's here in time to make breakfast. Remember the bratwurst and eggs with that lumpy bread you pull apart."

Tate nodded. "Cobblestone bread, I think he called it. Who could forget it? He left San Francisco yesterday afternoon, so he should be here tonight."

"Who's manning the Chez Shea's kitchen while he's gone?"

Tate shrugged. "Didn't think to ask him. Look—" Tate chose his words carefully, but he felt compelled to speak them. "At the risk of being told to get lost, would you mind finishing the story about your second week back on the job?"

"Oh, yeah." Mike replied almost absently. "It was the usual bank thing. Three perps, four customers and six employees on their faces, the guard with a bullet in his shoulder and the police brought there by an alarm someone managed to push."

Tate was mentally counting people. Fourteen, not counting the police. He tried to imagine the responsibility weighing on a negotiator's ability to reason with individuals crazy or desperate enough to do such a foolish thing in the first place.

"And they called you."

"Right." Mike took a moment to merge into the freeway traffic, displaying the skill of a man accustomed to the nerves and speed required, then settled into the middle lane and picked up his story. "I think everyone was trying to prove that they hadn't lost faith in me, that the farmhouse was forgotten and they knew I could handle this one."

He drew a deep breath, then blew it out.

Tate took that as an indication that it hadn't been that simple.

"I'd been talking to the leader of the three perps for almost an hour," Mike said, glancing away from the road to the dash.

"Where the hell are the windshield wipers on this thing?"

"The end of the stalk on the right side of the steering column. First position's delay, down for slow, down again for fast. Cruise control is the button on the end."

"Jeez. You even studied the manual on a rental car?"

"No, Einstein. I used to have a Toyota."

Mike took a few minutes to adjust the wipers to his satisfaction, while Tate thought it fortunate that all those years with clever daughters had taught him to be patient when he wanted to learn their secrets.

"Anyway, I'd assessed them as felony stupid," Mike went on, his glib comment suggesting the outcome hadn't been the tragedy Tate had worried about. "I'm ten minutes into the second hour, and I'm thinking, 'I've had it with asking them what they want to eat and what'll keep them happy. All the while trying to get inside their perverted little brains.' So I marched into the bank with my Glock and got the hostages out myself."

Tate was able to imagine him doing that but considered it best for his own mental health if he didn't think about it.

"Ticked everyone off, I'll bet," he guessed.

"Seems I'm a danger to myself."

Tate laughed. "I could have told them that when you were seven and climbed the maple tree to get a closer look at the lightning."

"It didn't hit me."

"No, but you fell out of the tree and broke your arm."

"Well, big deal. *You* broke *your* arm."

Tate turned to him to correct the story. "No, *you* broke my arm when you hit me with the butt of Uncle Jack's rifle."

Mike grinned, watching the road. "I was Jean Laffite repelling boarders."

"You were standing in the middle of *my* bed."

"Well, I always wanted your bed. It was a double, and Shea and I had those dinky twin beds."

Tate willingly let the argument wither, remembering how wild and adventurous the three of them had been in those days. How brave and contentious and certain they would grow up to save the planet and rescue beautiful, large-breasted women from dastardly villains.

He smiled thinly to himself. But Sandy had only been an A cup, and in the end she'd rejected him.

"They didn't fire me," Mike continued. "But I'm on extended leave. I know it's time for a change, because all of a sudden I'm really tired of talking. And I'm tired of listening. I just want to do what I want to do."

"And what is that?"

"I was thinking about the hotel business." Mike checked the rearview mirror, then passed a slow-moving pickup filled with lumber. "It'd be a nice change to see people when they're happy and on vacation instead of in crisis for whatever reason. I wouldn't have to worry about their psychoses and their rap sheets."

Tate carefully withheld any suggestion of surprise. "You think you'd like that?"

"I'm trained to protect and to serve. I'm a natural."

"And where would you do this?"

"Haven't decided. Somewhere tropical, maybe."

Tate had to agree that had a certain appeal. During cold Januarys in Boston, he thought about the Tropics himself.

They stopped for coffee in Newberg and pulled into French River just before dark.

"Is this the long road I remember?" Mike asked Tate, indicating the stop ahead of them. The road seemed to wind into the hillside.

"I think so." Tate pointed to the even rows planted along the slope of the hill. "There are the grapes." The gnarled and naked vines curved gracefully over the terrain like lengths of crumpled lace.

Mike turned the Camry up the road and followed its easy incline to the top, where it opened onto a meadow that brought memories of the summer they'd spent here flooding back.

Tate remembered that when he first saw the place he'd thought it resembled something he'd seen in an old period film. The town was built around a central square, and although the proportions were smaller and the buildings had a distinctly simple appearance, he'd been struck by the fundamental security created by a world that turned toward itself.

That had probably been Jack's downfall, Tate thought, as Mike followed the road between several decrepit buildings until they reached the square. He'd lost a woman to another man very early in his life and, according to Tate's father, had spent the rest of it longing for her.

He'd spent his younger years in solitary travel, backpacking all over the globe. At forty-five, almost thirty years ago now, he'd bought the winery from a man who'd given up on it, and then worked to bring it to life.

When Tate and his brothers had visited, Jack had worked alone, with occasional, part-time help from town. And more help was always brought in for harvest. But several years before Jack had disappeared, he'd hired a French wine maker to live on the property and help him raise the standard of the crop and production to a place where he could compete with the other wineries now becoming successful.

Mike pulled to a stop in the middle of the square. "Where to?" he asked. "The house is across the compound, right?"

"Yeah." Tate climb out of the car. It had stopped raining, and cold, damp, honey-sweet air hit him in the face, filled his lungs and chilled his body. He felt intoxicated by the purity of his surroundings.

Boston had its charms, but perfumed air wasn't one of them.

"God!" he said as Mike, too, got out to look around. "Take a deep breath."

Mike complied, then coughed and laughed. "My lungs are lined with car exhaust. I'm not sure I can take this."

"Don't you remember it from that summer?" Tate took a few steps forward, beginning to feel better than he had in ages. "I remember taking a deep breath and feeling my fear evaporate."

Mike turned to him in surprise. "Fear?"

Tate was startled to discover he'd actually said that. As a boy, he'd refused to admit to fear, especially to his brothers. He'd had an image to maintain and it didn't allow for terrors and indecision.

He'd done much the same when his marriage had fallen apart. He'd maintained a confident, cheerful demeanor for Susan and Sarah, until with uncanny wisdom they'd seen through it.

He applied the same principle at the office, where planning and design often generated great chaos and confusion before the result was achieved.

Someone had to have confidence in the outcome—even if he was pretending.

So, if his life had been all about pretending, he wondered why he'd suddenly admitted fear? The freedom he was feeling? The wilder surroundings? A clearness of vision brought about by clean Oregon air?

But before he could come up with an answer, he felt something nuzzle his ear. He turned in quick surprise and found himself staring into a woolly white face with large, limpid brown eyes. Tate blinked, certain the near-dusk light was playing tricks with him.

Then Mike, just behind him, muttered an expletive, grabbed his arm and drew him back. They slammed up against the car. A football-shaped head with a long nose, big lips and donkeylike ears was leaning toward him inquisitively. The head was perched on a long neck attached to a large horsy body with four relatively short legs.

"What is it?" Mike asked in a startled whisper as the animal moved to study him, then turned back and looked Tate in the eye. "Oh, God, it's going to taste you!"

Tate remained absolutely still. It didn't look hostile, but up close he could see very large, square teeth. "Well, you're a cop!" he said to Mike. "*Do* something."

"We just had this discussion," Mike reminded him. "I'm not a cop anymore. And I didn't pack any tranquilizer darts. *You* do something. Oh, Jeez!"

Mike's exclamation came as the big lips opened to permit the escape of a pink tongue that licked Tate's face from chin to hairline.

Concerns somewhat allayed by that friendly if smelly gesture, Tate put a tentative hand to the furry neck and patted. "Apart from a case of halitosis that could dissolve steel," he said quietly to Mike, "it seems friendly."

"It looks like a camel without the hump."

"I think it's one of those South American things." Tate groped for the right word as he continued to pat, gaining a little confidence in the beast's peaceful intentions. "A...a llama!"

"What's it doing in Oregon?"

"Must be a wine connoisseur."

The animal turned, then gave Mike a lick.

Mike emitted a high-pitched gasp. "I'll bet his last meal was skunk!"

"It was not skunk," a female voice said from behind them. "It was grass hay and vitamins."

A slender young woman in jeans and a red down vest over a blue-and-white plaid flannel shirt materialized out of the dusk. Tate noticed a complexion that was like moonglow in the waning light, a curly pile of bright-red hair and long-lashed gray eyes that looked over him and Mike with a sort of superior disdain lightly masked by cool courtesy.

"The Delancey boys?" she asked, wrapping an arm around the column of fur. The llama whickered and lipped the top of the woman's hair.

Tate thought he detected a subtle gibe in the question and wondered who *she* was. It surprised him that he could come all the way to Oregon and still run up against a facial expression often seen at high-society cocktail parties in Boston.

"We like to think of ourselves as full-grown," he said, offering his hand. "I'm Tate Delancey. This is my brother Mike."

She shook his hand. "Colette Palmer. My father is Armand Beauchamp, who's kept the place going in your uncle's absence." She reached for Mike's hand. "Hello. I thought there were three of you."

"Our younger brother's due later tonight." Tate noticed that she had a good grip and her hands were calloused—a detail at odds with the cocktail-party impression. Judging by the llama's reaction to her, she wasn't a newcomer.

"You live here?" he asked.

She met his gaze steadily as the llama sniffed her ear. "I don't know," she replied. "Do I?"

TATE DELANCEY WAS just what Colette had expected, from his cashmere coat to his undoubtedly Italian shoes. Big-city gloss was all over him, though his gaze was direct and more annoyed than condescending.

He was her worst fear realized. The Delancey boys, she suspected, were about to corrupt her haven.

"If you lived here yesterday," he said, "you'll live here tomorrow. We just got word about the inheritance and we're meeting with Mr. Reynolds tomorrow to learn the details. Once we have the facts, we'll decide what to do about the property." He glanced at Mike, who agreed with a nod. "Until then, everything remains the same."

She found little comfort in that reassurance. Tate

was from Boston, Rachel had told her, and didn't look as though he had a small-town bone in his body.

His brother also looked very big-city, though in another way entirely. Where Tate had the polish of metropolitan wealth and power, Mike looked street-smart and a little dangerous. She couldn't imagine either man wanting to live here, considering the state of the place.

That suggested they would either change things in a big way, or sell out to a developer who'd put up an outlet mall or a trailer park.

Whatever happened, the place that had been her safe harbor since her husband had died two years ago would be gone. She'd brought her daughters here because Megan, six at the time, had been shocked by Ben's loss and cried all the time. And Katie, who'd been five and just beginning to blossom, had been rendered mute.

The beautiful surroundings and the personal attention in the small country school had helped Megan learn to cope and adjust. But Katie, who appeared in other ways to have recovered, had yet to speak a word.

Colette was in a continuous state of panic over it, but did her best to appear calm and convinced that one day Katie would find her voice. She just hoped she could live with the worry in the meantime. And that her home wouldn't be sold before it happened.

Colette had shared her concerns with her father and Rachel, but they'd both been excited about the Delanceys' arrival. Her father had met Tate when Tate had come with *his* father to investigate Jack's disappearance.

Though Colette warned him that seven years had passed and Tate might have changed since then, her father insisted that he'd liked Tate and thought he'd seemed kind and astute.

Rachel had been away when Tate and his father had visited but, despite her concern for the future of her small animal preserve, felt the Delanceys were trustworthy. Colette, on the other hand, wanted proof up front that they deserved it.

"VICTORIA?" a high-pitched woman's voice called from somewhere ahead of them. "Victoria! Where are you?"

Colette Palmer tipped her face up to the sky and returned the call. "Over here, Rachel!"

Tate frowned at her. "I thought you were Colette?"

She smiled, hooking a finger in the llama's bridle. "*This* is Victoria."

A short, stout woman appeared out of the darkening blue of evening. She wore wire-rimmed glasses and her thick white hair was braided and wrapped around the crown of her head. She had a lined but softly featured face and lively blue eyes. Tate thought she would have looked like a throwback to another century except that she was dressed in blue denim overalls and high rubber boots. She had a real air of competence.

"Well." She smiled from Tate to Mike. "The boys."

"They like to think of themselves as full-grown," Colette told her as Victoria went to the old woman and took a treat from the palm of her hand.

Tate turned to Colette, challenging her smart reply with an arched eyebrow. She gave him a look of innocence in return.

The old woman wrapped her arms around Tate and hugged him. "I'm your aunt Rachel. Well, technically, I'm not your aunt, because I was just Jack's friend and not his sister, but we don't stand on ceremony around here and everyone calls me 'Aunt.' Welcome home. Which one are you?"

"I'm Tate." One part of Tate's mind thought the 'welcome home' had a very nice sound, while another part was thinking, 'She lives here, too? With Victoria?' "Thank you."

Rachel moved to embrace Mike. "And you are?"

He leaned down to her. "Mike," he said, laughing. "The llama's yours?"

She stepped back to pat the column of fur. "Yes, she is. She was abandoned when some gentlemen farmers lost their shirts and moved out a couple of years ago." She gave the word *gentlemen* scornful emphasis. "She's very happy here with the others."

"Others?" Tate asked. "You have other llamas?"

"Other animals," she corrected. "A couple of dogs, a lot of cats, a raccoon, a deer, a white mouse and a pair of Canada geese. I have a shelter at the back of the property. You boys had dinner?"

"Yes, thank you."

"Is one of you the chef?" she asked. Tate shook his head.

"That's Shea, who's on his way." He looked doubtfully toward the house. "We spent a summer here with Jack, but that was a long time ago. Is the kitchen still operational?"

She nodded. "I've tried to keep the inside tidy, but things are pretty old and Jack never replaced anything. The stove's ancient, but it works. So's the fridge. Everything else is old and rickety, but it'll serve until—" she smiled brightly, and a little forcedly, Tate thought "—until you sell or buy new, or whatever you're going to do."

"They don't know yet," Colette said in a pleasant tone that belied the taunting gleam in her eye. "They're meeting with Mr. Reynolds tomorrow, and once they have the details about the will they'll decide what to do about the property."

Tate turned to her with a mild frown. "You must be the winery's official recording secretary."

"She's the one who kept your grapes alive," Rachel put in, "when Armand's arthritis got too bad to allow him to work in the winter. If it wasn't for her, your vines would be in the same shape your buildings are in."

Tate swallowed his annoyance with the young woman. This relationship would be of short duration after all, and whatever her problems were with him, they didn't matter. One of them would be gone very soon.

"Thank you," he said to Colette. "We appreciate that."

"It was my pleasure," she replied, and this time he heard sincerity in her voice. "Before I came here I was a bank teller with a degree in horticulture. It was nice to be able to use it.

"I have to go," she said abruptly, giving Victoria a final pat. "The girls'll be eating Pop-Tarts for dinner if I don't hurry.'' She gave Tate and Mike a quick, half-smiling glance. "Good night."

"Good night," Mike called after her.

Tate watched her walk away, his eyes going to the gentle sway of her hips under the hem of her vest. She disappeared into the shadows.

"What girls will be eating Pop-Tarts?" he asked Rachel.

"Her daughters. Megan is eight, Katie is seven."

Mike slapped Tate's shoulder in pretended sympathy. "She's married. Darn. And you seemed to hit it off so well."

Tate deflected his sarcasm with a look.

"She's widowed." Victoria nudged Rachel, who gave the animal another treat. "She lost her husband just a few months before Armand's doctor told him his condition was going to get worse and he should think about retirement—or another line of work. But he and Jack had been friends, and he felt he couldn't just abandon the vines until Jack's disappearance was somehow resolved." Rachel sighed and looked around her at the old buildings surrounding the square. "I guess we'll never know what happened. We'll just have to trust that Jack's at peace. Come on." She tucked one arm in Tate's and the other in Mike's and guided them across the square to a path that led to the house. Victoria followed. "I've kept the utilities connected all this time so there'd be heat in the house and the pipes wouldn't freeze. We have an occasional serious cold spell."

"I apologize if this is a personal question, Rachel," Tate said as they all trooped up the path. "How were you able to afford to do that?"

"Jack made me a signatory on his bank account," she explained. "So I could write checks if he was gone. He used to go to the coast every once in a while to visit friends. Sometimes he'd stay a few weeks."

Tate remembered now. That habit had come up at the time of Jack's disappearance. But a careful retracing of the road between French River and the coast had revealed no evidence of him or his car.

They approached the house Tate remembered from that summer. It was now considerably older and in desperate need of paint. But a glance revealed no buckling, sagging or other evidence that the structure had been compromised.

It was a four-square Victorian, plain but sturdy, with a porch across its narrow front. Even spruced up, it would never be one the famous "painted ladies" old-home lovers across the country were restoring. But it looked strong and unpretentious, qualities he'd always admired in people and buildings.

"You stay here, Victoria," Rachel ordered over her shoulder as she started up the porch steps. "I'll be right back." She dug into the side pocket of her overalls for a key.

Tate and Mike followed her up.

She fitted the key in the lock, opened the door and reached in to flip on a light. "Home, boys, for as long as you need it to be."

Tate stood on the threshold, Mike slightly behind and to the left of him so that he could see over his brother's shoulder.

Rachel stood just inside, holding the door open.

"How long do you suppose it'll take you to decide what to do?"

Tate remained in the doorway. "I'm not sure, Aunt Rachel. Depends on the details."

Memories of that summer flooded over him. Once the child he'd been admitted the fear to himself, he'd gotten over it, found so much to explore and so much to enjoy about life in the country.

That curious comfort was pulling on him now, drawing him into the house. He found himself resisting, knowing something was about to change his life, change him. It was a little scary.

But he'd learned a lesson here as a twelve-year-old. Fear was dependent upon its host for sustenance. If it wasn't fed, it couldn't survive. And what was there to be afraid of in the concept of an architect turned vintner? All he had to do was buy his brothers out and head in a whole new direction.

He felt a small internal shock as the idea took form in his mind.

He stepped into the living room. "There are three of us," he told Rachel with a smile, "and we never agree easily on anything. Right, Mike?"

Mike stepped in after him. "I hate to make a liar out of you, but I agree."

# CHAPTER TWO

"It looks like the Addams Family lives here," Mike said, following Tate, who followed Rachel.

Tate grinned at him over his shoulder. "What do you have against water lilies?" The fir floors were worn but clean, and the fifty-year-old furnishings in the living room had been vacuumed and fluffed, but there was peeling blue wallpaper patterned with large white water lilies all around them. They contributed to the Morticia-Gomez atmosphere. It amused him that he'd forgotten the water lilies.

Tate went through to an adjoining dining room, papered in the same way. He noticed pocket doors and tugged on one to see if it worked. It did. "Nice detail," he said absently to Mike. "I forgot about those."

Aunt Rachel pointed to her left. "Kitchen," she said, then indicated the small room ahead of her that held an old pine nook. It had a cozy aura despite more of the water-lily wallpaper. "And the breakfast room."

She then redirected them toward the front of the house and a stairway that led to the bedrooms.

Here Tate's memory came sharply into focus. He remembered that he'd had his own room—with the maple four-poster double bed Mike had considered his pirate ship when he'd broken Tate's arm. There was also a tall dresser with five drawers, a mission-style lamp with a stained glass shade atop an end table and an ugly wardrobe to add storage space sadly lacking in the little room.

And it all remained. He walked into the room, feeling as though he'd left it yesterday. That strange sense of renewal filled him again.

"Great. You get the big bed again. I knew it," Tate heard Mike grumble good-naturedly as he trailed Rachel down the hall to the room he and Shea had shared. "Guess what? I get the twin beds and the girlie dresser and the little dinky closet. Again."

Tate wandered out to stand in the doorway of the room Mike had been given. "You could always take second-brother privilege and move into Jack's room. It has a double bed."

"The roof leaks," Rachel cautioned. "Right over the head of the bed. So the bed's in the middle of the room for now. Jack meant to fix it but never did. He just moved all his things in here—it's the only one where all the windows open."

Mike looked around him with a sigh. "At least they ran out of water lilies up here. What color would you call this?"

Tate tried to put a positive spin on it. "Guaca-mole?"

"I was thinking in less delicate terms."

"It's only for a couple of days."

Mike met Tate's eyes, his expression indecipherable. Then he went to the window and looked down. "Can't see anything, but as I recall, this room overlooks the grapes."

"You're right," Rachel confirmed. "I put an extra blanket at the foot of your beds, and I just had the oil tank filled. I'll turn up the thermostat when I leave, so you should be nice and toasty. Anything else I can do?"

Tate gave her a quick hug. "No. Thanks for making it comfortable for us. As soon as we know what's going on, we'll let you know."

"Good." She smiled, but Tate could see the concern in her eyes. "I'm not family. My husband and Jack were friends in their youth and when Bill died and left me very little to live on, Jack invited me to stay at the cottage. I do my best to pull my weight, though, and I have the animals to provide for. I know Colette's worried about her children and her father. We'd both appreciate a little time to pull together a plan if we have to move."

"I understand."

"I'll walk you out, Aunt Rachel," Mike said with a glance that just skimmed Tate. "I'll move the car while I can still see it and bring our things in."

Tate went to follow him. "I'll help."

Mike stopped him with a hand in the middle of Tate's chest. "No need. There isn't that much to carry. Shall I just park behind the house?"

"Sure."

Tate watched his brother lead the way down the stairs, then stop at the bottom to take Rachel's hand. Tough guy with a heart, he thought.

Tate went down to the kitchen, scrounging for a coffeepot or a pan for boiling water, thinking there was something going on with Mike. Those skimming glances definitely suggested something. Mike always looked you in the eye. It was a cop thing, Tate guessed. Presence was all important.

A quick perusal of the overhead cupboards revealed no foodstuff. They must have been cleaned out long ago. But there were several shelves of the old beige diner-type crockery Tate remembered from their childhood visits.

There were also utensils in the drawers, and pots and pans under the sink. He pulled out a medium-size saucepan, rinsed it out under the hot water, then half filled it with cold water. All the while thinking about Mike.

What was he hiding? Was he considering something he didn't think Tate would approve of?

No. Mike wouldn't care who approved or didn't.

Tate looked out the window over the sink at the sound of a motor behind the house. He saw Mike drive the station wagon into the shelter of a grove of trees. Mike stepped out, removed their bags, then simply stood there for a minute, looking up at the sky.

There were no stars and no moon, so Tate guessed that whatever Mike was seeing was within himself.

Then another figure got out of the car, a slightly thinner version of Mike. Shea!

Tate opened the back door, flipping on the back porch light.

Mike and Shea turned toward it. Shea, in black slacks and a peacoat, waved at Tate.

"Look what I found being dropped off by a cab!" Mike called, transferring the two bags he held to one hand so that he could take the fat suit bag Shea held out to him.

Tate started down the steps. "Cab? I thought you were driving down?"

"I did." Shea reached into the car and handed Tate a bulging suitcase. "My car broke down this side of Eugene. I took a bus to McMinnville, and a cab here."

Shea pulled a very large box out of the back of the car, then closed the door. Tate met Mike's eyes as Shea secured the lid of the box, then hefted it in both arms, and knew they were sharing a thought.

Shea hadn't packed for a three-day trip to talk over the will. This seemed like everything he owned.

"Okay." Tate moved toward the steps. "I was just about to boil water."

"Someone having a baby?" Shea asked, leaping up the steps beside Tate. "It's got to be Mike. You're too disciplined."

Shea went through the open door and into the middle of the kitchen, then set down his box.

Tate followed him and dropped the suitcase, groaning at his joke. "Don't tell me. You do your own dinner theater now? No one's having a baby. I have instant coffee in my briefcase. I thought you might welcome some after your car-bus-cab ride."

Shea put a hand on Tate's shoulder and assumed a serious expression. "If the day ever comes when I welcome instant coffee, you have my permission to end my misery."

Tate folded his arms. "How about if I don't wait and just do it now?"

Shea laughed and wrapped his arms around him. He did it quickly, then appeared embarrassed, but Tate felt the urgency in the embrace.

"But I brought a cappuccino maker," Shea said, pulling away, "and a grinder and five pounds of coffee."

Tate wondered if he was wrong to think that his usually cheerful and independent younger brother actually seemed to need him. If it was true, he was sure Shea wouldn't appreciate having it pointed out.

"Will you look at this thing?" Tate parted the top of the box so that Mike could see the ornate brass contraption it contained.

Shea pulled it out while Tate held the box down and Mike searched for a place to put it. The cupboards above the counter left no space for the two-foot-tall piece of machinery.

"What about on the table in the breakfast nook?" Mike asked, beckoning Shea to follow. "There's even an outlet there."

"All right. Lead the way. I can't see where I'm going."

Mike helped support one side of the machine as Tate guided their blind steps into the breakfast room and flipped on the light. The spot was perfect and still left much of the table clear.

Coffeemakers made to appear antique had been popular in Boston, but this one was beyond anything Tate had ever seen. It was a very fat brass cylinder polished to perfection and trimmed with filigree work and enamel-handled spouts. The domed top was crowned by a brass eagle, wings outspread in prideful display.

"Do you always pack this way for a long weekend?" he asked.

Shea's eyes locked on the brass for a moment and

a kind of despair was reflected in his eyes. Then he closed them and shrugged. "I had no place to put it, so I thought I'd bring it with me."

"You couldn't put it in the restaurant?" Tate asked. Shea wasn't like Mike; he didn't mind answering questions. But you had to ask them, because he never volunteered anything.

"No. It isn't mine anymore." Shea went back into the kitchen for the coffee.

Tate and Mike sat in the nook and frowned at each other.

Shea returned with a pound of coffee. "Anybody got a knife?"

Mike produced a pocketknife. "Who does the restaurant belong to?"

"The bank," Shea replied, making a surgically precise slit on top of the bag. "I was working my tail off and one day about a month ago, I looked up to see Marty being arrested for fraud. The assets of the restaurant were seized, and I was out of a job and mostly everything I owned."

"I tried to tell you at the time—" Mike began in exasperation.

Tate attempted to stop him with a look, but he was too late.

"Thank you!" Shea snapped at Mike. "What I really need right now is an 'I told you so.'"

"No, you needed it *before*," Mike snapped back, "but you wouldn't listen."

"Marty and I had been friends since high school!"

"Clearly that didn't impress the bank!"

"Could you save it until we get our coffee?" Tate asked Mike quietly. "And until he's done with the knife. Or did you lose all your survival instincts when you went on leave?''

Shea frowned crossly. ''I thought you were back on duty,'' he said to Mike.

Mike put a hand to one of the enamel handles on the cappuccino maker. ''If you get this damn thing going so that we can actually have coffee,'' he said, ''I'll explain it all. And you can tell us what happened to you. Meanwhile Tate and I'll carry our things upstairs.''

''I remember the girlie dresser,'' Shea said, a reluctant smile seeming to lighten his mood. ''I'm not sleeping in the room with the girlie dresser. And I'm not sharing a room with Mike!''

''Relax.'' Mike stood and stretched. ''We assigned you Jack's old room.''

''Really.'' Shea looked from Mike to Tate suspiciously. ''How come?''

''''Cause it leaks,'' Mike reported cheerfully. ''Right over the head of the bed. Be back in a few minutes.''

Tate went with him to pick up the bags and heard Shea's whiny, ''Maaan!''

Mike laughed and headed for the stairs with one bag under his arm and a bag in each hand.

Tate picked up the last one and laughed to himself. However full-grown they liked to think themselves, their roles were too firmly established to change.

They reconvened fifteen minutes later in the breakfast room, where the aroma of fresh coffee had Tate salivating. In the middle of the table was a plate of oatmeal-and-raisin cookies.

Tate and Mike stared at them in disbelief.

Shea filled three of the diner mugs with coffee. "Did you know we have an aunt?" he asked. "Rachel. She just brought these by. Or maybe I hallucinated the whole thing because there was a llama waiting for her at the bottom of the stairs. She assured me I wasn't seeing things, but I've been doubting my sanity lately."

Tate put an arm around his shoulders. "We've been doubting your sanity for years, but we do have an aunt Rachel. We met her when we first got here. And yes, she does have a llama named Victoria."

Mike slipped into the nook, helped himself to a cookie and took a bite. "And these are very genuine and very delicious, so you haven't hallucinated anything." He pulled a cup of coffee toward him and took a sip. Then he closed his eyes and made a sound of ecstasy. "Shea," he pronounced, "much as I hate to admit this to you, you make the best coffee in the entire world. You could be made president for this coffee alone."

Shea sat beside him and toasted him with his cup. "Thanks, but I do not choose to run. Now—what's this about your being on leave?"

Tate sat in the nook at a right angle to them and took a cookie from the plate as Mike told Shea about the hostage incident in the bank. Shea appeared older, he thought. Being seven years younger than Tate, he'd always seemed like such a kid. But now he looked as though life had worked him over a little, as though there was some mileage on the handsome, even features reminiscent of their mother.

"When are you going back?" Shea asked when Mike had finished with his story.

Mike shook his head once and took a long sip of coffee. "I'm not sure I am," he said finally, that skimming glance going to Tate again.

"But you've always wanted to be a cop," Shea said, leaning toward him, apparently worried. "You talked about it all the time when we were kids."

"He wanted to be a pirate, too," Tate said to lighten the atmosphere. Shea's earnest concern seemed to be making Mike grim. "You're too young to remember."

"No, I'm not," Shea returned. "You two try to keep me out of everything by saying I'm too young to remember. But I remember everything. He broke your arm playing pirates, and he accidentally skewered the plumber's butt using Mom's meat knife as a cutlass."

Loud laughter filled the small room. Even Mike was helpless with it for a minute.

"Wasn't my fault," he said, catching his breath. "He backed into me. I was just standing at the ready. He looked like Captain Kidd with those cuffed rubber boots!"

They roared again, then finally quieted.

"But as a career choice in the millennium," he said, sobering, "piracy is a little chancy."

"I don't know." Shea took a cookie, snapped it in half and studied it as though analyzing its ingredients. "Business is full of pirates. Isn't it, Tate?"

Tate nodded. "But it takes too much energy to be tricky. Piracy on the high seas is more honest. At least your victims can see you coming." He let a moment pass, then he asked, "You want to tell us what happened with Marty?"

Shea popped half the cookie in his mouth as he nodded, now apparently analyzing it with his taste buds. "Madagascar cinnamon," he said, holding up the other half of the cookie. "And white raisins. Our aunt's a gold mine, guys."

He quickly dealt with the second half, took a long pull on his coffee, then leaned against the back of the nook's bench and made a self-deprecating face. "To cut to the chase," he said philosophically, "it's all my fault. I should have been watching him—I know that. But he had the connections, he got us the location, did all the word of mouth. He knew all I wanted was a clean kitchen and full refrigerator. And I knew all *he* wanted was to hobnob with the clientele, wheel and deal with the suppliers, schmooze. We understood each other." His gaze swung from Tate to Mike again. "Not like the three of us, who really don't have a clue about each other. I can't imagine going to the office every day and being responsible for designing something into which people put millions of dollars. Or walking into the middle of some hostage nightmare and bargaining for people's lives. I think you're both nuts!"

"Thank you," Tate and Mike said simultaneously.

"I wanted life on a less cosmic scale," he continued earnestly. "A little restaurant on a busy street where people could come for a quick lunch and leisurely dinner and meet friends and be comforted and spoiled and go away feeling as though they'd had the best meal of their lives." Again, the brother-to-brother look. "Does that sound small to you?"

"The fact that you ask us that," Tate said quietly, "seems small to me."

Shea gave him an exasperated look. "What I meant was that you two had major and heroic aspirations. *My* dream's enough for me, but I've always wondered…how it seemed to you. You were larger than life when I was a kid, and that didn't change much as I grew up. No one ever made me feel as though I didn't measure up, I just always wondered privately if I did."

"Measure up to what?" Tate demanded, now really annoyed with him. "I have a thriving business, but my personal life fell apart. And anyway, your skills are different and unique and I was always pretty impressed with them."

"And I'm considered a threat to myself and others," Mike said rather proudly. "But I brag about you all the time."

Shea nodded, then smiled briefly. "I always worshipped both of you, but I never understood you." He sighed and played with the handle of his cup. "Then, when I'd lost everything and there was no one to turn to, I thought about the two of you and realized that your family counts—even when you don't really have a clue what they're all about."

Not only had he become a man, Tate thought, but a smart one.

"If anyone breaks into 'Hakuna Matata,'" Mike said with a quick sip of his coffee, "I'm out of here. Though Mom and Dad would be pleased to know that we've finally accepted one another."

They were silent for a moment, each lost in thoughts of the two people who'd tried so hard to make them friends.

"I still forget they're gone," Shea said, his voice

soft and distracted. "I think about them in that house in Santa Barbara, retired and really happy."

"Yeah." Mike sighed. "Me, too."

Tate remembered clearly the telephone call from Shea three years ago telling him their parents had taken their small boat out and then capsized in a sudden squall. It had surprised him that even at thirty-six he could feel like an orphan.

Tate had become close to his father when Jack had disappeared and he'd helped with the investigation. Edward Delancey had been an organizer, an executive for a retail chain, who was sent from place to place to open new stores and get them established financially.

Their mother, Andrea, started one small catering business after another that eventually had to be closed and reopened in a new location as she followed her husband around the country.

Edward had always attributed his success to the careful management of details, and he'd anguished over not knowing what had happened to Jack. Tate knew that he'd harbored the hope that one day, Jack would simply walk back into their lives.

Shea poured everyone another round of coffee and the three of them refocused on the present to polish off the cookies.

Then Tate asked, indicating the cappuccino machine, "So, you're thinking maybe you'll stay here awhile?"

"If that's not a problem for either of you," he replied, pushing his empty cup away. "I know you'd probably like to sell it, but I imagine a property of this size will take a while, and I have no place else to be right now. I'm cleared of any involvement in Marty's doings, and I'm supposed to remain available if the State of California needs me. But apart from that, I'm a free spirit. So I can hang around after you guys are gone, tidy up a little, maybe, show any prospective buyers around. What do you think?''

''Sounds all right to me.'' Mike rested an elbow on the back of the booth. ''If you don't mind company. I need a change of place, too, and I was about to offer to stay behind and see to things.''

Shea looked at once pleased and horrified. ''You mean, stay here together?''

''Yeah.''

Shea laughed lightly. ''We'd kill each other before Tate got to Portland Airport.''

''I'm not going to Portland Airport,'' Tate said, a sense of amused foreboding developing along with his excitement over being in French River. ''I was planning to stay, too.''

Shea ran a hand through his hair. ''But, why? How can the firm run without you?''

''It can run very well. Bill and Gina are brilliant. I just…'' He hesitated, doubtful he'd be able to explain to two single men what it was like to be without your family. Moving away from Sandy had been a relief after more than a year of continuous disagreement, but having the girls live an ocean away left him feeling as though he'd been run over by a tank. ''With the girls gone, I'm sort of at loose ends. As if I'm watching my life rather than living it. I have to find something new to do.''

Mike and Shea eyed each other, then Tate. ''You mean we're *all* staying?'' Mike asked.

Tate nodded. "Seems we're all looking for a change."

Mike closed his eyes. "There is no way this is going to work."

"Sure it is," Tate replied. "We just have to decide."

Mike opened his eyes again and asked suspiciously. "Decide?"

"Between piracy," Tate replied, "or the wine business."

## CHAPTER THREE

WHILE SHEA, who'd had the most harrowing trip, had the first shower, Tate helped Mike move the very ordinary square dresser with the round knobs out of Shea's room and replace it with the girlie dresser.

"He's going to cream you when he sees this," Tate warned as they placed the French-provincial dresser in the middle of the empty wall. "He hates it as much as you do."

"Serve him right," Mike said, dusting off his hands with great satisfaction. He turned to Tate, his expression grave. "I can't believe he thought we considered him inferior."

"We do consider him inferior." Tate watched a big drip fall into a plastic washtub where someone had placed a sponge to absorb the sound. The double bed—a brass thing in a clamshell pattern—had really been moved to the middle of the room. "Just not in the area of marketable abilities."

"Are you serious about running the winery?" Mike asked as they returned to his room with the other dresser.

"We'll have to see what the will says. And we'd have to all be in agreement. But I don't see why it wouldn't work."

Mike waved a hand in front of Tate's face as

though seeing if he were paying attention. "Hello? We don't know anything about wine. Drinking it, maybe. Growing it, no."

"We'll learn. And we have Colette."

"Tate, she didn't like us. She didn't like you, in particular. What makes you think she'll even stay if we decide to?"

"She has two little girls and a father who loves this place. She can't just up and move."

Mike expelled a gusty breath. "I hate it when you go all Pollyanna on me. You've always done that. You think just because *you* want to do something, you can make it happen."

Tate had found that philosophy usually succeeded, though he knew luck and fate had contributed greatly to his success in business. If only they'd intervened in his personal life, as well.

"It's all premature," he said, heading for the door, "until we know exactly what the will says. But wouldn't it be good if Aunt Rachel didn't have to move?"

"Yeah. But can this place support the three of us, much less our...dependents?"

"I don't know. I'll have to figure what yield and production will be, and what other potential opportunities we have."

Mike sat on the side of the nearest bed. "Right now, it looks like a winery-cum-petting zoo."

"Well, whatever brings in the tourists." Tate turned to leave the room and found himself face to face with Shea wearing a towel and a grim expression.

"The girlie dresser's in my room."

"Right."

"I'm not amused."

"Darn. And we did it just to make you laugh." Mike sidled past them and headed for the bathroom.

"I'll get you!" Shea warned after him.

Mike laughed scornfully and kept going. "Yeah, right."

The moment the bathroom door closed behind him, Shea turned to Tate and asked eagerly, "You want to help me move it back?"

"You bet," Tate replied.

Tate was putting away the meager contents of his bag when he heard Mike's voice from the doorway.

"You're playing both sides! You're double-dealing."

Tate turned around, keeping a straight face. "No, I'm not. I'm just refusing to *take* sides. I'm like a neutral country. Excuse me." Tate walked past him toward the bathroom.

"I hope the water's cold!" Mike shouted after him.

Tate half expected to find the French-provincial dresser in his room when he finished his shower, but the handsome colonial dresser remained in place, his shaving kit sitting atop it.

All right, he thought. Stalemate. For the moment there was nothing to argue about.

He pulled on the old sweats he slept in, flipped off the light, turned back the threadbare chenille coverlet and climbed into bed. That is, he tried.

His brothers had short-sheeted it.

COLETTE WALKED DOWN a row of chardonnay vines, buttoned the collar of her jacket against the midnight wind and lifted her face to the frosty quarter moon. It provided more beauty than light, but she was growing used to the darkness. Her world had been very black since Ben died.

Sometimes she felt as though she could reach him at night. As though time had rolled back and it was three years ago and she could stretch out a hand and connect with a muscled arm. It would gather her close and hold her until whatever had awakened her was forgotten and she could sleep again.

That would never happen, of course, so she simply talked to him. She told him about her fears for the future—what would happen to the winery, wondering where they'd be a year from now. And she told him how she worried about their daughters.

"Katie hasn't spoken since we found you," she said finally. "And every time she nods or shakes her head instead of saying yes or no, I want to scream and make her tell me what she's thinking, why she's muted herself."

Colette hunched her shoulders as the wind blew with more force. She turned back toward the house. Her father and the girls were asleep, but she hated to be out of earshot.

She started walking again, thinking that the road ahead of her looked very long and dark.

"Is that a metaphor for the rest of my life?" she asked no one in particular.

Nobody was listening anyway. Tate Delancey could hardly be considered an answer to prayer.

LLOYD REYNOLDS WAS short and slender and looked as if a sneeze would blow him over. But he had a voice like James Earl Jones—deep, resonant and majestic—that made one feel as though he made law rather than simply practiced it.

"'To my brother, Edward,'" he read to the people gathered around the old mahogany table, "'I leave my lifelong love and affection, knowing that his cleverness and industry and his wonderful Andrea have left him a comfortable retirement and a happy old age.'"

Lloyd cleared his throat and went on. "'I leave the winery and all its structures and property to my nephews, Tate Brian Delancey, Michael Anthony Delancey and Shea Xavier Delancey to share equally.'"

The brothers sat at one side of the table, and Rachel and Armand Beauchamp, a strong-looking man of medium height, were across from them. Armand's hands, Tate noticed, were arthritic and he rubbed absently at one shoulder. Tate guessed he was in his late sixties, and thought also that Colette must have gotten her gray eyes from him.

"'My only stipulations in the transference of this property are,'" Lloyd read on, "'number one, that a home be made for my friend Rachel Harwood and a comfortable space provided for her animals.'" Lloyd looked up at the brothers over the rims of large, square glasses. "Have you met the llama yet?" he asked in an aside.

"We have," Tate answered with a light laugh. "Scared Mike and me until we realized it was friendly."

Lloyd nodded sympathetically, then shook his

head at Rachel in what appeared to be teasing reprimand. "Ate my pocket handkerchief the first time I met her."

"It smelled of bay rum," Rachel said with a small smile. Despite the solemnity of the occasion she wore her overalls, a red flannel shirt and her rubber boots. "She thought it was a treat."

Lloyd smiled at her, then seemed to draw himself forcibly back to the matter at hand. "All right, to continue. 'Number two, whether or not Armand Beauchamp chooses to remain in the employ of the new owners, I leave him the house he's rented from me since the day he arrived at French River and the three acres on which it stands. Since that property adjoins the winery on two sides, I want the boys to be good neighbors to Armand, and to allow him access to and from his place on the winery's road free of charge.'"

Armand looked down at his hands on the table, his mouth tightening. He was apparently grateful for Jack's gesture.

Lloyd went on to read the physical description of the property and all the buildings bequeathed.

Tate let his mind wander and looked around the room. Then a movement in the bay window opposite him caught his eye. Framed in the bottom half of the old double-hung window were two young faces, both female.

One was very round, frantically freckled, had the same gray eyes as Armand and Colette and was framed with strawberry blond hair.

The other was a little paler and less freckled but had a pair of enormous blue eyes, a bandage on her chin and a bright smile. Her platinum-blond hair was shoulder-length and disheveled.

Megan and Katie, Tate remembered Rachel telling him the night before, were Colette's daughters. But he couldn't remember which was older.

He felt an immediate pang. Life had been good when his girls were that small. Well, he and Sandy had always had problems because of their different approaches to life, but they'd loved the girls unequivocally, and that love had pushed disharmony into the background.

They'd done a lot together on the weekends in those days—hikes, museum trips, beach vacations in the summer, ice skating in the winter.

The pang became an awful, aching emptiness. Paris was such a long way away.

He was distracted from the pain as he caught the eyes of the little girls beyond the window and they waved at him. A planter stood under that window, as he recalled. But he doubted that it would have raised them high enough to see into the house.

He was just beginning to entertain the uncomfortable thought that they must have placed something else on the planter, when he heard a strange metallic sound and saw looks of surprise on the small faces just before they disappeared from view. There was a clatter, followed by cries of distress.

The others looked out the window as Tate excused himself.

He found the girls, wearing fleece pants and berry-red down jackets, in a tangle on the walk that went around to the back porch. The younger one was crying and the older was trying to help her to her feet.

An old oval wash bucket lying nearby on its side must have been responsible for their untimely descent.

Tate took the older one's arm and looked her over quickly. No rips in her clothing, no visible injury.

"Megan or Katie?" he asked her, while scooping the smaller girl into his arms.

"Megan," the older one replied, then pointed to the child he held. "She's Katie. She always wants to do what I do, then she gets hurt. She doesn't talk."

Tate looked into Katie's puffy red face and wiped away her tears with his fingertips. "You mean she doesn't like to talk?" Sarah had always been quieter than Susan, more private.

Megan shook her head. "No, I mean she used to talk, but she can't anymore. It's kind of a sickness, like the flu. It's got a long name, but the doctor says she doesn't talk 'cause she's not ready."

Katie looked into Tate's eyes and he saw an unsettlingly adult expression there. "She used to talk, but she can't anymore." What had happened, he wondered grimly, to still something as irrepressible as a child's voice?

He smoothed Katie's tangled bangs and smiled at her. "Well, I bet when she *is* ready, she'll have all kinds of interesting stuff to tell us."

"That's what Mommy says."

Tate noticed the knee of Katie's sweats was torn and a very small smear of blood was visible. Her little porcelain face was smudged and teary, but she sniffed heroically.

"The tub got tippy," Megan explained, "and we fell."

He nodded. "That happens when you stack things up and try to stand on them. It isn't very safe."

"Are you gonna tell Mom?"

"No, but you'll have to when she asks how Katie got hurt."

Katie studied him with frowning interest, and he couldn't tell if he was coming off as a hero or a bad guy.

Armand appeared beside Tate and pushed up the hem of Katie's pantleg to assess the injury. "What happened?" he asked, as a very small knee with a very small scrape was revealed.

"I think they had the tub balanced on the planter to see what we were up to," Tate said. "But somebody must have shifted her weight, causing the perch to collapse."

Armand looked from one girl to the other in displeasure. "Spying in windows? Where are your manners?"

"No harm done." Tate, with Katie in his arms, led the way to the back door. "I have a tube of first-aid cream in my shaving kit. Let's go back inside."

Megan skipped along beside him. "How come you know our names?"

"Aunt Rachel told me," he replied. "And I met your mom last night."

"Are you the one that's gonna make us move?"

"No." He climbed the stairs and Armand passed him to hold the back door open for him. "And now the house belongs to your grandpa anyway. So nobody can make you move."

Wide gray eyes looked up at Armand. "Really?"

"Really," he replied, then ushered the child into the house behind Tate and Katie.

"Mom won't like that," Megan said seriously.

Mike came to take Katie from Tate. "Why?" Tate asked Megan in surprise.

She made a palms-up gesture meant to describe, he guessed, her mother's inexplicability. "She said she was looking forward to a fight."

Of all the things he might have looked forward to with a woman who resembled Colette, a fight wasn't one of them. At least not a real one. Which was probably the kind she had in mind.

"Spying casualty?" Mike asked, carrying Katie into the living room. "I saw them watching through the window."

"Yeah. I've got antiseptic upstairs. I'll be right back."

Tate returned with the tube and a bar of soap to find everyone gathered around Katie, whom Mike had placed on the sofa. He was washing off the scrape with a wet paper towel, as Armand held her hand.

Tate went into the kitchen to wet another one and apply the soap. He saw Shea and Megan in the breakfast room.

"What are you guys doing?" Tate asked.

"We're making mochas!" Megan said excitedly, holding a bag of coffee beans while Shea filled the grinder. "And he's gonna put caramel in mine."

Shea grinned at him. "I'm going to put caramel in everybody's. It's the only syrup I've brought. Fortunately, I think the kids will like it."

Tate winced. "Good idea. But no caramel in mine, okay?"

"Okay."

After Tate ministered to Katie's knee, Shea served the mochas and Armand allowed the girls to stay while Lloyd finished reading the details of the will. Megan stood by her grandfather, an arm hooked around his neck, and Tate found Katie leaning against him, her elbow resting on his chair as she stood like a stork, her sore knee raised.

Lloyd finished by saying, "Generally, it's all pretty straightforward, except for those two stipulations. Does anybody have a problem with one or the other?" He looked from Tate to Mike to Shea.

They looked at one another and said a firm, communal, "No."

"Good." Lloyd collected his papers and squared them against the tabletop. "Well, congratulations, gentlemen. You're now the owners of the Valley Winery. I imagine you'll be putting it up for sale?" It was a question.

Tate shook his head. "No, I don't think so. I think we're going to try our hands at growing grapes and making wine."

Lloyd stopped in the act of slipping his papers into his briefcase. "Seriously?"

"No." Shea laughed. "We never do anything seriously but with a sense of humor and probably a lot of foolish mistakes."

Armand glanced at the brothers with surprise, then approval.

"It is good to approach anything with a sense of humor. And if you will allow my daughter and me to help you, there will be fewer foolish mistakes—valuable, though they sometimes are.''

''Makes sense to me,'' Mike said.

Shea nodded. ''Of course.''

''Then it's unanimous.'' Tate stood and reached across the table to shake Armand's hand. ''We'll need at least a week to check everything out, consider our finances and come up with a deal. In the meantime, Rachel will continue to take care of the financial end of things.'' He turned to Rachel. ''All right?''

She rose from her chair and took his hand. ''All right. And as soon as you have everything straightened out, I'll happily give up the checkbook. I imagine one or the other of you will always be available to take care of it.''

''We'll see what happens.''

''Why are you shaking hands with everybody?'' Megan asked as she moved around the table to stand next to him.

''Because we're agreeing to work together,'' Tate replied. ''We're making a deal.''

''So...everybody you shake hands with can stay here?''

''Right.'' Megan gravely offered her hand, and Tate shook it just as gravely. Then Katie reached up to do the same.

Armand smiled at them affectionately. ''They are very good after-school help,'' he told Tate. ''And in the summer, we have a table at the weekend farmers' market, and they are excellent saleswomen.''

''I can well imagine,'' Tate replied.

Megan appeared to be bright and open, the way

Susan was. Katie glowed with an inner sweetness that reminded him of Sarah.

But could he develop a relationship with these two and not be tortured every day by the reminder of his own daughters so far away?

He looked down into the two eager faces and decided instantly that it didn't matter what it cost him. They needed desperately to know their world wouldn't change, and he'd been a father long enough to know that attention invested in a child always had a magical return for the giver, as well.

"Okay, that's the deal," he said, putting a hand to each fragile little shoulder. "You help out when you can. When you don't have too much homework or a date or something."

Both giggled at the notion of having dates. He listened appreciatively. His daughters had been gone only a month, but he'd moved out of the house a year ago, and though he'd seen them often, it had been a time of adjustment for all of them. A time that hadn't encouraged levity. He'd forgotten how warming a giggle could be.

"Rachel and I will take you on a tour," Armand offered. "You have brought boots?"

"No," Tate replied. "We just packed for a couple of days. But we have to go to town to stock our kitchen and pick up some other things. We'll put boots on the list and meet you after lunch for the tour. Would that fit your schedule?"

Armand grinned. "You now control my schedule, Mr. Delancey."

Tate frowned at that. "I'm not much for formality.

My name is Tate. And I'm not really into control, Armand. I think we should..."

Out of the corner of his eye, he saw Mike turn to Shea and knew they were exchanging a disbelieving look. He frowned in their direction.

"I'm not into control," Tate repeated with a roll of his eyes to Armand, "except where my brothers are concerned. And when you've known them a little longer, I'm sure you'll understand why. With respect to our relationship—yours and mine—we have a lot to learn from you, and I'd prefer to think we were all working together."

Armand nodded with approval. "I appreciate that. I will help all I can, but I do very little of the work now. Colette is the one whose help you will need. And I trust you are being honest about not wanting control, because she is a woman who does as she pleases."

"I detected a certain..." How did he put it nicely? Tate wondered. "Self-sufficiency," he finally said diplomatically, "in her manner when we met last night."

Armand nodded understanding. "Her mother was a Dane, you see, a proud descendant of Vikings, and though they stopped their plundering raids many centuries ago, I'm convinced the conquering spirit is as alive in that bloodline as it was in the days of Erik the Red." Armand's gaze lost focus for a moment and he heaved a wistful sigh. "That woman hunted down and found every feeling in my body and every thought in my head and used them to her advantage—and to mine."

Tate felt momentarily lost with Armand in

thoughts of a love that strong. Tate had once felt he'd found that with Sandy, only to discover their goals were totally different. He envied Armand his lasting relationship, even if it meant dealing with a difficult woman.

Then Armand seemed to call himself back and put an arm around each granddaughter. "She's been gone ten years and I miss her as though she'd left me this morning. But, as you see—" he squeezed the girls to him "—her legacy leaves me little time to pine. But I will be available to you this afternoon to take you through the vineyard."

Tate, Mike and Shea walked Armand and his granddaughters to the front door. Rachel's two dogs stood on the porch, tails wagging. One was large, gray and shaggy, and looked very much like a cross between a sheepdog and a Saint Bernard. The other was a small, friendly beagle with three legs.

The girls fussed over them and the dogs fussed back.

"Can we come on the tour?" Megan asked Tate as Armand tried to tug her down the steps.

"Of course," Tate replied. Then he remembered the parental kicker to all adult-child agreements. "If it's all right with your mom."

Clearly not expecting that to be a problem, the girls waved, then skipped ahead of Armand across the compound.

Rachel lingered on the porch as the dogs did their best to charm Mike and Shea.

"I'd like to say something." She tucked an arm in Tate's and drew him off to the side.

"Please. If you do have a problem with any—"

She shook her head. "No. It has nothing to do with the winery. It has to do with Colette."

Interesting, he thought, how the subject of the red-head kept coming up.

Rachel looked into his eyes. His mother used to give him that look. It probed where it had no real right to be.

"You've noticed her," Rachel observed.

Tate couldn't withhold a smile. "She doesn't exactly slip into the background."

"You know what I mean, Tate."

Strangely, he did. She meant that he'd been intrigued by her as well as annoyed.

"What did you want to tell me?"

Rachel put both hands in her pockets and sighed. Her breath curled away from her on the cold morning air. "That Armand oversimplified. He adores her, but he sees her as a father sees his daughter. I see her as another woman, another widow. She isn't just difficult—Viking history or not. However strong a woman is, when she loses the man she loves, she's terrified. And it isn't just fear of being unable to support herself and her children."

Rachel studied his expression, as though trying to assess whether she still had his interest.

"Go on," he encouraged.

"It's fear of having to do it without the love you've come to depend upon." She smiled lightly. "And when you're strong, fear makes you behave with bravado and push away anyone who tries to help because you don't want them close enough to see you are afraid."

He understood that completely. He'd operated on the same principle from time to time.

"I know you probably consider this none of my business," she said, but without apology in her tone, "and Colette certainly wouldn't thank me for analyzing her like this, but I mention it only because we need you here. And I think..." She met his gaze again, almost as if judging how he would take what she was about to tell him. "I think she'll make it hard for you."

He shrugged a shoulder. "Lately, everything's been hard. I'm in fighting trim."

Rachel nodded slowly, then punched him in the arm. "I'm going to like you," she said. She called the dogs to her. "Moose! Snoopy!"

Tate walked with her down the stairs. "We already like you," he said. "And your cookies."

"I notice you didn't serve any with the mochas."

Tate laughed. "Because there weren't any left."

Her eyes widened. "I brought four dozen!"

"I know. Sixteen apiece. They kept us going last night while we talked about running the winery instead of selling it."

"I'm glad of that." She stopped at the bottom of the stairs to squint up at him. The sun had broken through the dark clouds, though it was probably just a momentary respite. "I think Jack will like knowing you're operating it. Even though he didn't get to see you that much, he talked about you often. He told me about the summer the three of you spent here when your parents were at odds. He said you reminded him what he missed, not having a family."

"He was very good to us," Tate said. "That summer made a lot of difference in my life."

"What do *you* think happened to him?" she asked. The bigger dog whined, eager to be on his way, and she reached down to pat his head. "I know your father's detectives didn't discover anything."

"I can't even guess," he admitted. "There just wasn't a clue anywhere. They never even found his car. His checkbook and his credit cards weren't used, so it's doubtful he was robbed."

"It might have been for the car," she said reluctantly. "Since it was never found. I hate to think that, but it could be."

"Maybe." Tate looked at the horizon and smiled. "I prefer to think that he just got tired of the burden of everyday life and took off for somewhere else. Maybe somewhere warm and tropical—with coconuts and dancing girls. He used to tease me about doing that the summer we visited."

Rachel smiled, also. "Yes. I'd rather think about that, too. Well. Since you've been kind enough not to object to me and my animals on your property, my part of the deal will be a regular supply of cookies. But you'll have to ration them better than you did last night's batch."

"Right," he agreed. "We'll do that. Thank you, Rachel."

She walked away at a quick pace, the dogs loping beside her, happy to be on the move.

"Presuming that we're going to need high boots because the place is muddy," Shea said as he and Tate and Mike went back into the house to retrieve jackets and car keys, "maybe we should reconsider piracy. I mean, we never really voted."

# CHAPTER FOUR

"WE MADE A DEAL, Mom!" Megan said as she and Katie followed Colette to the kitchen table. Katie held a fistful of soupspoons. "He shook our hands!"

Colette tipped the saucepan of soup into the bowl at Megan's place. Her father hadn't come home since the will reading that morning, and she was dying to know what had happened. Her girls were a steady source of information on any subject, but their creative interpretation of events made them a bit unreliable. "*Who* made the deal?" she asked.

Katie held her hand high above herself while standing on tiptoe.

"They're all really tall," Megan stated. She never missed a detail. "His name is Tate."

Of course. The one with the superior look. "And what kind of deal did you make?"

"We get to stay!" Megan said, taking the spoon Katie handed her. "But we have to help after school."

As Colette poured soup into Katie's bowl, she looked up to assess Megan's expression. The child did not seem upset. "He said you *had* to help after school?"

She smiled happily. "Yeah! It's the deal."

She would have to get the particulars of the

"deal" from her father. She couldn't decide if the big-city boy was lording it over the innocent, or if her daughters had misinterpreted what he'd said.

In the meantime, she found their enthusiasm annoying. "Why are you so happy about it?" she asked as she served herself soup. "You hate to help me after school. You complain about it all the time."

"He's gonna be fun!" Megan said as Katie dispensed the rest of the spoons. The girls slipped into their chairs and giggled across the table at each other.

Oh, oh. The girls weren't fighting. Katie could maintain her end of an argument even without words. But now they seemed mutually delighted with Tate Delancey. This could be trouble.

"Yeah," Megan confirmed. "He didn't even get mad when we fell off the washtub."

Colette wanted to think that as their mother, she could read her devilish little cherubs like a book, but every once in a while they stumped her.

"What washtub?" she asked, about to put the saucepan back on the stove. But her father walked in and went to the sink to wash his hands. She went back to the table and poured soup into his bowl. "And where did you fall off of it? Hi, Dad."

"Well…" Her father smiled as her daughters exchanged guilty looks. Colette met it with her own I-want-the-whole-truth-and-I-want-it-now look. Megan swallowed and hurried on. "Well, you said we might have to move, and that those men would decide, so when Grandpa and Aunt Rachel went in to have the meeting with them, we wanted to know what was happening, but we couldn't see. So we found a washtub in the backyard and we put it on that box where the pansies are in the summer so we could see into the window.''

Colette closed her eyes. Wonderful. The new landlords had caught her children standing on the planter box like a pair of Peeping Toms. She drew a breath for strength, then opened her eyes and waited for the rest of the story.

Her father came to the table, his face carefully set in unrevealing lines. That meant he thought she was overreacting and he was determined not to interfere.

She ignored him. His determination seldom lasted longer than a minute anyway.

''He carried Katie!'' Megan said, her hair standing out around her head like a halo. It seemed electrified at the moment by her excitement. ''And the other guy—the second biggest one—''

''Mike,'' Armand stated.

''He washed her knee and Tate went and got some creamy stuff upstairs.'' She waited for a reaction, then added as a defense, ''She didn't cry!''

Katie came around the table and raised her knee for Colette's perusal.

Colette gently lifted one side of the bandage and saw a barely discernible scrape. And her knee was clean, too. She replaced the bandage and pointed Katie back to her chair.

''Girls, we've had this privacy talk before,'' she said, passing her father the dish of crackers. ''I know it gets lonesome for you out here, but you can't let yourself into Rachel's animal pens or peek into the windows at the big house. It isn't polite. We—''

''You're also not supposed to stack things up and stand on them,'' Megan said, eager to contribute to the lecture. "He said it isn't safe." Then the child's expression turned to one of concern. "You better shake his hand, Mom, or you won't be able to stay. Everybody made a deal. He lets you stay, but you have to do something for him."

"Really." Colette turned to her father, who was blowing on a spoonful of soup. He was blowing, she guessed, to reshape his mouth from the smile she'd glimpsed when she first looked at him. "This means they're not selling? At all?"

"That's right. They're staying to operate the winery."

"But…it'll never support all three of them."

Armand shrugged. "That's their problem, isn't it? Maybe they have plans. When we heard they were coming, you were worried they *would* sell. What's the problem now?"

"Well…do they plan on expanding to draw tourists? Are we going to have buses in the compound?" She frowned at her father. "Did *you* make a deal, too?"

"I did. I'm the new adviser on growing grapes and making wine."

"That's interesting," she said mildly, "considering I do all those things now."

He nodded. "I thought you'd want to make your own deal."

He was baiting her. She sidestepped. "The girls tell me they have to help him after school."

He passed the crackers to Katie. "They saw Rachel and me shake hands with Tate," he explained. "Megan asked him why we were doing it, and he told them it was because we'd agreed to stay and work together. Because they wanted to stay, they shook his hand. I mentioned they were good little workers, so their part of the deal is to help after school.''

"I see.'' So it was all very innocent on Delancey's part. That was too bad. She'd have liked something to use against him.

"About peeking through the window,'' she said to Katie and Megan. "I want you to promise me you won't do that again. It's rude. And nosy. Nobody likes a rude and nosy kid.''

"There was no harm done,'' her father said quietly. "And he was very kind about it. He seems very kind about most things.''

The crackers came back to Colette. She took several and crumbled them in her soup. "You'd think a kind man would have visited his uncle more often.''

"He runs a business all the way across the country,'' her father said. "And there was his family to consider.''

Rachel had told her he was a builder or something, but Colette hadn't heard about the family. "Then how is he going to run both a business and a winery when they're thirty-three-hundred miles apart? And how is his wife going to react to French River? It isn't every woman who'd be happy in this muddy little corner of the world.''

"The wife, I believe, is gone,'' Armand replied. "Lloyd said she moved with their two daughters and a new husband to Paris. But I don't know about the business. Maybe you can ask him when you make your deal.''

"Maybe I don't want to make a deal.''

Her father gave her an infuriating smile. "Maybe you don't know what you want."

TATE PULLED ON the ugly but functional rubber boots and decided he liked the feel of them, if not the look. They had none of the restrictions of the dress shoes he'd worn almost every day of his adult life.

On the old sofa across from him, Mike and Shea were doing the same.

"Jeez, these are ugly," Shea said, holding out one long foot to study the boot. "We're sure this is a better career move than piracy?"

Mike stood, tucking his jeans into the tops of his boots. "No, but the boots are pretty much the same. So if it's higher fashion you're looking for, I don't think piracy will do it. And they wear hats with plumes." He pretended to shudder.

Shea rose and walked across the living room, testing his footwear. Then he pointed to the pile of dark rain slickers on the other end of the sofa. "While we get to strut around in cow-dung-colored rubber with a hood that has a duckbill. Could that possibly be worse than a plume?"

Tate drew on a slicker. "Are you two going to whine every step of the way? Because, if you are, I'll take Megan and Katie as partners, instead."

"What are you going to do about your Boston partners?" Shea sat down again and readjusted his right boot. "Fly back once in a while to keep your hand in?"

Tate closed the snaps on the front of his slicker. "I'm going to sell."

"You're selling your partnership?" Shea and Mike asked simultaneously. They looked shocked.

Which surprised him. "How did you think we'd get this place on its feet?"

Mike started to speak, closed his mouth, then tried again.

"I don't know. I guess just...slowly. I have a savings account I can contribute, and a few stocks I can sell. I don't think you should let go of your partnership until we know this is going to work."

"I don't have a dime," Shea admitted, "but I was thinking I can cook in town evenings and add what I make to the kitty. I agree with Mike. I don't think you should go selling what it's taken you all these years to build until we know we're doing the right thing."

Tate was touched by his brothers' concern, but he couldn't approach this in a halfhearted way, because then the enterprise would definitely fail. And Shea and Mike were as much on a limb as he was.

He rejected their suggestions with a shake of his head. "We have to give this our full attention and dedication," he said, "or it isn't going to work. I'm not thinking about slow, steady growth, either. We need an all-out push to get this place on the map along with the other Oregon wineries—maybe even put us ahead of them."

Shea looked at Mike. "Is he delusional?"

Mike studied Tate worriedly. "Maybe his boots are too tight."

"Hey." Tate shook his head over their lack of faith. "Who made the neighborhood garage-cleaning business turn a profit when we were kids? Who turned Shea's popcorn balls into a money-making proposition at city baseball games? Who sold Mike as a bodyguard to the prom queen and—I might remind you—got him a date with Melissa Belmont?''

Mike shifted his weight to one foot. ''As I recall, the neighborhood garage-cleaning operation profits took a nosedive when you blew out Dad's Shop-Vac by inhaling Mrs. Gunderson's hamster, and we had to replace it and the Shop-Vac. *And* the Sports Club was going to take us to court over the popcorn balls because we were taking funds away from their concession. *And* Melissa Belmont dumped me for Bruce Kubik.''

''It isn't my fault that you had no sex appeal.''

Mike sighed tolerantly over the gibe. ''And all the other stuff?''

''Doesn't matter in light of the fact that each and every operation made us money. We had the best bikes, the best skateboards and the best cars—junkers though they were—in our group because I have a knack for making money. My partnership will buy us a face-lift for all the buildings, and probably whatever we need to update and streamline the operation. This time next year, we'll be open for tours. And if we work efficiently, by then we might even have a restaurant.''

Shea's expression turned from playful derision to complete seriousness. ''A restaurant? Here in the compound?''

''Yeah. So don't go taking any jobs. You'll be needed here full-time. And, Mike, we're going to require a PR campaign that'll bring every tourist in Oregon to our door. You're the smooth talker.

Sounds like a job for you. Can you delay the hotel thing for a while?''

His brothers looked at each other as he opened the front door. ''You coming?'' he asked.

Mike followed him onto the porch. ''You scare me when you get like this. I feel as though I'm related to Donald Trump.''

Shea came out and pulled the door closed, the look of stunned seriousness still in place. ''What kind of a restaurant?''

They paraded down the front steps and walked toward the road that led to Armand's place.

''Whatever kind you want,'' Tate replied. ''I was thinking something elegant and tasteful to highlight the wine. Which is what you do anyway.''

''Do we have any wine? I mean, has Armand been making it?''

''I don't know. That's a question we have to ask.''

A Jeep came up the slope from the far side of the compound, Armand at the wheel. He pulled up beside them and then held the front seat down while Mike and Shea climbed into the back.

''I thought the girls were coming,'' Tate said as he got into the front.

''They're with Colette, helping her prune,'' Armand replied with a grin. ''So that they can start keeping their part of the deal.''

''You know that was just for their benefit,'' Tate explained. ''They wanted to be part of—''

''Of course I do.'' Armand started down an easy slope, heading for the rows and rows of low vines. ''But it's a good object lesson for them. Deals require that you be responsible. And because they

made it with you, they're eager—at least for now—
to do their part."

Armand stopped in the middle of the rows of dormant vines. "I don't know how much you remember
from your visit as children."

Tate shook his head. "Not very much about the
vineyard. And, of course, during the summer there
was no wine in production. So you can safely assume
we know nothing."

He smiled. "I did not want to talk down to you."

Mike laughed. "That would be impossible."

Armand got out and encouraged them to follow
him up and down a row of vines. The earth was soft
and wet and sucked at their boots. "These are pinot
noir grapes," he said. "The same grape that produces *la belle France*'s famous burgundy. In the
spring they will be shoulder to shoulder with bright-
green leaves, then in the summer the grapes will be
royal purple in color."

Tate noticed that these vines had already been
pruned.

"It looks as though Colette's already been here,"
he observed.

Armand nodded. "We renew the two major limbs
each year by leaving the two strongest shoots and
cutting off last year's. The vines are generally very
healthy, though they haven't gotten the pampering
we would have provided if we'd had more funds at
our disposal."

"So you *have* been making wine?"

Armand shook his head. "No, we haven't. I
stopped the year Jack disappeared because it was too
much to handle on my own. But I continued to tend

the vines, and sold the grapes to other vintners. We've been able to at least pay the taxes and keep the buildings from falling down, though they'll need more attention than that if you're planning to make wine again.''

Tate nodded.

They piled back into the Jeep and Armand drove across the top of the hill and stopped again where the vines were divided by a much wider road. "That side is chardonnay grapes. They will be green, like a seedless table grape.''

Armand drove on, past a simple farmhouse. "My home,'' he said. Then he continued along the road to a place where bare trees were visible in a long, straight line. He got out of the Jeep again and they followed him through the naked trees to a fast-moving river about an eighth of a mile wide. "You cannot tell now, but those are cottonwoods. They are wonderful to sit near in the summer and picnic. This is French River.''

It was gray under a gray sky. Summer picnics seemed a lifetime away.

"It is one of my favorite places to think,'' Armand said, then he winked at them. "As long as I don't think too much. Come. We'll look at your buildings.''

He drove back up the hill until they reached the decrepit building nearest the road leading to the highway. It was barnlike, the outside weathered to bare wood, though the inside was treated.

A concrete floor seemed to stretch forever. On one side were tall tanks, and on the other large open vats. Tate had a vague memory of having once accompanied Jack into this room. He went to one of the square vats.

"This is the winery," Armand said.

"And these are fermenting tanks?" Tate asked.

The old man nodded. "The open ones are for the red wine because it is important that the skin and seed remain in contact with the must for flavor and body."

"Must?" Mike asked.

"Must is the thick liquid that is neither juice nor wine but a mixture of grape juice, stem fragments, skins, seeds and pulp that comes from the stemmer-crusher."

Armand pointed to a large red contraption with a wide mouth and what seemed to be a motor mounted on the side.

"We place it on supports over the tank or vat," he said, "and crush right into it." He pointed across the room to the tall, closed tanks. "For our chardonnay, we press right after crushing so that the must is squeezed from the skins for purity of color and flavor. With the reds, we press about a week after fermentation."

Shea looked around at the stainless steel with a frown. "I thought there'd be lots of big barrels."

Armand smiled. "I asked Rachel to sell them several years ago. They have only a five-year life—three for white wine, then two for reds. And once a barrel has held a red wine, it cannot be used for white again. When Jack disappeared, the cycle was in its fourth year anyway. So we cut the barrels in half and sold them for planters. The money allowed us to roof Rachel's house." He looked worried. "Replacing them will be a major expense. Seven hundred dollars a barrel for Limousin oak.''

Tate ran his hand over the staves on a very large press. ''I understand a lot of wineries are aging in stainless steel.''

''True. But Colette thinks nothing gives the char-donnay that buttery, nutty flavor, or pinot noir the perfect oakiness, like the barrel.'' He shrugged, a gesture that seemed very French. ''She has strong feelings but admits her experience is somewhat lim-ited.''

''And what do you feel?''

''That oak does add unique character, but I am open-minded enough to try new things. And we still have time to make that decision.'' Armand indicated the machinery. ''Some of our equipment is very old, but quite serviceable. Except for the barrels, we have what we need to start again.''

Tate grinned. ''You don't think Colette will be talked out of the barrels?''

That shrug again. ''She is less open-minded than I.''

''The Viking ancestry?'' Tate guessed.

''And the education. A dangerous combination in a woman—knowledge and a warrior spirit.''

Shea peered into the stemmer-crusher, then looked up, his expression wry. ''That's the way women are today,'' he said. ''They should all be wearing breast armor and carrying spears.''

Mike raised an eyebrow at that observation. ''That sounds like the voice of experience.''

Shea sighed, appearing suddenly bleak. ''You don't know the half of it.''

Armand led the brothers down a set of stairs at the side of the room and into a dim, low-ceilinged basement. "The cellar," he said.

The room yawned emptily and Tate thought it still smelled of wine.

"I like to dream of this being filled once more," Armand said.

Tate clapped him on the shoulder. "So do I."

When they were outside again, Armand escorted them to what looked like an old bunkhouse. It was wide, and a second level had three dormers. He pointed to the back. "There was a kitchen through those doors, and horse stalls on the side were converted to showers and a *toilette* in the thirties. I think in the old days, even before Jack owned the place, this was where the harvest help stayed."

Tate turned to say something to Shea, but he was missing. Mike pointed to the saloon doors at the back of the room through which their younger brother was about to disappear.

He'd had the same thought, Tate guessed. This building would be the restaurant.

Shea appeared at the doors a moment later, beckoning the group to join him. "Look!" he said, sounding rhapsodic. "A stone fireplace with a pothook!"

"Well, if you don't need a stove," Tate teased, "we can open tomorrow."

Shea didn't even notice the joke. Mike caught Tate's eye and grinned. They'd harassed Shea unmercifully all their lives, but they considered him good company, and even now it gave them pleasure to see him happily in his element. Particularly after what he'd just been through.

But his happiness was short-lived.

"It costs a fortune to outfit a kitchen, Tate. We'd better see how things go..."

Tate shook his head. "I'm an architect, remember. I have connections with wholesalers. And the restaurant would make money for us." He looked around at the bare wood and tried to imagine it power washed and finished, the roof and walls reinforced, the floor replanked. "You think this is the building for it?"

"I've got to have that fireplace."

"Okay. Start making plans."

Leaving the bunkhouse, they angled across the end of the central square, heading for a small cottage with a large penned area beside it in which Victoria strolled and several other animals moved and slept.

"How would you feel about running a B and B?" Tate asked, voicing an inspiration as they walked toward Rachel's place. "Along with your duties as PR person for the operation, of course. It's like a smaller version of the hotel business."

Mike blinked. "Ah...where?"

"Here."

Mike grinned and indicated the lowering sky. "This is hardly the Tropics."

"I know. But you might like it anyway. Besides, it'll be good training before you take over the Tahiti Hilton. We can put an office in it for your PR duties."

Mike looked around the compound. "But *where* here?"

Tate pointed to an empty plot of land on the opposite corner of the square. "We'll build it. Right there. We'll put up a Victorian with just seven or eight rooms. People can stay, have a place to eat, shop, buy wine."

"Shop? Where?"

"When we renovate the winery, we'll put in a tasting room and a gift shop. And an office upstairs."

"Of course. Why didn't I think of that? It's all so easy. Build this, restore that, move, add—"

"You're forgetting the garage-cleaning business."

"You're forgetting the hamster."

Tate looked him in the eye. "Do you have doubts about this? If we're going to invest time and effort, we have to be in agreement."

"Oh, I'm in agreement." Mike laughed. "At least until we see how it all goes."

"Fair enough."

Rachel came out onto the porch to wave at them. The dogs burst out after her and rushed over to the men, requiring attention from everyone.

"Is the tour under way?" she asked.

"Yes," Armand called, stroking Moose between the ears. "Do you wish to join us?"

She shook her head. "I have cookies in the oven."

Victoria came to the fence. Tate went to stroke her nose. She lipped his hand, then his chin, then his hair.

"How do you feel about construction noises?" Tate asked Rachel as he stroked the llama's long neck. "We're talking about making some repairs and putting up a building."

She came halfway down the steps. "A building? Where?"

He explained about the B and B, almost expecting her to protest the disruption it would cause.

Instead, she smiled widely. "That sounds wonderful. I'd love to see this place come to life. If the noise gets too bad, I'll get ear protectors."

He studied her solid but faded little cottage. There was moss on the roof, and two of the six shutters dangled. "How about if we spruce your place up a little on the outside?"

She joined her hands at her bosom. The vulnerable gesture was at odds with the overalls and the rubber boots.

"I'd kiss you!" she declared. "All of you!"

Tate waved, then blew her a kiss, as they moved on. "We'll be back to collect when the time comes."

"How's your place?" Tate asked Armand.

They all stopped in the middle of the compound. "Comfortable," Armand assured him. "Colette and I painted it last summer."

Was there anything Colette didn't do?

"Is there anything else you would like to see?" Armand asked. "Colette is at work pruning, if you would like to observe."

Mike reached out to shake Armand's hand. "Thank you," he said. "If you'll excuse me, I'll go back to the house to make a few phone calls. Tate, do you mind if I use your cell phone?"

"Of course not." He looked around at the wide-open valley. "There must be a signal to pick up around here. I haven't tried it yet. I think I left it on my dresser."

"You're welcome to use the phone at my house until yours is connected," Armand volunteered.

"Thanks." Mike waved as he started away. "I'll try the cell phone first."

Shea offered his hand to Armand, too. "I think I'll take another walk through the bunkhouse."

Armand shook his hand heartily. "It would be a blessing to have a fine restaurant within walking distance of my house. I was a waiter in my youth."

Shea laughed. "Maybe you should brush up on your skills. I might need help that would be willing to be paid off only in good food."

"Ah! I'm your man!" As Shea headed toward the bunkhouse, Armand turned to Tate. "Would you like to see Colette at work?"

She probably wouldn't like him watching her, he guessed, but that was unfortunate. He was now her employer. Though he had no intention of trying to control everything, he had a take-charge nature, and plans for making the winery functional again were tumbling around in his brain, encouraging him to act that way.

"I would," Tate replied.

"She has been up to her ankles in mud for several days," Armand warned with a smile. "She will be at her Viking best."

Tate shook his head. "I come from a long line of bloodthirsty Irish who fought the Viking raiders."

Armand elbowed him as they approached the Jeep. "Mr. Delancey, you are aware the Irish lost?"

## CHAPTER FIVE

COLETTE SAW the Jeep make the turn at the head of the row of chardonnay vines she was pruning and noticed there was someone in the passenger seat. Delancey, she guessed, inspecting his vineyards.

"Here comes Grandpa!" Megan called, running out between the rows to wave at him. "And Tate's with him! Now you can make your deal, Mom!"

Katie was perched on the tailgate of the old red truck into which Colette placed the pruned vines. She leaped down to join her sister.

Hands protected by thick work gloves, Colette gathered up a snarled ball of vines and pushed it into the back of the truck, determined to be polite but to make no deals. She had no intention of promising to work for him if he was proposing to turn this perfect little spot into some big-city venture.

She heard the Jeep stop. Both girls ran to welcome their grandfather and his companion.

"Colette," Armand said. "I've brought Mr. Delancey to watch you prune the vines."

"I've just finished with this load," she said, planning to turn and give her new employer a courteous but frosty greeting. Movement, however, was impossible. Something had caught the front of her jacket and trapped the bale of vines against her.

"I was just about to…take this load…home." She tugged, thinking her jacket had been snagged by the cane. But a piece of it had worked itself into the loop fastener on the front of her jacket and wouldn't let go. The end of it slapped her in the face as she struggled.

Her traitorous children laughed. "Mommy's stuck!"

Color filled her cheeks—half from embarrassment, half from exasperation. Her clumsy gloves made working with the small loop impossible, and she had to raise her arms high above the snarl of vines to pull them off.

"Let me help." Tate pulled her back against him, then reached a hand around her to push at the vines.

She leaned her head back to dodge a loose cane and connected with his shoulder. It was covered in a brown slicker, but she felt the tough bone and muscle underneath.

Before she could raise her head again, he'd leaned over her shoulder to assess the problem. His chin bumped the side of her face and she found herself imprisoned between his body and the tangle of canes.

Instantly, her lungs felt empty of air and she couldn't move.

Ben had been a very warm and physical husband, and though she'd learned to live without sex because their relationship had always been about so much more than that, she really missed the spontaneous hugs, playful swats and kisses for no reason.

And now, without warning or any real cause, her body reacted as though it was responding to a sexual overture. Deep inside her, a hot little pulse beat madly.

"Ah, here it is." He moved one hand around her waist to hold her still, while drawing the vine out of her button loop with the other.

The cane resisted, caught on a nubby eye, and he let go of her waist to use his index finger to push the loop open.

But the action caused his other three fingers to slip inside the opening of her coat. Quite inadvertently, they cupped the bottom of her breast.

Her body went into overdrive, tingles shooting inside her from her heart to her knees.

"There," he said, freeing her. "Dangerous stuff."

It was a full five seconds before she could move or draw in air to speak. Either he hadn't noticed that his fingers had touched her breast, or her double As had made little impression on him.

"Hi, Dad," she said finally, her voice deep and husky, like Lauren Bacall's. She cleared her throat. "Mr. Delancey."

He smiled. "I've just plucked you from the vine. You can call me 'Tate.' Do you burn what you prune?"

"No." She looked around for her gloves. Her father handed them to her. His gaze was questioning. She felt sure he couldn't have seen what had happened, but he could tell by her behavior that something had. She made a project of pulling on the gloves, giving her time to stiffen her somewhat jellylike demeanor. "We take them down to our place where Dad's cleared space and we cut them into eighteen-inch pieces and replant them."

"As a kind of nursery?"

"Sort of. After they propagate, we either plant them here or sell them to the home wine maker at Saturday Market."

"Saturday Market is a cooperative?"

"In town. Yes. Things from the garden, crafts, art, baked goods. It starts at the first sign of sunshine—usually May—and lasts until the rain—about October."

He smiled down at Megan and Katie, who were crowding close to him. "I understand the girls are the stars on your sale staff."

Mention of her children allowed her to loosen up for a moment.

"Yes. Katie charms customers with her smile, Megan gives samples of Rachel's baked goods, then I talk them into buying grapes for their home gardens." Then, because she couldn't loosen up too much, she added, "Probably not an event you'd find in Boston, so you won't have to worry about it."

She sounded very defensive, even to her own ears. When she saw her father frown at her and Tate Delancey raise an eyebrow, she wasn't sure if she was pleased with herself or disappointed.

Armand drew the girls with him toward the truck. "I'll take the vines," he said to Colette, opening the passenger-side door and helping them into the cab. "You drive Tate home."

Megan protested from inside the truck. "We want to ride with Mom."

Armand closed the door on Megan's complaints and walked around the truck to the driver's side.

Colette searched her mind desperately for a reason

why *she* should be the person to take the vines, and couldn't think of one.

In a moment, her father drove off and she was left alone in the middle of a muddy row with Tate Delancey looking at her in puzzlement.

"You have a problem with me," he said without preamble.

She certainly did. And not just the one he was suggesting.

She met his frowning gaze and reminded herself that he was her employer. "It's not my place to—"

"Oh, come now," he interrupted mildly. "I can't believe you've ever worried about your place. Tell me what's on your mind."

"All right," she said, facing him. She blurted it all out. "You're going to change everything. It happens all the time around here. Big-city people get tired of their lives and move to the country. Only they don't like it the way it is. They have to bulldoze or terrace or log. They buy animals they ultimately abandon—along with the environment they've changed—because they decide they really don't like it here after all."

"Have you seen me bulldoze or terrace or log anything?" he asked reasonably, though there was a spark in his eyes that suggested he could be driven *beyond* reason.

She folded her arms and shifted her weight. "Not yet."

"Then isn't it a little premature to accuse me of doing those things?"

It was, of course. It was downright ridiculous now

that it was out of her mouth, but she swallowed any temptation to admit that.

"You wanted to know where I stand," she said loftily.

"Mmm. Behind a verbal Uzi." He headed for the Jeep. "I'll remember." He opened the passenger-side door and held it, obviously waiting for her to get in.

The courtesy, she guessed, was intended to contribute to the guilt she already felt. It worked.

"Look," she said, as she climbed into the Jeep and he closed the door. She had to wait for him to walk around the vehicle and get in behind the wheel. "It's just that I like it here. I know that since you've inherited the place, you're entitled to do whatever you want with it. I just hate to see it filled with noisy machinery and crawling with people who consider us nothing but an afternoon's entertainment."

"I'm sorry," he said, turning the key in the ignition, then raising his voice slightly above the sound of it, "but if we let you stomp the grapes in an old oaken tub, we'll never produce enough wine to support your family and mine."

That startled her. "Your family's coming? I thought your wife—" She stopped herself, but it was too late to save him from the knowledge that his tenants had been discussing his private life.

"Yes?" he asked.

She had no choice but to finish. "That she'd re-married and moved to Paris. I'm sorry, but Dad, Rachel and I depend upon one another for everything, and Rachel always knows what's going on. I'm not always sure how, but she does."

"Yes, she does," he admitted. He drove to the road that ran around the hill, then up into the compound. "She's absolutely right. When I said 'my family,' I meant my brothers."

Colette nodded. "When I said 'noisy machinery,' I meant big equipment that was going to tear everything down so you could start over."

"Actually, we intend to just polish up what's already here." He glanced her way, his eyes holding less annoyance than they had a moment ago. "And aren't you a little young to be so stuffy about change?"

She ignored hurt feelings over the "stuffy" remark and tried to pinch his conscience. "My father's lived on this place for thirteen years, and all the time your uncle was missing, he did his best to keep the grapes alive at considerable cost to himself physically, disregarding the better money he could have made at another winery. He loves it here. My children love it here."

"I've discussed the changes with your father," Tate said with no evidence of guilt, "and he's not upset at all. Do you suppose that's because he's taken the trouble to actually learn what we intend to do and you haven't?"

She opened her mouth, prepared with a snappy reply, but before she could give it, he added, "And your girls seem delighted by the prospect of things happening around here. Using them as an excuse just doesn't hold up."

Tate pulled up in front of the house and cut the motor. He turned to her with a matter-of-factness she found unsettling in view of her own irritation with him.

"I presume," he said, "this means you aren't interested in spending time with me."

Her feeling of being slightly unsettled quickly changed to suspicion. "Spending time with you? In what capacity?"

He groaned and shook his head. "I meant in the vineyard, with you teaching me about all this. Come on, Colette, I can't believe that wild red hair and all those freckles come with no sense of humor or adventure."

Something about her own eagerness to jump to idiotic conclusions forced her sense of humor to emerge. "Like Bozo, you mean?" she asked.

It was clear he didn't understand. "Bozo?"

"When you have red hair, the other kids always call you Bozo. You get defensive about it."

He nodded slowly, as though he did understand that. Then he added, "But you're beautiful. Still, you're defensive about everything."

She was rendered momentarily speechless by the compliment. Everyone, Ben included, had always told her she was cute. No one had ever called her "beautiful."

"Well," she replied belatedly, "I'm defensive because you're changing my world."

"Just a little. And you'll still be the same."

She wasn't so sure about that.

They stared at each other for a moment, then he said, serious again, "I meant spend time with me to help me get acquainted with the vines, with the process, with everything I need to know to make this work.''

She drew a deep breath, hoping she wasn't putting herself out of a job. "I can help with the vines," she said, then added candidly, "but all I know about the wine making is what I've read in books. I've studied hard, but my father has all the practical experience. And the instincts. And anyway, I understand you've already made a deal with him."

"Deal?"

She told him about Megan and Katie, and their insistence that one had to have a deal in order to remain. "Dad told me you hired him as your adviser."

"That's true." Tate unlocked his door and pushed it open. "But I don't want to aggravate his arthritis by dragging him around the place during a cold, wet winter. I thought we'd save our discussions for the fireside. You, however—" he smiled suddenly "—are young and agile and could help me despite the weather. You can be my field adviser, if you have to tell the girls you have a title."

His field adviser. "I'll think about it," she promised as he got out of the Jeep. She stepped out, too, and walked around to climb into the driver's seat.

He pushed the door closed and leaned on it. "I'll pay you…" He named a sum that doubled what she'd been making for the past two years.

She barely withheld an unsophisticated gasp. She had Ben's insurance, and her father refused to take any rent from her, but health insurance took a big chunk out of what she allowed herself monthly. Also, she worried constantly about the girls' education. She held out her hand without thinking about the offer too long. "You now have a field adviser."

His hand engulfed hers and the contact caused her to have an instant and vivid memory of his fingers cupping her breast.

As she looked into his eyes, he leaned over her, and she knew that he had noticed her reaction.

"Yes," he said quietly. "With everyone watching, I thought it best not to say anything you'd have to explain. It was an accident, and I'd apologize, but it was too sweet a moment."

She discovered that the body working at double speed slowed performance rather than enhanced it.

She opened her mouth to disabuse him of any conclusion he might have jumped to, but he forestalled her when he straightened and nodded.

"I know. Just a field adviser. All I want right now, too." He slapped the palm of his hand down on the knob to lock her door. "I'll be leaving in a couple of days for a week or two, then I'll be back."

"Good." She struggled to pull herself together. "I'll have the pruning done by then and we can plant the mustard."

"Mustard?"

"Between the rows," she explained. "It's a green fertilizer and serves to aerate the roots of the vines."

"All right. I'll come by before I leave."

With a wave she drove away. As she followed the road home, she tried to reconstruct what had just happened and discovered that she couldn't remember much of their conversation.

Instead her memory had retained details of his face as they'd talked—a warm smile, the snap of temper in his dark eyes, humor struggling with it, eventually lightening them. The set of his jaw, the way his brow furrowed in concentration, the afternoon dampness beading in his thick dark hair.

She had a mushy sensation in the pit of her stomach that was at odds with the toughness she'd adopted to get herself from day to day when Ben died.

Ben. She couldn't forget Ben. He wasn't just the husband she'd adored, the father of her children, the reason for all her goals and dreams—he was her hero.

And it was becoming harder to remember all the details about him, which she'd held close for so long. She had to guard against losing them.

She let her excitement deflate and reminded herself that this was just a job. Just a job.

But it felt like more.

THE AROMA OF garlic and onions filled the house as Tate walked into the living room. Mike, sitting in one corner of the sofa with the cellular phone, his stocking feet propped up on the old trunk, waved at him.

"Okay, that's good, Whitey," Mike was saying. "I'll be home to pack what I'm keeping, then I'll set up the garage sale for you and the boys, and their club can have the proceeds if you'll take what doesn't sell to the thrift shop or the dump. Great. I'll see you day after tomorrow."

Tate removed his jacket and opened it out on the back of the overstuffed chair. Then he sat down and pulled off his boots.

Mike turned off the phone and placed it on the coffee table between them. "Thanks. Gave my landlady notice, and got a friend who works with teenagers to run a garage sale for me."

"You're not shipping any furniture?"

"No. Whitey's wife knows a secondhand store that can make me a little money on it. And we have what we need here." He looked around at the old but comfortable furniture.

Shea came out of the kitchen with two steaming mugs and set them in the middle of the coffee table. It didn't smell like coffee.

Tate picked up the mug and sat back in his chair. A sweet and spicy aroma wafted around him and the brew in his cup was a dark red.

"Mulled wine," Shea said, hands on his hips, obviously waiting for Tate and Mike to try it. "Be a good winter drink for the restaurant, don't you think?"

Tate sipped and felt the warm, lightly alcoholic, nicely spiced liquid ease down his throat and warm him.

"Good stuff," he said, relaxing almost instantly. The coziness of the house after the invigorating but chilly fresh air, and the delicious drink, were untangling his mind following his conversation with Colette.

She was interesting, he thought, but too complex. He was tired of complex women. Sandy had been wonderful on many levels but was too determined to have life the way she wanted it regardless of whatever anyone else needed.

Only, he hadn't understood that at first because

she'd been so charming, so sexy, so good at making him believe that he was the selfish one.

But he didn't want to think about that now. He raised his cup to Shea. "Definitely a winner."

Mike agreed, then asked Shea, "Where's yours?"

Shea pointed back toward the kitchen. "I'm cooking."

Tate frowned at him. "Can't you put it all on simmer, or something?"

Shea shook his head pityingly. "That's the reason *I'm* a chef and you're an architect."

"So, it doesn't come out Cordon Bleu quality," Mike said. "It's just us."

Shea gave him the same look. "I can't prepare bad food. That would be like you letting a perp go or Tate building something he knows will collapse. I have to do it right. That's my job here. And since I don't have the money to contribute, I..."

Tate put his mug down on the coffee table, walked past a startled Shea and into the kitchen, where he shut off the heat under a pan in which garlic and onions were simmering in butter. Then he found a pot filled with the spicy wine Shea had just served.

He ladled out a cup and turned to carry it back to the living room but found his way blocked by Shea, who stood in the middle of the doorway.

"You don't mess with my cooking," Shea said grimly.

Tate handed him the cup. "I didn't mess with anything. I just shut off the frying pan and—"

"It's a sautée pan."

"Whatever. It doesn't define what you are to this operation. The three of us are partners, and while you're wonderful with food and a clear asset to us, you can save the labor for the restaurant. In this house—where we're just us—you're not the cook. And you're not required to wait on us because we put up money, and you didn't."

A range of emotions passed through Shea's eyes, pride uppermost, followed by gratitude.

"All right," he said finally. "No need to sermonize."

"Then will you go sit down so that I can get to my wine before it's cold?"

Shea sat on the sofa in the corner opposite Mike, then moved in a little when he couldn't reach the coffee table to put up his feet.

Tate reclaimed the chair and reached for his mug. Then he focused his attention on Mike. "While I'm on the subject, you don't have to sell everything you have in the world to make a financial contribution to the place. Since the idea to try to get the winery running again is mine, let me foot the bill. If we need capital later, you guys can kick in."

Mike and Shea looked at each other before turning back to Tate to say simultaneously, "No."

"If we're equal partners," Mike said, "then we have to make the contributions we feel we can in order to carry our part of the load. And you have to let us do that."

"Yeah," Tate admitted, "but I don't want you to be penniless if I'm wrong about this."

Mike raised his head from the back of the sofa in feigned shock. "You? Wrong? Don't shatter our world." He rested his head again and grinned confidently. "Anyway, I like the idea, and the more I think about it, the more I think we can pull it off."

"Me, too." Shea sipped at his mug. "So we sink or swim together. If you are wrong, I can teach you and Mike to be waiters."

Mike recrossed his ankles on the table. "And I know triplets in Las Cruces who'll let us live in their trailer."

Tate smiled and nodded. "It's always good to have an alternate plan. Guess we have to come up with a name."

"You mean aliases?" Shea took a pillow from the corner of the sofa and leaned an elbow on it.

Tate sighed patiently. "I mean a company name. And we should use it whenever we do anything on behalf of the business. The something-or-other vineyards or winery or cellars. Or we could keep Valley Winery."

"I think it should be something new," Shea put in. "Since it's a new direction for all of us."

"What about just our name?" Mike suggested. "Delancey Vineyards." He tried out the sound. "Delancey Winery. Delancey Cellars." He paused, then said it again. "Delancey Cellars. What about that? The rhythm's good."

Shea frowned. "But we don't have any cellars. And we won't for a while. We're sort of starting from scratch."

"Picky, picky. Delancey Vineyards, then?"

"It doesn't have to be Delancey at all," Tate said. "We could name it French River."

Mike stared into his cup, thinking. "I like Delancey. Don't you?" he asked Shea.

Shea nodded. "Yeah. I like it."

"Delancey Vineyards it is." Tate sipped at his wine. "Now you have to come up with a design for our label."

Mike lowered his feet. "Isn't that a little premature if we won't have wine for a couple of years?"

"Well, you don't have to do it today. But keep the thought on the back burner and make it something brilliant. We should have it to go with our publicity info. And we'll want it represented on the wall in our tasting room. You can help him, Shea."

"I thought we were all in this together," Shea argued. "Equal partners et cetera. You're the one who makes those cool architect's renderings."

"With help from a computer and a pencil plotter."

"A what?"

"Never mind. You'll see it when it arrives. Meanwhile, you'll need something to do to fill the lonely evenings while Mike and I are settling things in Boston and Dallas."

Shea gathered up empty mugs. "You're going, too?"

"Yeah. A week ought to do it. I'm going to make arrangements for the sale of my partnership, close up my place and ship my office equipment and some of my furniture here. If it arrives before I get back, be careful with it, okay?"

"Okay. You want me to do anything while you're gone?"

"Just keep an eye on Aunt Rachel, be handy if Armand needs anything and relax. When Mike and I get back, we'll finalize plans for remodeling and restoring the winery, plan the restaurant and think about the B and B. So, get your rest now.''

"When are you leaving?" Mike asked.

"If you're going day after tomorrow," Tate replied, getting to his feet, "I'll do the same and we can drive to the airport together. When are you coming back?"

"I'll only be a couple of days." Mike grinned. "No partnership to sell off. I'll be driving my Blazer, though. Anything you want from Texas?"

"Good barbecue sauce." Shea headed for the kitchen. "I'll do some ribs when you get back."

"And I'll come pick you up at the airport," Mike said. "Or would you rather Colette did that?"

Tate studied his expression, looking for the taunt he was sure that remark contained, but he found only innocence. In Mike, that alone was proof of the contrary.

"Now, why would you say that?"

"I happened to be looking out the window when you drove up," Mike answered. "You two chatted for a while, stared a bit, then shook hands—a rather protracted shake, if you ask me. Do I detect a romance?"

Tate had to laugh. "I think it's quite the opposite. She doesn't like me. You noticed that yourself last night, remember?"

"Last night she didn't appear as interested as she did today."

"That's only because I doubled her salary."

"Generous. How do you know the winery can afford it?"

"She has two little mouths to feed and she works

like three men. *I* can afford it, even if the business can't.''

"Here we go, gentlemen.'' Shea appeared, three mugs clutched in one hand. He'd refilled each with the mulled wine. "This is an auspicious occasion. Calls for a toast.''

They held up their mugs and said simultaneously, hopefully, "To Delancey Vineyards!''

## CHAPTER SIX

TATE FOUND Colette pruning vines. He and Mike were leaving for the airport in fifteen minutes, and he had to say goodbye before he left. She was the one who was really in charge of the vineyard, after all. She should know how to reach him if there was a problem.

"Hi," he said as she looked up at his approach. She straightened and pushed the hood of her jacket back. A thick, wet mist hung in the air and smelled like an herb garden.

"Mike and I are taking off, but I wanted you to know where to reach me if you or your father needs anything." He handed her a business card, on the back of which he'd written his home and cell phone numbers.

Colette took the card, thinking that it had been ages since a man had offered to be available if she required help. Oh, her father was always nearby and would run to her defense in a minute, but generally he considered her quite competent and never thought to back her up unless she asked.

"Thank you," she said. She guessed she looked like Medusa, spirals of red hair sticking up everywhere like weirdly colored snakes. She raised a hand to smooth down the wisps, but from December to

May in Oregon, her hair was hopeless. Tate was a business associate, anyway. He probably didn't even notice.

"I appreciate that, but I'm sure we'll be fine."

His eyes roved her face, then went to her hair, and she saw a small smile form on his lips.

"Bozo?" she asked, smiling, too.

He laughed lightly. "No. Not at all. There's something very appealing about a tousled woman."

Tousled. The word suggested sheets and pillows and sleepy mornings. She felt herself beginning to get flustered.

"When will you be back?" she asked calmly, remembering that he'd said all he'd needed from her was field advice.

"A week from today." He put his hands in the pockets of his long cashmere overcoat. She was surprised to see he'd worn his rubber boots with it. "Mike's going to pick me up. He'll be back a couple of days before me. Shea'll be staying, though, so you can call him if you need something immediately. We got a phone yesterday. That number's on the card, too."

"All right." She smiled with the competent confidence she was so eager to reflect, because that was who she was at heart. This breathless, in-a-dither woman she became when he looked at her wasn't really her at all. She'd never been an airhead. Ben had loved her no-nonsense manner.

But she gazed into Tate's eyes and saw…concern. And something else. Something unclear, possibly not even completely formed. Something that looked like…desire?

An answering spark flared in her chest and her right hand made an unconscious move toward his sleeve.

Before she could even wonder what was happening, he had her in his arms and was kissing her with a slow, seductive deliberation that dissolved a budding thought of protest.

Her brain simply refused to engage and allow reason to function. She guessed later that it was because her senses were in control.

She tasted him—a hint of coffee and toothpaste. He had the cool, mobile lips of man who knew precisely what he was doing.

She heard wind in the vines, the call of crows and the whoosh of a cloud of starlings that were the enemy once the grapes came.

She felt the soft, expensive texture of his coat under her fingertips, and his hand at her back. The sensation was blunted by her coat, but gooseflesh rose along her scalp.

She caught a whiff of a cologne that made her think of smoking pipes and firesides.

He finally pulled away from her but held her for one extended moment while he studied her in frowning perplexity. Then he dropped his hands and opened his mouth to speak, but it seemed as though what he wanted to say wouldn't come. He looked up at the sky, then down at her again and finally said on a brisk note, ''Call if you need me.''

Then he was striding away—a fashion dichotomy in cashmere coat and rubber boots.

Her brain came to life and she was flooded with

reaction. She felt as if her heart followed him up the road.

*Oh, no,* she thought. *No!*

BILL MARKHAM WAS waiting for Tate at the airport that night. He was short and squarely built, a design genius with an enthusiasm that was infectious. He talked nonstop as they drove through the tunnel under the Charles River, headed for Tate's condo.

"I hope you don't mind, but I set a breakfast meeting for us with Charlie McCann. He's so eager to assume your partnership that he's changed into someone unrecognizable. He's usually so dour at cocktail parties, you know?" Bill made a dour face at Tate, then screeched to a stop as the traffic slowed. Driving through Boston was like driving through hell. Riding with Bill in Boston was like being stalled in hell.

"I guess he's tired of going it alone and knows he'll do bigger and more interesting jobs in a partnership. But I wasn't sure he had the money. And I mean, I know you need to cash out to be able to do this brewery thing."

"Winery thing," Tate corrected.

Bill glanced at him in surprise and almost took out a mailbox.

"Watch—" Tate began to warn, then Bill righted the car.

"I got it!" he said. "I got it! Gina wants you to come over for dinner while you're here, and she says when you get your stuff cleared out, you can stay at our place until you're ready to leave. Jacob's doing great, feeling a lot better. We're even getting a little sleep. Oh. About McCann's money. He has some. Gina says she heard his wife inherited. I mean, he's done some small jobs around town, and one on Long Island somewhere, but, you know, not enough to enable him to buy you out. Or so *I* thought. But Gina knows all, and damn if she wasn't right. He's ready with cash. So I thought we'd get him before he changes his mind. Okay? Eight o'clock?''

As Tate opened his mouth to reply, Bill passed a slow-moving van on the right and the outward push of sound became an indrawn gasp of panic as a pickup screeched to a halt in the process of exiting a gas station.

''I got it! I got it!'' Bill promised again, swerving around the truck just in time to save Tate's life, or, at minimum, the use of the right side of his body.

''You're quiet today, Tate,'' Bill observed as traffic eased. It was Tate's opinion that everyone within a four-block radius was now giving Bill space. ''You want to tell me what brought about this decision? Gina has a theory, you know. She doesn't think Sandy was ever the woman for you, that you two just kept it going for the girls, and now that you're free of her, you're looking for Mrs. Right. Is *she* on the money?''

The interrogation and the cheerful banter continued for six days—through the sale of Tate's partnership in Delancey, Markham and Free to Charlie McCann; the various arrangements made to ship some of his office equipment and furniture; showing the condo; and the surprise, last-minute sale of the condo to a friend of Gina's.

Tate studied his bank balance, and though he'd

been accustomed to a hefty salary and yearly bonuses from the partnership, he felt like a mogul of some kind.

Then common sense took over. He added to the college funds he'd set up for his daughters at the time of his divorce and made a contribution to the one Bill and Gina had started for Jacob.

The quiet dinner at Le Marquis de Lafayette, which Bill had promised him on his last night in town, turned out to be a farewell party that included everyone from the office and, it seemed, everyone they'd ever done business with.

For the first time since he'd made the decision to revive the winery, he felt uncertain. In this room filled with everyone and everything familiar, he thought about acres of grapes that would wither and die if the wrong decisions were made, of decrepit buildings that would cost a mint to restore, of big plans that would require unlimited heart and energy to see them through—and wondered what in the hell he thought he was doing.

Then his mind created an image of a woman dwarfed by an oversize coat, standing alone in a muddy row of grapevines under a heavy sky—and the insecurity subsided.

He stood still, tuning out what went on around him, simply wondering what on earth it meant. The panic had felt very real, and now it was gone. Vanquished by a mental picture of Colette Palmer.

She'd looked stunned and a little offended when he'd kissed her, though she'd been the one to make the first move.

He could have sworn she'd enjoyed it as much as

he had. But what did he know? Two weeks ago he'd been an architect with a solid business future; today he was a man who'd liquidated all his assets and was heading west to garden.

And he wasn't afraid.

Paradoxically, that was the scariest part of all.

Cece came to wrap her arms around him. She wore a short black cardigan, one button done up at the throat, and a pair of diaphanous black pants. She looked worried.

"Are you going to be okay?" she asked. "You're sure this is the right thing to do? Sometimes when people die, those left behind tend to get rid of everything and move away, but that isn't..."

"Cece." He put a hand to her arm to stop her. "Sandy didn't die—we got a divorce. And that really doesn't have anything to do with this. It's just an opportunity that's come up at a time when I'm free to take advantage of it."

She nodded, but he could see that she didn't believe him. She was convinced he was a broken man.

"Okay," she said, patting his hand. "Just remember that we're most vulnerable in the process of change. So be careful, Boss."

"Don't worry about me." He gently clasped the hand that was patting his. "What about you? How do you like Mr. McCann so far?"

She sighed mournfully. "Well, he's nice enough. But he asked me to only make *regular* coffee." She emphasized the word with scorn. "Imagine. In this age of being able to try a new coffee every day for four months running, he wants regular coffee. What do you suppose he designs? Storage units?"

Tate resisted the temptation to laugh. "He probably has other qualities you'll learn to appreciate."

"Maybe. But what I admired about you was your adventurous soul. You gave me a job in spite of my not very good references because you knew how much I wanted another chance. You didn't worry about what would happen when I eventually screwed up—you just thought about the importance of giving me a chance."

He wondered if that had been true or if she was giving him more credit than he deserved. Actually, all he remembered was that she'd seemed so eager, and he'd seen in her the spark of someone who connected with people and cared about them.

Toward the end of his marriage, when Sandy had stopped even pretending that it meant anything to her, he'd watched her at parties, kissing the air, tossing compliments and making promises, all in the interest of business, and he'd begun to question whether his life was real at all.

Then Cece had walked in and restored his faith.

She hugged him again. "I'm gonna miss you."

"Well..." Was he going to regret this? Probably. "If you decide you can't stand to make regular coffee, Mr. Markham knows how to reach me. Maybe I can help you find a job in Oregon."

She smiled appreciatively. "Thanks, Mr. Delancey. But that's not going to happen. There's my mom, you know, and I can't leave. I'm all she's got."

"I understand. Call me even if you just need someone to talk to."

"Okay." She walked away, leaving him feeling as

though he should quickly add a footnote to Mc-Cann's contract forcing him to let Cece make flavored coffees at least one morning a week.

Bill, Gina and Jacob saw him off the following morning. Gina cried and Bill pursed his lips. He embraced them both for long moments. There was nothing left to say when you'd reshaped a skyline together.

He kissed a squirmy Jacob on the cheek, then walked through the gate, buoyed by the friendships that distance couldn't break.

He made notes to himself on the plane, committing the scores of ideas swirling in his head to paper.

Between Boston and Chicago, he redesigned the winery building.

Between Chicago and Portland, he made a restaurant out of the bunkhouse—at least in rough form.

At PDX Tate went to the baggage carousel where Mike had promised to meet him. Intent on finding a tall, dark-featured figure in a leather jacket, Tate looked right over the top of Colette's head.

Then a hand came into his peripheral vision and he looked down. Colette. He'd never seen her in anything but work clothes, and stared for a few minutes before recognizing her in slim jeans and a white shirt under a Black Watch tartan jacket. Her red hair was free and stood out brightly against the chic but dark jacket.

She'd come to get him! Maybe he'd been mistaken about her reaction to that goodbye kiss. Maybe she'd actually missed him.

His blood was beginning to heat, when he looked

into her eyes and saw that she appeared far less enthused about spotting him.

So she was here against her will and he'd been right. She had hated the kiss. He couldn't decide if he was relieved or disappointed. On one hand, she was beautiful and interesting, but on the other, she was moody and enigmatic. And there was enough mystery in his life at the moment.

"Hi," he said, doing his best to sound friendly and employer-like. "Where's Mike?"

"Lots of industry going on at the winery," she said, reaching for his briefcase. "And none of the men wanted to leave. I couldn't even get my daughters to keep me company. I'll hold this while you get your bags."

"Industry?" he asked.

Before she could explain, there was the thunk of luggage hitting the carousel, and travelers waiting to claim their things converged on the offerings.

"I'll stay here," she said.

Tate pulled off a blue nylon suit bag filled to bursting with things he might never wear again, and waited several more revolutions until a soft-side case in the same color appeared.

He turned toward Colette and she started for the exit signs. After they'd negotiated the escalator and headed for the terminal doors, he asked again, "Industry? They're not trying to build anything on their own, are they?"

She looked as though she didn't want to smile, but she did anyway. "No, they're not. But they are busy. I'm not supposed to spoil the surprise."

"Colette, it's an hour home," he said, sidling

through the doors as she held them open for him. "My peace of mind is at stake here."

He noticed the sweet air and breathed it in. And there was no rain. The sun was feeble, but it was there.

Colette shook her head firmly, looking professional as she walked across to the parking structure with his briefcase in hand. She might have been a lawyer or a corporate vice president, instead of a vintner who was usually knee-deep in mud.

"I *can* tell you that dinner is beef bourguignon. My father happened to mention to Shea that he loves it. And Shea said it'd be a good recipe for the restaurant since it requires a robust red wine and brandy." She led the way across the parking structure to the elevator and pushed the up button. "He's invited all of us over as kind of a christening of the winery and your plans for it."

The doors parted on an empty car, and she held them open until he was inside. Then she got in and pushed three.

The doors closed and tension seemed to suck the air out of the small space. He was sure it was something only he felt, until he saw Colette drag in a breath, then fan at her face as though trying to stir a breeze.

She stared into the other corner of the car, apparently determined to avoid his gaze.

"Pruning finished?" he asked, wondering if he was imagining her discomfort.

"Day before yesterday," she replied, still not looking at him. She watched the floor indicator above the door. "Did you get everything done at home?"

He nodded, then realized she wouldn't see that. "Yes," he said. "Home is now officially French River."

The doors opened on the third level and she put a hand out to hold them so that he could pass through. "You look exhausted," she observed.

He frowned teasingly as she followed him out. "Men don't like to hear that any more than women do. You're telling me I have bloodshot eyes with bags under them?"

"No," she replied, smiling at him over her shoulder as she moved past him. "I'm just saying you look as though packing up your old life wasn't as easy as you make it sound."

"You're presuming that."

"No, I know that."

"How could you possibly?"

She stopped at the back of a blue Blazer with Texas plates, dug a key out of the pocket of her jacket and pulled down the tailgate. He tossed in his bags, she handed him his briefcase, which he also put inside.

When Colette looked up after unlocking the doors, he was waiting for an answer. She didn't want to get into this with him. She hadn't wanted to get personal at all, but she'd seen him striding through the baggage area, tall and strong looking and confident and she'd felt the attraction that had gotten her into trouble the day he'd left.

Her hand had moved toward him seemingly of its own volition and he'd kissed her.

She'd regretted it all week long. Regretted that she'd liked it.

This tension wasn't going to go away unless she confronted the attraction and bested it. Because *he* wasn't going away.

"I'm a mother," she said, assuming a friendly demeanor that she hoped said she had no sexual interest in him whatsoever, despite the goodbye kiss. "I can read eyes."

"Now, how can you do that," he asked, "when you haven't looked into mine since we met at the baggage carousel?"

He had her there. Friendly, she reminded herself. Disinterested in anything else.

"It doesn't require staring if you're good at it." She tried to distract him from this line of conversation by holding up the car keys. "As I recall from our brief ride in the Jeep, you like to drive."

He wrapped his hand around the keys, catching the tips of her fingers and holding her in place. "All right," he said. "Let's see if I'm as good at this as you are." He looked directly into her eyes. She looked back, doing her best to appear undisturbed, but she had the most unsettling feeling he was seeing things she'd hidden carefully from everyone else.

After a moment he frowned and dropped her hand. "You like me. You don't want to, but you do. And you're worried about that," he said.

She put her hands in her jacket pockets and wondered if that was too self-protective a gesture. "I thought I'd made it clear that I don't like you. Remember that discussion before you left about all the changes you're making to the place I love?"

He nodded, his eyes still on hers, as though he were continuing to read her. "I think that's the root of the trouble. You're upset with yourself because you're attracted to me in spite of what you think I'm going to do. *You* reached out to *me* for that goodbye kiss.''

She closed her eyes for an instant, embarrassed. When she opened them again, he was smiling.

''It would have been gentlemanly of you not to mention that,'' she said. ''And I might have reached a hand toward you, but you certainly made the most of the opportunity.''

He laughed softly. ''That's what I'm all about, Colctte. I never waste an opportunity.'' Then the humor left his voice. ''But it was more than that. It felt like a gift. Come on. It's getting cold out here.''

He let her into the vehicle, then walked around and climbed in. He backed out of the parking spot and followed the arrows to the exit.

A gift. She struggled against a little glow of warmth.

They were on the freeway before he glanced her way again. Noticing the sun in her eyes, he reached over to lower her sun visor.

''Where did you live before you came to French River?'' he asked.

''Seattle. I went to school there.''

''You met your husband in school?''

''No.'' She watched the shopping malls and industrial complexes speed by and thought it strange that the pain of Ben's loss could be so fresh when the life they'd shared seemed as though it had taken place in another lifetime. ''I lived in a dorm with a bunch of other girls, and somebody's hot plate started a fire and before we knew what had happened the whole floor was engulfed in flames."

He looked at her with a frown. "You were in the building?"

She nodded, smiling ruefully. "I was in the shower, so I didn't even know anything had happened until I opened the bathroom door and found my room filled with smoke. I tried to go into the hallway, but the smoke was thicker there and I couldn't see anything. So I ran to the window, but I couldn't open it. Most of the crowd's attention was focused on the corner of the building where the other girls were coming out, but one fireman saw me, and he ran for the entrance."

Her sigh reflected the relief she'd felt at the knowledge someone was aware she was in the building.

"The smoke was so thick. It hurt to breathe. I opened the door to go out into the hall and stayed down on all fours, trying to head for the door the fireman had used to come in. Then I heard him calling me."

"He knew your name?"

She smiled. "No. He was shouting, 'Where are you, gorgeous? Speak to me!' I could hear him opening doors. I tried to shout, but I couldn't. Then he fell over me. When I woke up, he was carrying me outside. One of the other firemen was yelling at him for going into the building without telling anybody. And he said, 'I saw this face in a third-story window, like Juliet looking for Romeo.' Then he asked me out."

Tate laughed. "My kind of guy. Clearly one to take advantage of an opportunity."

She nodded. "We were married two months later. I would have never made it out of the building on my own. If he hadn't seen me and come for me…I wouldn't be here today."

Tate studied the road. The guy had saved her life. He'd truly been her hero as well as her husband. Not a claim many men could make.

There'd been a point in his marriage when Sandy had considered him an asset to her career; then, when he'd taken a stand against the every-night cocktail parties, she'd told him he was detrimental to her plans for the future.

While he'd been convinced he was right, it had hurt to hear that. And he'd felt the loss of all they'd once meant to each other.

"Did he die in a fire?" he asked gently.

"He died because of a fire. The roof of a warehouse collapsed when he was trying to drag out a friend who'd become disoriented." She said it unemotionally, as though she'd taught herself to hear the words without flinching. "He was hit by a beam. Just a glancing blow—so he thought he was all right. He got up and pulled his friend out. But a blood vessel had been broken…" She sighed and leaned her head back. "A *subdural hematoma* is the proper term. He was everything to me," she added, a little defensively, he thought. "He was a hero and there just aren't that many today. I can't simply get on with my life as though everything we had together isn't burned into my brain." He felt her looking at him and turned quickly to meet her gaze. "And I don't want to."

That was clearly put. She was entitled to have things the way she wanted them.

But, damn it, so was he. The last couple of years had been about living Sandy's life because he'd been trying to protect his children.

Then it had all fallen apart and he'd felt all angry and resentful. He'd considered it grossly unfair that he'd had to lose his children because he and their mother could no longer deal with each other. But he'd tried to do the noble thing once he'd met Dudley and learned that he was decent if eccentric. He'd tried to upset Sandy's plans—and therefore his daughters'—as little as possible.

This was his second chance. The winery was his opportunity to start over, to have things the way he wanted them for a change.

And he wanted at least the opportunity to get to know Colette. She might be emotionally paralyzed by her husband's death, and Tate might find the attraction between them was no more than that, but he had the right to make the discovery for himself.

He wanted to ask her if Katie's silence was somehow related to Ben's death, but Colette looked as if she didn't want to talk about that anymore.

"I once rescued a mean tomcat from a tree," he said, setting out to lighten the mood. "I know it's not as good as a burning building, but the cat must have weighed thirty pounds at least. And he'd been up there a couple of days. He was pretty ticked off."

"How'd you get him down?" Her voice had lightened.

"Charm," he replied.

"No, really," she said. "How'd you get him down?"

He pretended hurt feelings. "You don't think I can be charming?"

"Yes, I do. But only in the interest of getting things your way, which wouldn't work with a cat."

He gave her a deliberately superior glance. "It'll work with anything—or anyone."

She shook her head doubtfully. "You'll have to prove that."

He smiled. "I intend to."

## CHAPTER SEVEN

As he drove the Blazer up the hill and into the compound, Tate gazed around him and felt a surge of excitement. He loved looking at a blank piece of real estate and figuring out its potential.

But this wasn't a museum or a high rise or a mall built to someone else's specs. This was his—well, theirs; his and Mike's and Shea's. But his brothers were willing to follow his lead. The Delancey Vineyards. Jack would like that, he thought.

When he pulled the vehicle to a stop in front of the house, Tate saw the front door open cautiously and Megan and Katie step out. Seeing the Blazer, the girls ran quickly back inside again.

Even with the windows rolled up, Tate heard Megan's high voice call, "They're here!"

"Looks like your daughters are visiting," Tate observed.

Colette nodded and smiled. It was a mysterious smile, he thought. But, then, she was a mysterious woman.

"They've been baking with Shea while you were gone," she said. "I've had to pry them out of your house every night to get them home for dinner. They've taken a real shine to your brothers."

"Thanks for coming for me," he said when they

were out of the vehicle, expecting her to hurry off. "I'll take the girls home later."

She pulled his briefcase out of the back. "I'll help you carry your things in."

"That's not necessary," he protested, but she was already striding up the porch steps.

He followed, and as she stepped aside to let him open the door, he turned the knob and walked into the living room.

At least, he thought it was the living room.

The dingy interior had been painted a soft creamy white that made the ugly furnishings appear far less horrible. A colorful, richly textured throw had been placed at an angle over the back of the sofa, and there was a grapevine wreath on one wall, dried leaves still attached at the bottom. Grouped around it were framed photographs.

The smell of fresh paint hung in the air, and the house had a sparkle that hadn't been there when Tate left.

He turned to Colette, stunned. "Did you do this?"

She shrugged. "I contributed. But I think I hear most of the culprits whispering upstairs."

Tate paused to listen, and heard scurrying and unsuccessfully suppressed laughter from the top of the stairway.

He put his bags down and headed up.

Megan and Katie met him at the landing, beside themselves with excitement, and walked the rest of the way with him.

Armand and Rachel stood with Mike and Shea in the newly painted hallway. It was now a light blue-gray that was carried into the bedrooms, as well. The woodwork was a crisp white, and someone—Rachel, he guessed—had made curtains. Tate's were a bold gray-and-red plaid, Mike's dark-blue-and-gray paisley, and Shea's a teal-and-gray stripe.

These rooms, too, had been scrubbed, and each had a smaller wreath and more pictures on the wall.

"Mommy made the wreaths," Megan told him, "and Aunt Rachel found all the pictures in the attic and went to the junk shop for frames."

Tate was surprised to find himself almost overwhelmed with emotion. This was a testimonial to their belief in the project, proof to him that they were behind him and could work together toward what had become a common goal.

He caught Mike's eye and saw the silent promise there that had always been a part of their relationship. It had seen them through schoolyard fights, their parents' deaths, Tate's divorce and Mike's first leave of absence from the police department.

It said simply—I'm here.

Shea's gaze said the same thing, only more aggressively, because as the youngest brother, he'd always had the most to prove.

Armand shook Tate's hand, and Rachel threw her arms around him. "I can't tell you how happy I am that you boys have decided to come home. Well, I know this isn't technically home, but Jack enjoyed you boys so much he would have stolen you from your parents if he could have. When you're loved that much, that makes it home."

Colette's eyes told him one thing and then another. 'You're right, I do like you, but that's all. There will never be anything else so forget it.'

Megan and Katie, however, dragged him into his room to show him what they'd made him, a sure sign of their affection. "It's our handprints," Megan said, pointing to the baked clay disks hanging on the wall with loops of red ribbon. "Shea made the stuff, then he baked it for us. It's like our handshake, and means that we'll always work really hard."

Tate hugged them both, thinking they made up in a small way for the absence of his daughters. He straightened and looked at everyone.

"Thank you," he said. "I don't know what to say."

"Good." Mike gestured him toward the stairs. "You talk too much, anyway. Come on. Dinner's on and the aroma's been driving us crazy for the past few hours."

Someone had set the dining room table with a lace cloth, and the clunky diner dishes had been placed on it like the finest china. Rachel had brought candlesticks and Armand had brought his kitchen chairs so that they all crowded around the table to eat the beef bourguignon Shea had made.

They lit the candles and ate in the warm shadows as though it were a formal occasion of great importance.

Tate thought it was. The work everyone had done while he was gone reinforced his already strong determination to give the Delancey Vineyards his all.

He'd lost one family, but he'd been given another.

"This," Armand said some time later, pointing to his empty plate, "must go on the restaurant menu. I haven't ever tasted it prepared this well, even in Paris."

Shea inclined his head, accepting the praise graciously. "Thank you, Armand. We'll have to serve a light fare, also, for those watching their waistlines and their cardiovascular systems, but for those of us who simply love to indulge—some hearty recipes, as well."

"Excellent!" Armand leaned back with a contented sigh. "The French, you know, do not believe that life should be lived in moderation. One must give everything, and to do so, one must be fueled by the best food."

"Amen to that," Rachel concurred. "I've always believed in putting real butter in cookies."

Mike raised his glass to her. "And we believe in your cookies."

"So, what's our first step?" Shea asked Tate after they'd all helped clear the table.

"I sketched out a plan on the plane." Tate put his napkin down beside his empty plate and got to his feet. "It's in my briefcase."

"I'll get it!" Megan cried, leaping out of her chair.

Katie mouthed a protest and followed, trying to overtake her, clearly wanting to be the one to provide the small service.

The sound of a tussle could be heard at the bottom of the stairs.

But when the girls returned, each was holding one of the double handles.

Tate thanked them and put the plans down in the middle of the table. Everyone leaned toward them.

"It's rough," he said, "but this is how I see it. Of course, it's only cosmetic, and the real work—and the source of our success—will be on what we do inside. So, what I'll need from each of you is a list of what you'd like to have for your area—Armand for the winery, Colette for the vineyard, Shea for the restaurant, Mike for the B and B. Maybe make two lists—the first a practical one and the second a dream list. We'll try to fill the first and work at eventually filling the second. Okay?''

Everyone nodded, still studying the sketches.

''We'll meet here once a week for business discussions and planning until we have an office in the winery.''

''I'll provide the pastries for our meetings,'' Rachel volunteered, then turned in sudden concern to Shea. ''Or is that stepping on your toes?''

Shea shook his head. ''Not at all. In fact, if you feel up to it, once the tasting room's open, maybe you could bake the sweet things to go with the wine.'' He turned to Tate with a look of bliss. ''She makes a peach tart that's to die for.''

Rachel looked astonished.

''Well, then she'll have to split her time,'' Tate said, ''because I was thinking that children visiting with their parents might enjoy visiting with her menagerie. Sort of like a petting zoo. We could spruce up the pen a little. What do you think, Aunt Rachel?''

She put a hand to her heart and patted it. ''I…think I'd like that. Both things.''

''I don't mean to create problems,'' Mike said, ''but are we going to have some sanitation problems because there are animals on a property where a product is being prepared for consumption?''

''Good point,'' Rachel agreed, ''but Jack already looked into it. My pens are on a hard surface that's washed into a septic tank and draining field at the bottom of the north side of the slope. We're covered.''

''Excellent.'' Tate felt an arm come around his shoulders and glanced up to find Katie leaning against him, reading his page of notes. Apparently aware she'd been noticed, she looked into his eyes and smiled.

He'd spent enough time with his daughters to understand that while time stretched eternally for children, emotions were immediate. Temper was loosed instantly, pain decried hotly and love given without hesitation.

The small gesture touched him. In the past couple of years he'd lost so much, and Katie's little smile was very welcome. He lifted her onto his knee and the dinner table discussion continued.

COLETTE WATCHED Katie sitting on Tate's knee, looking like the queen of the universe, and tried not to worry. It was a simple case of hero worship. Children got that all the time.

But Megan, who loved her sister dearly and also resented her desperately as a contender for attention and affection, sat across the table, arms folded, face set in a pout.

She, too, had come to worship Tate in the two brief days he'd been at the compound before going back to Boston. She'd talked about him all the time he was gone, reciting over and over what he'd said, what he'd done, how wonderful it would be when he returned.

Despite the inconvenience of having her children

adore a man who seemed ready to become a problem in her life, Colette was willing to put up with it because their father's death had left a gaping hole in their little lives.

Colette's father was always there for them, but his age and his arthritis prevented him from being the strong arm that guided their explorations and kept them from harm.

They'd identified that quality in the Delancey brothers, particularly Tate. That was no surprise. He was the experienced one, the one who talked about his daughters with longing in his eyes.

*God*, Colette thought, the word both an oath and a prayer. This was a complication she couldn't afford.

Her only hope was that he wouldn't be as adept with her girls as he'd been with his. Megan and Katie were strangers to him, after all. He and her children had no common history.

Besides, he'd already managed to alienate Megan.

Colette was determined to talk to her about it tonight. She would simply reiterate what Megan already knew, that because of Katie's silence, strangers often thought she required more attention, while Megan's competence and lively personality simply earned their admiration.

Colette was just gaining a little comfort from her thoughts when Tate pointed the pencil he held at Megan.

"You'll have to be in charge of the Saturday Market department," he said with the same seriousness with which he'd approached everything else.

Megan caught his eye in complete surprise, then

unfolded her arms, coming out of her pout like a flower in the sunlight.

"When does Saturday Market start?" he asked her.

Colette was aware he knew the answer to that; she'd told him herself. He was trying to draw Megan out, give her equal footing. Clever.

"May," Megan replied, her voice still reflecting surprise and uncertainty.

"Okay." He made a note. "I was thinking we should make a bigger booth. You and Katie can plan what you'd like to have, but you have to write it all down so I have something to work from. And though one of us will be with you at the market, you'll have to keep track of what sells and what people say about it and report back to me. Okay?"

Megan's eyes grew huge, then she squared her shoulders. She looked quickly to Colette for confirmation that she could indeed do what he asked.

Colette felt a groan form in her throat but held it back. This didn't mean defeat; it just meant that he *thought* he knew what he was doing with her elder daughter. Whether he did or not remained to be seen. She gave Megan a nod.

"Yeah." Megan's voice rose a decibel. "I can do it."

Katie did not appear upset that she was now her sister's employee because Katie, after all, had the coveted spot on his lap.

Tate focused on Katie. "You'll have to do your best to help her," he said, "because she'll have a lot of responsibility and she'll need to be able to depend on you."

Katie nodded vigorously.

Colette felt whatever smugness she'd held on to during this display of parental tactics begin to disintegrate. The man was good.

Tate looked around the table. "Any questions?"

Armand shook his head. "But I'm sure many will arise when I try to formulate my plan."

"That's fine." Tate put Katie on her feet and stood. "Bring them all to the next meeting, or pass them on to Colette. I'll probably be seeing her every day."

Wonderful, Colette thought as they all got to their feet. An impossible situation made worse by constant proximity.

After her family and Rachel had pulled on jackets to go home, Tate took Katie's hand, then reached out for Megan's. And that was the clincher.

Megan ran to take it, physical contact the only thing so far lacking in her sudden promotion to *entrepreneuse*.

And Colette's smugness vanished altogether.

She didn't want to analyze what she was feeling in its place. It was a lot like terror, with something else attached.

"Tomorrow," Megan said excitedly to the Delancey brothers as they stood in the cold darkness around the Jeep, "we're gonna bring you a present!"

"You helped paint the house." Tate closed and locked the passenger-side door as Colette settled in. "That was a great present!"

"But we've got another one!" Megan said as Katie giggled. "Three of 'em!"

Tate glanced from Mike to Shea for a clue. Both shrugged to indicate their lack of knowledge.

Colette smiled, a little of her good humor restored. Along with some of her smugness.

"It's a surprise," she said, looking into Tate's eyes. "The girls really want to do this for you. We'll be over in the morning, if that's all right. I'll pick up the chairs then."

"We'll be here."


TATE, MIKE AND SHEA filed up the steps and back into the house.

"Looks like you've broken a few hearts." Mike stopped at the table and started stacking the vinyl chairs that belonged to Armand.

Tate helped, while Shea hooked his two index fingers in the remaining coffee cups.

"That's the extent of my charm." Tate laughed lightly. "I'm liked by children and animals."

Mike glanced over his shoulder at him as he carried the chairs to the kitchen, where he placed them by the back door.

Tate followed, with Shea bringing up the rear, cups in one hand, tablecloth balled up in the other.

"Now, how can that be true," Mike asked, "when Colette volunteered to pick you up?"

Tate stacked his chairs on top of Mike's. "Because none of you wanted to leave to come for me."

Mike grinned. "Well, that's partially true. We all voted and decided our lives over the next few months would be far less hectic if we left you stranded at the airport."

"Then we remembered an important detail." Shea

placed the cups on the counter and pitched the tablecloth into a basket at the top of the basement stairs. He smiled winningly at him. "You have all the money."

"Ah. Reminds me." Mike reached into a clown-shaped cookie jar on the counter and withdrew a slip of paper, which he handed to Tate.

The slip of paper, Tate noted, was a check for forty thousand dollars. Made out to him on Mike's Dallas account.

Tate looked up at him, horrified.

"You put a check for forty thousand dollars in a *cookie jar?*"

Mike raised an eyebrow at his tone. "Yeah."

"You're a cop, for God's sake!" Tate retorted. "What kind of security is there in a cookie jar?"

Mike rolled his eyes. "A lot," he replied. "Nowadays thieves stand across the street from banks with binoculars to watch you punch in your ATM number." He turned to Shea and added significantly, "And there are never any *cookies* in the cookie jar to attract anyone."

Shea opened the dishwasher door. "If you're going to eat them by the dozen, you can't expect them to stay there for very long, can you? In the three days since you've been home, you ate the three dozen Rachel brought you and the madeleines I was trying out for the restaurant."

Tate tried to arbitrate by handing back the check. "Why don't you keep it until we need it?"

But all he did was start a battle of another kind.

Mike folded his arms. "No. You take it or I don't show you my brilliant plans for the B and B."

"But we have a good stake…"

"Glad to hear it. Now it's improved by forty thousand."

Tate pocketed the check to keep the peace, then went into the living room to open his soft-sided bag. He drew out a fairly large plastic-wrapped package, for which he'd had to abandon a favorite old down jacket in an airport rest room.

He carried the package back into the kitchen and handed it to Shea.

Shea recognized the contents immediately and hooted his approval. "All *right!* Copper bowls!" He pulled out the three bowls nested inside each other.

"Crepes for breakfast," he promised, then met Tate's gaze with gratitude. "Nice of you to remember these."

Tate shrugged. "There was a gourmet shop with those bowls in the window at the airport and I was an hour early."

"And you've nagged and whined," Mike reminded him. "How could he forget?"

Shea sighed with forbearance. "If we'd decided on piracy, I could slice you into sandwich meat with my cutlass right now."

Tate patted his shoulder consolingly. "But you couldn't open a restaurant."

"Sure I could. Somewhere on Ocracoke during the off-season. In the summer we'd simply post a note on the door that says Closed. Gone Plundering."

Tate knew it was chauvinistic of him, but plunder made him think of Colette in a neat little blazer and jeans.

"Mike...about Colette volunteering to pick me up at the airport."

Clearly surprised by the return to their earlier conversation, Mike took a moment to refocus. "Yeah. I had my keys in my hand and was ready to go, when she showed up all spiffed up and said she'd be glad to get you if I'd rather stay and keep working. She even added that she was more familiar with the roads than I was, and that she hadn't left the property in months."

Tate was inordinately cheered by that news. "Really. She told me she was the one who came because none of you was willing to leave your work—not that she would tell me what that was."

"She wanted to spend some time alone with you."

It sounded as though she did. But she hadn't behaved that way at all.

Which should be no surprise to him, he told himself. He'd watched Sandy in action often enough to know how effective subtle manipulation could be.

What he didn't need was more of the same from another woman.

For a moment he was annoyed, but that changed to satisfaction when he thought about Colette's motivation again. She'd wanted to spend time with him!

That was more than interesting.

Tate patted the pocket in which he'd placed the check. "So, do I get to see these brilliant B and B plans?"

Mike stretched his long arms overhead, looking weary. "How about over breakfast. I'm wiped out."

"Sure. Thanks for all the hard work." Tate turned to Shea. "You, too. Need help cleaning up?"

"Nope." Shea swiped the counter with a sponge. "Almost done. You must be beat. All that traveling, thinking, romancing. I'm used to late hours. I'll hang around for a while and watch TV if it doesn't bother anybody."

Mike shook his head. "I'm used to talking for a living. This manual labor's wearing me to a nub."

"Mmm," Tate said. "What happened to your claims of being so much younger than I am?"

"Oh, shut up. Good night."

"Poor baby," Shea called after Mike as he left the kitchen. "That's what you get for having only verbal skills."

Mike turned, intent on retaliation, but Tate caught his arm. "We need him. Remember the beef bourguignon. And the empty cookie jar."

"But I have to kill him."

"Now, think. If you kill him, all our money goes to pay your lawyers and we're out one winery and three futures."

Mike considered that for a moment. "But we're also out one brother. Come on, Tate," he implored. "It's what we've wanted since we were kids."

"Only until he learned to cook."

"I thought," Shea said, faking injury, "that I wasn't to be viewed as cook and bottle washer around here."

"Right now it's keeping you alive," Tate warned. "Good night."

Mike helped Tate carry his bags upstairs. Tate dropped the suitcase on the bed, and Mike stopped in the doorway, handing him the suit bag and the briefcase.

"A thousand of that," Mike said, keeping his voice down while pointing to Tate's pocket, "is from Shea."

Tate frowned. "I thought he didn't have anything."

"A package arrived by mail yesterday. Something he'd given someone." Mike leaned a shoulder against the molding, looking perplexed. "I don't know what it was. Something small. I asked and he bit my head off. Anyway, it had gone to his apartment in San Francisco, and his landlady had forwarded it. He took it to town and came back with a thousand bucks he insisted on adding to the pot."

"How small?"

Mike made parallel lines with his index fingers, first horizontally, then vertically, about three inches apart. "About so."

"A piece of jewelry?"

"Could have been. He burned our lunch when he came back from town."

"He was upset."

"I'll say. It was canned soup. See you in the morning." Mike straightened lazily and headed off to his room.

Tate closed his door, wondering about Shea's package and the pride that had required he contribute his last thousand bucks to their plan.

Then he smiled, thinking it had taken a lot of work and abuse on their part, but he and Mike had raised a comrade.

He unzipped his bag, pulled out a stack of underwear and turned to the dresser. Then he swore and laughed simultaneously.

He had the girlie dresser.

## CHAPTER EIGHT

THE "PRESENTS" ARRIVED promptly at 9 a.m. the following morning in Colette's truck. Megan and Katie, dressed for school, struggled up the front porch steps with their burdens. Katie had a large paper bag and Megan managed a small pet carrier.

A niggle of foreboding made Tate turn toward the cab of the truck. Colette sat at the wheel and gave him a casual smile and wave that he didn't trust at all.

He braced himself and got down on his haunches to investigate the contents of the carrier. He heard the forceful little mews of protest before he saw three small kittens.

One was a bright calico with colorful splotches. Tiny claws gripped the carrier door and needlelike teeth showed as she decried her incarceration.

Behind her, also complaining, was a classic gray tabby with big green eyes. Finally, in a corner was a black kitten, a little larger than his siblings, and apparently not at all concerned about his fate.

Megan put the carrier down and waggled her hand. "They're getting heavy!" she said, a broad smile lighting her face. "Somebody left them at the Ledbetters' and they brought them to Aunt Rachel. We've been bottle-feeding them for her."

"Well." Tate had to inject enthusiasm into his voice. He liked cats. He'd shipped Misty Emmaline, a fat and spoiled seven-year-old white Persian, to his daughters in Paris. He'd loved her, too, and had hated to see her go, but he remembered what his life had been like when she'd been a kitten.

She'd frolicked while they'd tried to sleep, and his arms had resembled a road map until she'd learned to retract her claws during play.

But he looked up at the bright-eyed expectancy in the little girls' faces and gave his thank-you everything he had.

"This is one of the nicest gifts we've ever gotten," he said, pushing himself to his feet, then leaning down to hug each girl. "We're going to go to town and buy food and bowls and…"

Katie handed him the paper bag, her pleasure in his reaction clear.

"It's all in there," Megan said. "And a litter pan. Mom bought everything."

Mike and Shea wandered out.

"What's this?" Mike asked, going down on one knee to peer inside the carrier.

"It's your presents!" Megan said. "One for you, one for Tate and one for Shea."

"Ah…" When Mike looked up at Tate, as though hoping his brother would find them a tactful way out, he shot him a fierce frown that told Mike he'd better react as expected.

With grudging acceptance of the silent edict, he gave each little girl a genuine smile. "This is really cool. Thank you!"

"They're great!" Shea picked up the carrier, and

the calico screeched at him. "Cats are good company. Don't you guys want to keep one?"

"We wanted to keep all of them," Megan admitted with a confirming nod from Katie. "But Mom
thought you would feel like this was home if you
had kittens."

Tate walked the girls back to the truck and opened
the passenger-side door for them. He lifted them in,
then smiled across them at their mother.

"They like their presents, Mom!" Megan snapped
her belt into place, appearing very happy. "Grandpa
was wrong after all, and *you* were right!" She turned
to Tate then and added with a frown, "Grandpa
thought you would think they were too much trouble
and you already had too much to do to worry about
taking care of kittens. But Mommy said it would be
good for you."

Tate suspected a slight there and challenged Colette with a direct look. "Good for us?"

She kept that innocent smile in place. "Good for
you, particularly. Kittens are like quicksilver—you
can't pin them down and make them conform or
force them to listen. You can't make a deal with
them—" she gave the three middle words special
emphasis "—and expect that to mean all will happen
according to plan."

Tate detected a new toughening of her defenses.
He couldn't decide what had brought it on.

Unless she resented her attraction to him. He knew
it was there, though she had been doing her best to
conceal it from him.

"Do you think that's what I'm about?" he asked.
"That I make deals only to suit myself?"

She opened her mouth to reply, then changed her mind and checked the watch at her wrist. "I have to get the girls to school. Do you need anything from town?"

He shook his head. "No, thanks. When are we putting the mustard in?"

"As soon as I get back?"

"I'll be ready."

"I'll pick you up."

Tate smiled at Megan, then at Katie. "Thanks again for the kittens. You can come and visit them anytime, okay?"

Katie, in the end seat, wrapped her arms around his neck and hugged him.

Megan waved from the middle.

Tate stepped back and closed the door, then watched as the old pickup rumbled away.

"What are we going to do with three kittens?" Mike asked as Tate walked up the porch steps.

Shea took the carrier inside. "You don't have to do anything with them," he said, depositing the cage in the middle of the living room. "A little food and water and a convenient litter pan and they fend for themselves very well."

Tate closed the door as Mike wandered after Shea, appearing doubtful.

Shea got down on the floor and opened the wire door. "Let's see what we've got here."

The calico burst out of the carrier as though she'd been shot from a bow. She went straight to Mike, the tallest vantage point around, and raced up the left leg of his jeans.

"Hey, wha—?" Mike's gasp of surprise was followed by a complete turn, arms held out, as the cat scrambled for purchase on the leather of his belt. "I don't... What is he...? Ouch!" The cry of pain came as the kitten pulled herself up to his shoulder using all four agile feet. After one quick look around, she decided to settle there, tucking her feet under her and peering forward to inspect her host's earlobe.

Shea laughed as he ran in pursuit of the tabby that was headed for the kitchen. "He's a *she*," he called back to Mike. "All calicos are female."

The black-and-white kitten sauntered out of the carrier, yawned and sat down.

Tate picked it up. "Bored with us already?" he asked, drawing the small bundle to his chest.

A purr began much louder than the kitten's size should have allowed. Tate stroked the little head with the tip of his index finger and the kitten closed pale-blue eyes and leaned into him.

"Ow, ow, ow," Mike complained, steadying the kitten on his shoulder with one hand and wincing. "Whose idea was this?"

"Colette's," Tate replied, reaching up to gently unfasten one tiny claw from the skin at Mike's temple. Then he scooped the calico off Mike's shoulder with one hand. "Here. Pet her and she'll relax. She just wants to know you're friendly."

Mike looked as if he held a pinless grenade. "I'd be more friendly if she wasn't bent on shredding me." He cradled her to his chest and stroked her gingerly between the ears with his thumb. "What have you done to tick off Colette?"

"I'm not sure," Tate evaded. He grabbed the paper bag with the supplies in it and headed for the kitchen. "But we can do this. A bit of food, a bit of attention, and cats are great."

They found Shea sitting in the nook, chin rested in the palm of his hand as he watched the tabby lapping milk out of a saucer with speedy efficiency. Shea batted lightly with his index finger at the white tip of the straight-up tail.

"We fed a family of cats at the restaurant in San Francisco," he said moodily. "One of the waitresses took them all home with her when we closed the place." He smiled. "They liked sole almandine night the best."

Tate worried about the grim set of his jaw.

"You been thinking about what you're going to need for the restaurant?" He opened the fridge and pulled out the milk.

Mike opened the cupboard in a search of saucers. The calico leaped out of his hand and onto the shelf. He chased her through three cupboards, then pulled her out of a colander, her four paws flailing.

"Jeez, this thing's motorized. How did I end up with the kinetic one?"

The cat retrieved, Mike came to the table with two small bowls.

"You're the one with the ability to talk bad guys into surrendering." Tate poured milk into the bowls. "And she's clearly a perpetrator. It was fate."

"Great." The kitten scrambled off Mike to get at the milk. "Fate can't send me a leggy blonde or a rich redhead with nymphomaniacal tendencies."

"There're always those triplets in Las Cruces."

Tate filled the litter pan and set it in the hallway near the basement door. Shea dug farther into the bag

Colette had provided and, after finding several cans of a kitten formula wet food, added three more saucers to the middle of the table. Mike pulled out a note and read aloud: "'Kittens have had their shots but should return to the vet's in a month for boosters.'"

He attached the note to the same nail that held a calendar Shea had put up.

"We talking about restaurant and B and B plans today?" Shea asked, packing away the rest of the food in a lower cupboard, then folding up the bag.

Tate shook his head. "Colette and I are planting mustard. Seems it's a green fertilizer. We can talk about the plans tonight, though."

"Ah. Green as in natural."

"Right."

Shea smiled suddenly. "A month ago did you have any idea you'd be running a winery and know that mustard was fertilizer for vines?"

Tate laughed. "Not a clue."

"Well. Just to feed your knowledge, I'll make honey-mustard chicken for dinner."

"I told you you don't have to..."

"I'm trying it out for the restaurant. Oops! There goes Sterling. Close the basement door! Quick!"

Mike hurried around the corner to comply as the tabby jumped onto the floor and scampered off. His siblings continued to eat.

"Sterling?" Tate asked.

"Yeah. Sterling Silver. I thought it was clever. What are you calling the black-and-white?"

"I don't know. I'll have to think about it. You got a name for the calico, Mike?"

Mike came back around the corner. "Bonnie," he replied without hesitation.

Tate missed the joke for a moment, then it occurred to him. "I get it. The Bonnie and Clyde Bonnie with the criminal mind."

"That's the one."

"Okay, I'm out of here. You guys staying home?"

Mike hitched a thumb toward the door. "I'm going to the library." He looked at Shea. "You want to come, or do you want me to bring you back anything?"

"Thanks, but I've got things to do. I'll keep an eye on our 'brood.' God." Shea groaned. And his brothers stopped at the door, questioning looks on their faces.

He scooped up the tabby as it ran to him then said, "Isn't sharing a place filled with cats supposed to happen to old-maid *sisters*?"

COLETTE DROVE the Ledbetters' tractor home under a bright-blue sky filled with friendly white clouds. She hated to admit to herself that she was excited about spending the day with Tate. And it wasn't just simple anticipation. She was excited.

She felt a tingle in her chest, her cheeks were warm, and she wouldn't be surprised to learn there was a sparkle in her eye. That would never do.

But it did. And it seemed determined to despite all the warnings she ran over and over in her mind.

She couldn't simply push aside the memory of the man who'd saved her life and been such a wonderful husband and father, just because she was lonely.

She didn't want her daughters to become even

closer to Tate Delancey in case nothing more came of it.

She should never have agreed to be in charge of field operations, knowing he intended to expand the winery and bring tourists to their quiet little hillside.

But as the tractor bounced across the compound toward the Delanceys' house, she admitted to herself that was stupid and narrow-minded.

He wasn't bringing a theme park to French River, just expanding the winery and adding a tasting room, a restaurant and a B and B. She would have to see the results in order to be able to complain about it with a clear conscience.

Of course, by then it would be too late.

But by then she would have had double her salary for several months, and could take her father and daughters away if they decided they didn't like it here anymore.

Good, she told herself. She was being flexible. She sometimes had trouble doing that. Particularly where her heart was involved. It usually engaged so completely, so forcefully, that once she decided on something she couldn't change her course. That was what had happened with Ben.

So Tate knew she was attracted to him. She could live with that. Like was a very long way from anything that would put her memories in jeopardy.

And this excitement was just the result of not having much company her own age. Her father was a good companion but talked a lot about the past, and her daughters were delightful and though sometimes profound, appropriately childish in their interests.

It was a novelty to have someone around who was interested in what she thought and what she did.

She was entitled to be excited about that.

She pulled up at the foot of the Delanceys' porch steps.

Tate appeared immediately at the door, probably drawn by the rumble of the tractor. He hesitated for one surprised moment, then started down the steps, laughing. He looked wonderful in snug jeans, a gray sweater and the rain slicker.

"I guess this means you don't have a day of romance in mind," he said, stopping doubtfully at the bottom of the steps. The tractor had only the seat she occupied. "Do I get on somewhere or just run along behind?"

She tipped her head to the right side of the tractor. "There's a step on this side you can stand on, then hold on to the back of the seat."

He did as she asked, his body crowding her. "Just promise you won't plant me," he teased.

She smiled and put the tractor in gear. "I won't. We only get ninety-nine cents a head for architects."

THE MOTOR ON the old tractor chugged and the machine's teeth dug into the iron-rich soil, chewing it up and spitting it out again in a rich form ready to welcome seed.

They took turns driving. Sometimes she coached him on the controls, torturing him with her nearness as she leaned over him to explain or indicate something.

It was no easier for him when she drove because

her hair flew into his face and there was a light purity to her scent that reminded him of the perfumed air.

But he did his best to concentrate on the work.

Mike had been right when he said the vines looked dead, with their gnarled trunks and withered branches. Colette had explained they were simply dormant.

"They'll bud in late March or early April," she shouted over the sound of the machinery. "They'll be fuzzy, kind of like pussy willows. That produces something that looks like a tiny grape, but the actual blooming from which the grapes appear doesn't take place until a month later. By the end of April we'll begin to see the first new leaves."

"According to everything I've read," he said as they bumped slowly along, "that's when everything's most vulnerable. And anything can happen."

She gave him a self-deprecating look. "That's when we'll have to call in the expert."

He smiled. "Your father?"

"My father."

Tate, riding the step and holding on to the back of the tractor seat, watched the rich earth churning behind them.

"The soil looks so fertile," he said, "as if it should produce something close to perfect."

She eased the tractor to a stop at a juncture with the lane to Armand's home.

A sudden silence surrounded them, and all they heard was the sound of birds, a sigh of wind and one of Rachel's dogs barking in the distance. He stepped off the tractor and took in the peaceful moment.

He turned to Colette to share it and found her

watching him with longing very clear in her eyes. She didn't look away.

It was only when he took a step toward her that she straightened in the seat and tightened her coat around her.

"Actually," she said on a brisk note, "we're lucky to have it, but rich soil is not a requisite. The French say the vine must be made to suffer. Dry and stony land that would support no other crop suits grapevines just fine. Their roots go deep down to find the moisture they need."

"Is that what you're doing now?" he asked.

She looked puzzled. "What?"

"Digging for old memories to keep going?"

She looked momentarily unsettled, then she admitted, "I am. That's what memories are for."

He had to grant her that. "But do you want to build the future on old experiences?"

She swept a hand toward the vineyards and the compound above. "Your big plans are going to fill all our lives with new experiences. I won't be able to avoid that even if I might want to."

He nodded. "But I was talking about experiences for the soul." He met her eyes and added quietly, significantly, "For the woman."

She looked away, her hands clenching the steering wheel. He got the impression she was avoiding his eyes because of something she didn't want him to see in them, rather than because he'd horrified her.

When she finally met his gaze, he could read nothing revealing there. She'd retreated.

"That's all over for me," she said. "Do you want

to break for lunch, or would you rather work through?''

"Come back to the house with me,'' he offered. "Maybe Shea could be charmed by your presence into fixing us something.''

She pointed to her father's house. "I made a couple of extra sandwiches when I packed the girls' lunches. And my father said he intended to spend all day at the winery, making plans.''

"All right.'' While a sandwich was not normally preferable to something Shea had prepared, a little time alone with Colette without the rumble of the tractor in his ears would be welcome.

Mostly, he thought in light of the conversation they'd just finished, because he enjoyed torturing himself.

COLETTE POINTED Tate toward the living room as she draped their jackets on the back of the kitchen chairs. "Have a seat on the sofa, and I'll bring your sandwich out. I'll build a fire. Oil heat's great, but nothing warms your bones after a morning outdoors like the real thing.''

"Is there anything I can do?'' he asked.

"Not a thing. It's all ready—I just have to add a few refinements.''

He stopped in the doorway. "Refinements?'' he asked with a surprised smile. "For me? I'm touched.''

"It's only potato chips.'' She shooed him off. "Go sit.''

The moment he was out of sight, she felt her heartbeat relax. Jeez. A moment ago it had seemed like a good plan to invite him to the house, even to build a fire, to prove that no matter how intimate their conversations got, no matter if he talked about the nonexistence of her womanly experiences, she wasn't letting him any closer. She was an island unto herself, and she was doing fine.

But her body was trying to betray her. Her pulse was fast, her breaths a little strained, her hands unsteady as she distributed chips and poured coffee.

And her concentration was scattered. That was what worried her most. She was usually very focused, and her determination never wavered.

She drew a breath and reminded herself that *she* controlled her body. Then she carried the tray of sandwiches and coffee into the living room.

Tate was not on the sofa but on one knee in front of the fireplace, a bright little fire hungrily feeding at the kindling he gave it until finally it licked at one of the big logs.

"I didn't know fire-building skills were required in Boston," she said, taking their plates off the tray as he came to join her.

He sat beside her, leaving a comfortable space between them. She didn't like that she'd noticed the space and not the comfort it should have provided.

"We had a weekend cottage with a fireplace in New Hampshire." He took an eager sip from his mug. "Coffee's also good for the bones. Damp cold has a way of getting right to the heart of you."

She nodded. "Sometimes, by the middle of February, it gets to your attitude, too. You'll do anything for sunshine. And then there'll be a miracle day that's crisp and cold but sunny, and you're fueled to make it through another couple of months.''

He picked up a half of his diagonally cut sandwich and studied the layers. He turned to her with a grin. ''Bologna and cheese. I used to love that as a kid.'' He sat back. ''Then suddenly everywhere I went served only canapés and caviar and I found myself craving bologna and cheese, and hotdogs and kraut.''

''The girls love that, too.'' Colette snapped a chip in half and popped one piece into her mouth, chewed and swallowed. ''Well, Megan likes kraut. Katie makes terrible faces, so she usually gets her hotdogs with chili, instead.''

Tate turned slightly sideways to face her, wondering if she'd mind if he asked a question about Katie.

She sipped her coffee, then leaned back with it. She raised an inquiring eyebrow at him.

''Megan told me that Katie doesn't speak,'' he said. ''But she also said that she used to, and you said that one day she would again.''

Colette did not seem to resent bringing up the subject, so he continued. ''So, the problem isn't physiological?''

Tate saw a sadness and frustration in her eyes that she must have lived with since the problem first developed. He knew how stricken he would feel if one of his daughters was unable to speak.

Of course, such a condition was horrible for the children, but to a parent, their children's voices were music. Sure, they could use it to anger you or frustrate you or challenge you, but none of that mattered when they laughed or chattered or simply said, ''Dad.''

Colette shook her head. "Katie found Ben," she said quietly, then took another sip of coffee. "He was off the day after the warehouse fire." She smiled distractedly, caught up in thought, eyes glazed. Then her brow puckered and she refocused on Tate. "He seemed fine. Was home alone all day, fixed dinner, complained of being tired and went to bed early. I followed soon after because we'd had an auditor at the bank and I was tense and exhausted. Katie got up during the night to go to the bathroom and found him on the floor. When she came to wake me up..." Colette's voice tightened. Tate took her hand, wanting to tell her she didn't have to go on but guessing that she probably did. That wasn't the kind of thought one could keep inside for very long and still be able to function.

"She just kept shaking me and pulling on me," she went on. Her voice steadied, but she was grinding his knuckles to powder. "And I could see in her eyes that something terrible had happened. When she pulled me into the bathroom and I saw Ben, I knew immediately that he was dead. And I think she did, too. She hasn't spoken since."

One tear slid down her cheek and she swiped it away with the palm of her free hand. He wondered if she even knew she still held his.

She heaved a sigh. "We've been to see everyone our doctor could recommend, and the diagnosis is unanimous. There's nothing physically wrong. It's traumatic aphasia." She gave him a weak, insincere smile. "I've learned more medical terms in the past two years than I've ever wanted to know. All we can do is love her and pray that she'll want to talk again.''

"She seems so happy," Tate said. "It's hard to believe she wouldn't just shout if she wanted to."

Colette nodded and reached for her coffee again. Tate freed her other hand and gave her a napkin. "That's most of the frustration for me," she said, dabbing at her eyes. "I keep expecting her to speak to me, but it's just not happening. I wonder if I'm doing something wrong...."

Tate frowned at her. "You can't believe that. I'm an experienced parent and I've seen you in action. You're not doing anything wrong. You know how kids are. Who can tell what complexities are at work in her little mind? Maybe she thinks because she found him and couldn't help him that she's to blame."

She nodded, putting her coffee back on the table and pushing the napkin against her mouth.

"Intellectually, I know that," she said, her voice high and frail. "But in my heart—" Tears brimmed in her eyes and spilled over "—I just want her to...talk."

Tate wrapped his arms around her, the gesture more instinctive than conscious. For an instant, she stiffened, and he was afraid he'd done the wrong thing and upset her further.

Then she leaned into him and wept.

ON SOME LEVEL, Colette realized that in accepting Tate's comfort she was only sabotaging herself. Tears shed by a woman and wiped away by a man took a relationship to a level beyond the struggles for power or the riddles of attraction.

And that was when either could be most vulnerable.

But right now she didn't care about that because the tears weren't about her so she wasn't really risking anything. They were about Katie, who was going through life without the ability to comment on it, criticize it or rail against it.

As her mother was doing now.

When Colette felt Tate's arms close around her, she didn't want to resist the harbor they provided. It had been a very solitary two years—even in the company of her daughters and her father.

She'd seen her daughters through the worst of their grief, tried to shoulder her father's burdens and keep the vineyard productive while he coped with his arthritis, and wearing on her every moment of every day was the terrible worry of whether or not Katie would ever speak again. Whether or not she herself was doing all she could to help her child.

It was like falling into a warm-water bath to be able to abandon her worries in a noisy spate of tears and let Tate Delancey hold her up.

Moments later, when she'd cried herself out and was left exhausted, it occurred to her that she'd deluded herself. This *had* been about herself as much as it had been about Katie. And yet she'd done it anyway.

Selfish, she told herself. Unprofessional. Exploitive.

No matter what she called it, she couldn't make herself regret it. She was wrapped in his arms, he was stroking easy circles up and down her back, and the knot in which she'd been tied all these long months seemed...to...be...

COLETTE AWOKE to six pairs of eyes looking down at her in grave concern. Katie and Megan leaned very close to her, and her father was above them.

Had she hit the snooze alarm? she wondered in confusion, since everyone else was up and she wasn't?

No. She clearly remembered driving the girls to school, leaving the truck at the Ledbetters' and borrowing their tractor—

She sat up suddenly as memory brought her fully awake. Everyone around her drew back in surprise.

The tractor! Tate! Lunch, conversation, tears. Oh, God!

He'd put the afghan over her. Great. Not only had she cried in front of him, but she'd wimped out and fallen asleep! Asleep! In the middle of a workday. In the middle of an important project!

All right, that was it. She was reclaiming control. She didn't care how good it felt to relinquish it, she had things to do and she wasn't going to get them done playing the pale heroine in a Victorian novel.

Her resolve wavered when she got to her feet and realized he'd pulled off her boots. How had he done that without waking her? She must have been very tired—and he must have been very gentle.

"What time is it?" she demanded.

"Not very late," her father replied, putting a hand to her shoulder. "I came home and found you asleep, so I went to the bus stop to pick up the girls." He followed her as she looked around and under things for her boots.

"I'm fine, Dad," she said, ignoring his speculative look and kissing each child's cheek. "Good day at school? Has anybody seen my boots?"

"Tate said to tell you he set them behind the chair," Megan reported. "He's putting the tractor in the shed."

It was time to take a stand, Colette thought as she retrieved her boots and sat down to pull them on. She'd told him how it was before, but she was going to have to tell him again. In words he would understand this time.

Boots on, she put an arm around each daughter and brought them with her into the kitchen. "Have some cookies and milk," she said, shrugging into her jacket. "I have to talk to Tate for a minute."

"Can't we come?" Megan asked hopefully.

Colette shook her head. "It's business, sweetie. I'll be right back."

Then she slammed out of the back door, reiterating privately that it was business, all right.

Personal business.

COLETTE SAW Tate walking out of the shed and heading up the road to the compound.

"Tate!" she called, running to catch up with him.

He turned, hands in the pockets of his jacket. Even from several yards away, she saw the tenderness in his eyes.

"You're up," he said as she stopped a foot away from him. His eyes went over her face and she saw a sort of rueful acceptance edge aside the tenderness.

"And somehow the fact that you fell asleep is *my* fault, isn't it?"

"No." She spoke firmly, abruptly, wanting him to know she was serious. "I'm not blaming you for anything. It was kind of you to pull off my boots and cover me with a blanket. But I would be much happier if you'd just leave me alone."

"That's going to be hard to do if you're working for me."

"I mean, leave me alone personally."

"On a two-person job that requires we spend hours together far away from everyone else, that's also hard to do." He shifted his weight and his eyes went to her hair as the wind caught it.

She captured the ends impatiently in one hand and held it down.

"Are you upset because I saw you cry?" he asked, his expression suddenly set in tougher lines.

"No," she lied. "I'm upset because we keep drifting into..." She made a helpless gesture with her right hand, groping for a word.

But he didn't seem to be paying attention to her words. He looked as though he'd read something in her eyes that was a revelation to him. "You're upset," he said, "because I held you while you cried. And because that relaxed you enough to fall asleep. How long has it been since you've slept the night through? Since Ben died?"

"That's not what we're talking about," she said coolly.

"Oh, yes it is," he insisted. "You just don't *know* that's what we're talking about. Because you don't know yourself very well."

"And you do?" she challenged. "Based on our brief acquaintance."

"How long did it take you to feel as though you knew Ben?"

"Well, of course that was quick. He saved my life!"

He nodded. "And you're saving his, aren't you? Trying to make it last forever. But if I hadn't been sitting on the sofa when you started crying, you would have been alone. He wouldn't have been able to hold you because he isn't here."

"If you hadn't been sitting on the sofa," she said stiffly, "I probably wouldn't have been crying. You're the one who brought up Katie."

"And you didn't need to talk about it?"

She began to deny that she did, then decided lying was futile.

"There are a lot of things I need that I can't have."

He looked heavenward in exasperation. "You mean you need them, but you can't get them by yourself, so you don't want them. Because that would mean asking for help or suggesting that you're not in control. And you can't do that because you have to do everything by yourself."

"I do not," she said impatiently. "I'm just trying to survive and move on. And men like you who are used to having control of the deal don't like players who can manage without you."

He ran a hand wearily over his face. "You're surviving," he said finally. "But do you really think you're moving on?"

"How far can I move," she demanded, her voice

rising. Then she put a hand over her mouth, apparently realizing she could be heard from the house. She took several steps away, grabbing Tate by the shirtsleeve and pulling him with her. "How far can I move," she asked again, speaking quietly, "when my daughter is speechless because a horrible image is burned in her brain? Where can I go until I fix that?"

Tate felt as though he'd been gut-punched. Of course. How far away could a widow get from her husband when her child's problem was somehow tied to his death?

But there was a connection here she wasn't seeing.

"Maybe she'll be able to get over it," he suggested gently, "when you do."

She looked as though he'd wounded her. "I have done everything I can think of—"

He stopped her with a raised hand. "I know. But you're holding on to him and she's holding on to you, which means he's got a grip on her. It's a circle, Colette. There's no way out from there."

"And what do you think is the solution?"

He smiled thinly. "Let somebody else in."

"I can't," she said.

Tate felt his heart ache. He wasn't entirely sure why this woman had become so important to him so quickly, but she had.

"Okay," he said with a sigh. "I'll help you plant the mustard tomorrow, then anything else is up to you. What do we have to do then? Watch for mold? Keep the vines warm?"

She studied him suspiciously for a moment, then she shifted her stance and replied. "Yes. We're relatively pest-free, but we look out for mold and frost. Later, bees and birds are a problem, but most of the work is at harvest.''

"All right. I'll be wandering around a lot to try to learn things, but I'll spend most of my time at the compound. The work crews are coming next week. I hired a couple of them so we can get things done quickly. Call me if you need me.''

She didn't seem to like his plan.

But she said quietly, "I think that's best.''

"All right. You're picking me up in the morning?''

"Yes.''

"See you then.'' He turned and started up the road, thinking that the rest of the winter was going to be very long.

COLETTE WATCHED HIM GO, his name on the tip of her tongue. He was only steps away, but she already missed him.

# CHAPTER NINE

"WELL, WHERE IS HE?" Tate frowned at Shea, who'd just told him he hadn't seen Tate's kitten since late morning. "I thought you were keeping an eye on them."

Mike glanced up from the table where he'd spread a book and some papers. Sterling and Bonnie were sound asleep in a gray and colorfully spotted knot atop something that resembled a drawing. "What happened? Trouble in paradise?"

"Please don't analyze me," Tate snapped at him. "I'm not a wacko holed up with hostages. And it's purgatory, not paradise."

He strode toward the stairs, seeing out of the corner of his eye a surprised look pass between Mike and Shea. That annoyed him even more. He was the one who'd always watched *them* for telltale signs of some need he could provide. He was never the one in need.

Until he'd met Colette Palmer.

"You're acting like a wacko on the loose," Mike called after him.

Shea followed Tate. "We've searched everywhere. He must have found a comfortable spot to curl up and catch some Zs."

Tate ignored him, feeling irritated and irascible. If

the kitten was missing, he'd lost what little foundation he had left.

*God*, he told himself. *You're pathetic. You survive the breakup of a Æfteen-year marriage, the absence of your daughters, the sale of your condo, the house in New Hampshire and your share in a ten-year business partnership—but you go crazy over being dumped by a woman who was never all that interested in you anyway, and the disappearance of a kitten you saw for the Ærst time this morning and that probably wasn't a good idea anyway.*

He walked into his room and slammed the door— only there was no sound. He turned to see that Shea had intercepted it with the flat of his hand and stood in the doorway.

"I'm sorry," Tate said in a tone that sounded anything but. "I didn't know you were behind me."

"It's okay." Shea flexed his right hand. "Five working fingers are really more than you need. I was trying to talk to you."

"I know." Tate yanked off his jacket and tossed it at a chair. "I was trying not to listen."

He turned, wondering how he could ask Shea to get lost without sounding like a complete sociopath, when he noticed the partially open second drawer of the French-provincial dresser.

He approached it, spotting something black in it and knowing he had never owned anything in the way of black underwear. Closer inspection revealed a very gentle rise and fall of a furry black body. White whiskers quivered, and four tiny white paws twitched, as though chasing dream mice.

Relieved beyond explaining, Tate scooped out the

little kitten, who opened one eye and started to purr as Tate placed him on one of his pillows.

The kitten stretched, curled up again and went back to sleep.

"Well, that solves that," Shea said. "He disappeared into your poor housekeeping. And now you know what to name him."

"What?"

"Jockey. He likes your underwear drawer."

Tate laughed, thinking Shea was technically wrong but on the right track. "Actually, it's Joe Boxer."

Shea laughed, too. "Better yet. It's not every cat that has a first and a last name." Then he sobered and braced a hand in the doorway. "Colette dump you?"

Tate sat in the room's only chair and pulled off his boots. "No. She never let me close enough to have to dump me. She just…walked around me."

"Worse. Makes you feel like you're not even there."

Tate put the boots aside and sprawled in the chair. He didn't want to confide in anyone, but Shea didn't seem to have any inclination to leave. "I feel like that in general. Like I'm nowhere familiar. I'm no longer what I was, not yet what I intend to be. Just stuck somewhere in the middle—really nothing of any consequence."

Shea dropped his arm from the molding and leaned his back against the opposite side. "You're somewhere—it's just somewhere new, right? Like Mike and me. Like Colette, too, if you think about it. I mean, she's been here for two years, but she's a widow now and a single mother. I can't imagine that ever gets comfortable. Life's a journey. Who said that, anyway?''

Tate shook his head, a little surprised by Shea's philosophical turn. ''Not a clue. But that's a good attitude, especially if you have to deal with losing everything.''

Shea placed the sole of his tennis shoe against the opposite molding and flexed his knee as though he were on a piece of exercise equipment. ''It's humbling, but it teaches you just how much you can do without. All the things you think are so essential to live and be happy, don't really mean that much.''

Tate could only suppose that was true. He still had many material things. He'd chosen a different lifestyle on a less affluent level than what he'd grown accustomed to, but it hadn't been forced upon him— nothing had been stolen from him. Unless fate could be considered a thief.

''My losses were more personal,'' he said.

Shea lowered his foot and brought up the other. Tate got the impression he was doing it to avoid a reply. Then he finally said, ''Yeah. I know a little about those, too. Nothing makes up for that.''

He lowered his foot and chinned himself on the overhead molding.

Tate grinned. ''Do we need to get you a gym membership?''

''How about a NordicTrack we can all share?''

''Where would we put it?''

''The dining room?''

''That would look very *Architectural Digest*.''

Shea rolled his eyes. ''You're not an architect anymore—you're a vintner. So it doesn't matter. I doubt that *Wine Spectator* would care what you put in your dining room. You going to be ready for dinner sometime soon?''

''You going to go bother somebody else and let me take a shower?''

''Fine. See if I try to comfort you again.''

Tate went to the doorway as Shea started down the hall. ''Hey!'' Tate called. ''You did. And I appreciate it.''

Shea waved without turning. ''I know. Dinner in ten minutes.''

FRESH FROM THE SHOWER, Tate reached into the still-open drawer for fresh socks and was surprised when something scratched his hand.

He felt blindly in the back of the drawer and realized that a folded square of paper was caught in the cleats of the drawer above it. He judged by the ragged quality of one end of it, that the kitten had been playing with it. He got down on one knee to look into the drawer and free the paper.

He opened up the white sheet of notebook-size paper and found a photograph wrapped inside a handwritten letter. The photograph was of an attractive young blond woman and a boy about four years old.

The woman wore a simple dark coat that fell to midcalf. The little boy wore a cowboy hat and a thick coat and held a huge gray cat in his arms. The three were posed before a storefront covered in small signs that advertised various grocery products and several gift items.

Tate guessed by the woman's hair and the car reflected in the store window that this was taken in the fifties.

He placed the photo on top of the dresser and read the letter written in a loose and fluid hand. It was dated January 19, 1952:

Dear Jack:

Hi. It's Daniel's birthday today. Mom gave me the money you sent for him. Thank you. I told you that isn't necessary, that we're fine, but you've never listened to me before so I don't know why I expect you to be any different now.

I bought this cowboy outfit with it. He loves it! Doesn't he look proud? I told Robert it was from my mother.

Thank you for abiding by my decision. I know how hard it is because I, too, live with it every day. But what kind of happiness could we hope to have if we trampled on the happiness of others?

Fate has a way of poking fun at us—of putting the people we've looked for all our lives into our paths at a time when we can't possibly connect with them.

I wish you were here in Cave Beach. What sustains me every moment of every day is knowing you're out there somewhere, loving us.

All my heart, Tess

Tate stared at the photograph again. Jack and this woman had to have been lovers and this had to be their child. He couldn't believe it.

Jack had always seemed like such a crusty bachelor, and all the time there'd been a woman who loved him and a son with Jack's blood in his veins. And for reasons that weren't entirely clear in the letter but that might be explained by the presence of a husband, they hadn't been able to be together. How had Jack dealt with that without going insane?

Tate looked at the letter again, then an important detail of it struck him like a sledge.

January 19, 1952.

Jack had disappeared January 19, 1992!

What did that mean? Had he set off to find his son on the boy's birthday? The boy would have been forty-something then. But where would he have been?

Tate studied the photograph. Were the woman and the boy connected to the store in the photo, or were they simply posed there?

Intrigued, he grabbed up the letter and hurried downstairs to dinner.


"Wow." Shea said the word quietly, fingering the photo as he and Tate and Mike sat in the nook drinking cappuccinos, their dinner finished. The kittens played under the table with a wad of paper. Shea's expression was grave. "Tough to love a woman you can't be with."

Tate noticed that Mike was frowning at Shea. Then he looked at Tate as though he, too, knew there was something Shea wasn't willing to share.

"Yeah," Tate agreed. "And to have a child you can't parent."

Mike was rereading the letter. "What do you think? Did he hide this in his dresser because she was married to someone else and he didn't want anyone to know?"

"Sounds that way." Tate passed Mike a plate of peanut butter cookies Shea had put in the middle of the table. "I can't imagine what else could have kept them apart. But I don't know if it was hidden or not. It might have just gotten stuck. That's happened to me when a drawer gets too full."

"I wonder how they met? Where is this Cave Beach, anyway? Oregon?"

Tate shrugged. "My office equipment should be here tomorrow. I've got road atlas software."

"So you think Uncle Jack might have been going to see his boy when he disappeared?" Shea handed the photo to Mike and reclaimed the letter. "It's the same day, only forty years apart. That has to be more than coincidence."

Tate nodded. "That's what I figured. And I'll have a couple of days before I have to get ready for the construction crews. What do you say we find out where Cave Beach is and see if we can pick up any clues about Jack."

Mike looked up from the photo, frowning. "Tate, the trail's seven years cold. We don't have this woman's last name. We don't even know what state she was in when this was taken. All we have are first names—Tess and Daniel."

Tate agreed with a single nod. "I know. I just keep thinking that he wouldn't have disappeared on purpose. And if there'd been foul play, wouldn't something have turned up by now? His car? His body? Something?"

"Yeah, you'd think so. But this state has so many

remote areas, deep ravines, cliffs, rivers. You could hide a body anywhere.''

''But a yellow Cadillac?''

Mike grinned. ''You got me there. Okay, I'm for it. I just don't know how far we'll get.''

Shea took the photo from Mike and studied it. ''There must be something here that'll tell us where it is.''

''But even if it does,'' Mike said, ''that was forty years ago. They could have moved to Mars by 1992.''

''Or maybe they stayed. There's no way of knowing. Ah! Here's something.''

''What?'' Mike and Tate asked simultaneously, leaning toward the middle of the table.

''See this sign?'' He pointed to a white square on the storefront window.

''Yeah,'' Mike replied.

Tate squinted, thinking he should see about getting glasses for reading. ''What does it say?''

''Salmon cheeks,'' Shea replied.

Tate and Mike looked at each other.

''You're sure?'' Tate asked.

''Yeah. It's a regional delicacy.''

''I didn't even know salmon had cheeks.'' Mike peered closer. ''You mean like the loin in pork?''

Shea closed his eyes and groaned, then looked up at Mike. ''Not those cheeks, bright boy. Facial cheeks. There's a lot of meat in them, and they're particularly tasty.''

''Jeez. How many does it take to make a meal?''

Tate patted Shea on the shoulder before he could explode. ''You're missing the point, Mike. It's a regional dish. From salmon. So we're probably looking at Oregon or Washington. Maybe Alaska or Canada. Good work, Shea.''

''Sure. So where do we start?''

''Wherever Cave Beach is.''

Mike raised a hand to get their attention. ''Something else just occurred to me. If Jack had a son, why did he leave the winery to us?''

Tate had to admit that was a good question. ''Maybe Tess's husband was still alive. Maybe the truth still had the potential to ruin her life.''

''If that's true, then why was he going to *find* his son?''

''Maybe he wasn't going to introduce himself or anything,'' Shea suggested. ''Maybe he just wanted to see him. You know. From afar.''

Mike considered that, then nodded as though agreeing that could be likely. ''All very strange,'' he said.


''I'LL TAKE THE TRACTOR back to the Ledbetters,'' Tate told Colette after they'd finished planting the mustard. He stopped the tractor on the edge of the compound on the side opposite his house.

''I'll take it back,'' Colette argued mildly. Tate sat in the seat and she rode the step. ''I borrowed it. And I have to bring the truck home from their place anyway.''

''I'll bring it to you.''

''That's foolish. Then you'll have to walk all the way back.''

He'd been contrary all day long in little ways that didn't really matter. Or maybe she'd been contrary and saw everything he did as annoying. She couldn't be sure. She'd been in a bad mood since their argument the night before, and it bothered her that it didn't seem to bother *him*.

She wasn't getting those all-seeing looks anymore. Or even the concerned ones she hadn't enjoyed quite as much but that told her he was interested.

She recognized that as absolute contrariness on her part. She didn't want to be involved with him. That attraction made her feel as if she were being torn in two. Ben had been her everything, and too much of her continued to be tied to him because of Katie.

But it wasn't as easy as she'd thought to push Tate back to his side of the line. His presence in her life had provided her with something indefinable that she was having difficulty doing without.

Which was absurd, because she'd only been without it for a day. But that had been long enough to show her she might have to find a way to deal with her past because she seemed preoccupied by the future. Last night, she'd dreamed about it.

Grape-heavy vines, a busy winery, gourmet dinners in the restaurant, carloads of tourists.

She wasn't sure she liked that part, but she would reserve judgment until the time came.

Mostly, she didn't like the manner in which Tate was treating her. She couldn't decide if his friendly but impersonal behavior was punishment for her inability to let him any closer, or if this truly was the way he conducted an employer-employee relationship.

Whichever it was, she didn't like it.

"You're being arbitrary," she accused.

He gave her an arrogant look. "I'm also being your employer, so watch it."

"You really think you can get through a wet spring without me to watch for mold and frost?"

"As long as I have your father."

"If I go, he goes."

"You sure about that?" he asked with an easy confidence that unsettled her. "He and I shook hands on a year's work. I don't think he'd put it all aside as lightly as you're doing."

"I'm not—" she began to deny hotly, when a blood-chilling scream filled the silence around them. It came from the direction of the winery.

Tate leaped off the tractor and headed for it at a run.

Colette followed, puzzled by the sound. The scream had sounded female—and not that of a child or an older woman—but a woman her own age. And she was the only one on the compound.

As she reached the winery in Tate's wake, she discovered Victoria had pinned a small but very buxom blonde to the side of the building and was kissing her.

# CHAPTER TEN

COLETTE STRUGGLED valiantly to hold back a laugh. Felicia Ferryman was backed against the board-and-batten wall of the winery, pale with terror, eyes closed tightly against the amorous assault of Victoria's tongue.

Victoria seemed completely oblivious to the screams issuing from Felicia's throat.

Colette lost all amusement in the situation when Tate ran to Felicia's rescue, getting between the screaming woman and the affectionate llama. The mayor of French River was dressed in her usual sexy-chic business suit, the skirt four or five inches above her knee.

Matching heels gave her shapely legs every advantage, and the vee neck of a silky blouse betrayed only a shadowy suggestion of the fulsome curves inside.

A straight veil of sunshine-blond hair fell past her shoulders and was seductively rumpled from her brush with Victoria.

Tate pushed the llama a safe distance away, patted her neck and told her very unoriginally that she was a "good llama," before turning to Felicia.

Colette was not a bit surprised when the woman who had the city council, the county commissioners, the school board, the industrial development committee and even the mosquito abatement district in her pocket—the pocket of her tailored silk pajamas—flew into his arms with a torrent of tears.

Tate looked at Colette in amazement over the top of Felicia's head.

Colette rolled her eyes and went toward them. "You okay, Felicia?" she asked briskly. She put a hand to the mayor's shoulder and on the pretext of taking a diagnostic look at her face, pulled her out of Tate's arms. "It's terrifying to be mauled by a kissing llama."

Felicia focused on Colette, probably remembering last year's winery association banquet when Felicia had sampled too heartily. She'd gone into the ladies' room and stood in the stall a moment too long, trying to decide whether or not she would lose her cheese twisties.

Colette had hurried in on an urgent mission of her own, pushed her way into the same stall and sent Felicia chin first into the wall.

It had taken a full ten minutes and Rachel's smelling salts to revive her.

Felicia had awakened enraged, no doubt embarrassed in front of the little crowd that had collected, and she'd called Colette "the trashy squatter from the Valley Vineyards."

"I'm terrified," Felicia replied, her expression injured but heroic. "One doesn't expect to visit a vineyard to welcome the new owners to the community and be assaulted by wildlife." She turned to Colette and the look became lethal. "I thought you'd be gone by now."

"You two know each other?" Tate asked.

"Tate Delancey," Colette said, indicating Felicia with a sweep of her hand, certain the woman must have heard the new owners were handsome and eligible bachelors and that *that* was the reason for her visit, "may I introduce Felicia Ferryman, mayor of French River? Felicia, Tate Delancey, master of the vineyard."

Tate quirked an eyebrow at Colette's theatrical introduction, then took Felicia's arm. "Maybe you'd like to come to the house for a cup of coffee. I'm sorry you were frightened, but I assure you Victoria is harmless and was just saying hello."

Felicia's pout was nauseating but probably attractive to a man like Delancey. "How can you be sure?"

"Well, I can't imagine she would try to chase *you* away," he said with a smile. "Come on. My brother makes the best coffee anywhere."

Colette noticed the emphasis on the "you."

Felicia fell for it like a bowling pin.

Tate turned to Colette with a bland smile. "So, you're taking the tractor back to the Ledbetters?"

She looked into his eyes, trying to assess whether he was getting her out of the way to devote his complete attention to the mayor or simply getting back at her for pushing him out of her life.

She found it impossible to tell.

"Yes," she said, angling her chin. "That's what I wanted to do in the first place, if you recall?"

"I do," he replied politely. "And I appreciate it."

He hadn't appreciated it five minutes ago, but she was courteous enough not to point that out.

Colette performed that small chore and then drove

the truck home. Once inside, she greeted her family, who were gathered around the coffee table, poring over a drawing her father had spread out. Then she went upstairs to shower and change.

In old black sweat bottoms and a black T-shirt, she pulled out hamburger from the refrigerator and an onion and a garlic bulb from the cooler, ready to prepare spaghetti.

Katie wandered in, put the step stool against the counter on Colette's right and climbed up to watch her work.

Colette reached out to pinch Katie's chin. "Hi, sweetie. Have a good day at school?"

Katie dipped her head from side to side in a gesture probably intended to indicate it had been nothing special. Then the child held her hand high above her head and gave Colette a questioning look.

"Tate?"

Katie nodded.

"Ms. Ferryman came to welcome him. He took her into the house for a cup of coffee." Colette now allowed herself to giggle. "Victoria frightened her. She had her backed against the wall and was licking her."

Katie laughed musically, then held her nose between two little fingers.

Colette had to agree. The mayor would never be a favorite around here.

Then she held up the index and little fingers of her right hand, the middle ones folded down and made her tall sign for Tate. "I love Tate."

"He's a very nice man," Colette agreed, though thinking privately that was an insipid description for the man who alternately irritated and excited her beyond words.

Katie erased her thought from the air with a swipe of her small hand. Then she pointed to Colette, made her sign for tall, then her sign for love.

Colette chopped onions and garlic for all she was worth. "No, Katie, Tate doesn't love me and I don't love him. Love takes a while to grow and we haven't known each other very long."

Katie leaped off the counter and went to the refrigerator, where a dozen magnets pinned notes and recipes to the door.

One of the magnets was a small picture frame, containing a photo her father had taken when Ben had still been alive. It was of the four of them, sitting in front of the Christmas tree.

Katie brought the photo to Colette's side and pointed to Ben's face, her expression questioning.

"Daddy?" Colette asked. "Do I still love Daddy?"

A nod.

"Yes, I do." She put down the knife, dried her hands on a towel and crouched down beside Katie. "We talked about how he's never coming back, remember?"

Another nod.

"And how we have to plan new things for the three of us to do together and with Grandpa, because Daddy isn't here anymore. But love is a very special thing, and I'm just not ready to give that to someone else yet."

Katie made the tall sign again, an expression of disbelief on her face.

"No, not even to Tate."

Katie looked crestfallen. She took a last glance at the framed photo she held, then returned it to the refrigerator.

"Katie." Colette caught her child's hand and lifted her up to sit on the counter. She recalled her conversation with Tate yesterday afternoon and wanted to make sure she wasn't missing something.

She smoothed strands of platinum hair from Katie's face and smiled at the still-unhappy little girl.

"You know I love you very much."

Katie nodded, her brow furrowed.

"And you know that your daddy loved you very much."

Nod.

"Katie…can we talk about that day?"

Colette's meaning was clear. Katie's withdrawal was slight but definite. As was the shake of her head.

Colette was a little surprised. She thought that had all been handled. Megan brought up the subject every once in a while and Colette had presumed that because Katie was always with them when they discussed it, those conversations somehow addressed Katie's concerns, too.

But, of course they hadn't. Colette realized she should have known that. Megan couldn't speak for Katie, though she tried to often enough.

"Well, may *I* talk to *you* about it?" Colette asked. "I'm worried about something and it would help me if I could tell you."

Katie studied her, wide gray eyes reluctant. She finally nodded.

"Okay." Colette leaned an elbow on the counter,

one hand on Katie's knee. "Sweetie, I'm worried that because you were the one to find Daddy, you think what happened was somehow your fault. But we talked about that, remember? Something hit his head when he was getting Uncle Brad out of the fire, and even though he thought he was all right, he wasn't. Only, the problem didn't show up until that night."

Katie's lips trembled and her eyes were filled with a complex message of pain and misery Colette couldn't interpret, but it was enough to tell her Tate had been right. Katie seemed to feel responsible.

Colette wrapped her arms around her. "Katie, it's not your fault. It was just a terrible accident. Something that isn't at all fair. But you didn't do anything wrong, Katie. Remember? You came and got me, and *I* couldn't do anything, either."

Katie wept, clinging to her with the strength of a child twice her size.

"What's the matter?" Megan appeared at Colette's elbow, putting an arm around her waist and wedging herself in between her mother and her sister. "Why is she crying? What's wrong?"

Colette opened her mouth to try to explain without going into unhappy detail, but Katie took care of the problem by making her sign for Tate.

"What about Tate?" Megan wanted to know.

Katie pointed to Colette and shook her head.

Megan, too, looked dejected. "You don't like him anymore?" she asked Colette. "Katie and I were kinda hoping you'd get married."

Colette was delighted that her daughters still managed to share thoughts and feelings with each other despite Katie's silence—she just wished they'd discuss something else.

"You don't marry someone you've known less than two weeks," Colette explained patiently as Megan hiked herself up onto the counter beside Katie.

Colette moved her knife and cutting board out of the way.

"Your mother and I were married after a very brief acquaintance," Armand said, walking into the kitchen. He noticed Katie's puffy face and went to lift her onto his hip. "What are those tears for? Have you been chopping onions?"

"Mom's not gonna marry Tate," Megan revealed, her voice heavy with disappointment. "Just because she hasn't known him very long. Me and Katie love him, doesn't that count?"

"If I got married again," Colette explained with a cautioning glare at her father, "it would have to be to somebody I know would be a good husband, too, not just a good father. Because when you go away to school someday, I'll still have to live with him."

"I don't think you have to worry about Tate Delancey concealing anything," her father said, drying Katie's eyes with his handkerchief, then making her blow her nose. "I believe that he is precisely what he seems to be. You could know him for ten years, and that wouldn't change."

Colette got the frying pan from the back of the stove and began to crumble the hamburger into it. "Then based on what I've seen so far," she said, "I know I couldn't last a week with him, much less a lifetime."

"Based on what?" her father asked. "His concerns for all of us or his working agreements that are both thoughtful and generous? His talent and his eagerness to try something new? His ability to admit that he doesn't know everything? His kindness with the children? His pleasant disposition?"

Colette looked up at that. "He's bossy and contentious."

Armand raised an eyebrow. "*You* are bossy and contentious."

Colette pointed the girls toward the living room. "Megan, take Katie and see if you can find the red-and-white checked tablecloth. I think it's in the credenza in there."

The moment the girls disappeared, Colette faced her father, hands on her hips. "I know I'm not the heroic adventurer Mother was because she took off with *you*. They don't make men like you anymore."

"*He* is a man like me," Armand said with a smile. "Only, you know me as your father, not the man with whom you have to match wits to maintain your position. He's strong and solid and principled." He put his hands on her shoulder, suddenly serious again. "This is your time, Colette. Fight the bonds that hold you back."

She wanted to protest that she couldn't claim freedom from something that might continue to hold her daughter. But the girls were back with the cloth and she was forced to drop the subject.

That night she lay in bed and wondered if Felicia was still at Tate's house. It was almost midnight, so if Felicia's call had truly been about business, she would be long gone.

If it hadn't... Colette got a mental image of the two of them locked in a passion-filled embrace and winced.

She turned over, punched her pillow, fluffed it up again and dropped her head onto it.

The image remained.

To make it less painful to contemplate, she put her own face on Felicia's body. There. That was better.

She experienced one indignant, what-do-you-think-you're-doing?! then let herself admit she was being selfish and self-indulgent. Then she simply relaxed and allowed her little dream to play out.

"I am deeply attracted to you," she heard herself admit. "I want to love you. But I'm all wrapped up—insulated against the pain of loss, the worry about Katie, the terror of being wrong about the grapes."

"Do you think I would blame you if you were wrong?" he asked her, running his hand in long strokes down her back. "Don't you understand I could lose everything and still be the happiest man in the world if only I had you?"

Colette sat up and threw her pillow. Now she was delving into major fantasy.

She'd been right when she'd pushed him away, and she'd been right when she'd made it clear to Megan and Katie that a romance between their mother and Tate simply wasn't going to happen. Ever.

He was free and liked things his way, and she was all trussed up with responsibilities and old baggage.

It was hopeless.

She found her pillow in the dark, tossed it back

into place and climbed back into bed. She settled into the pillow and pulled the blankets up, as though they could protect her from the chill caused by her loneliness.

Tate had diminished that for a while, but that was over now.

Damn it.

"OKAY, HERE WE ARE." Mike pulled the Blazer into a parking spot in front of a sign that read Saint Peter's by the Sea Catholic Church, Cave Beach, Oregon. The church itself was up at the top of a little bluff, and across the street were a gas station and a grocery store. "Do you think this is all there is?"

Shea, in the back seat, ducked down to see out. "Seems to be. There's a grocery store, but it looks too new."

Tate shook his head. "It's a rehab."

"A what?"

"It's been renovated. Look at the Italianate detail on the second story. I'm going in to ask some questions. Anybody want to come?"

"They'll probably think we're casing the joint," Mike grumbled, but he was pocketing his keys and opening his door.

"I could use a mocha," Shea said, following them across the empty street. "You suppose they have one?"

They didn't. The market was relatively small, though it did have a deli with several kinds of meat and cheese, fried chicken, something called "salsa bites," and onion rings.

Shea walked past the display case looking as though his culinary sensibilities were offended.

The young man behind the counter glanced up with a smile. "Help you?"

"We're looking for a lost relative," Tate said candidly. "I wonder if you know anything about the history of this store."

The young man wiped his hands on the front of a white apron and moved to lean against the side of an antique-looking cash register. "Not very much. I bought it three years ago from a guy named Tully. Was in his family for a while, I think."

"Is this Tully still around?"

The clerk shook his head. "He moved to Florida with the money from the sale."

"How old was he?"

"Sixty-two. Said he wasn't waiting till sixty-five."

"And he left with his family?"

"No. He didn't have any. He was kind of a grump. I worked with him summers through college so I knew how to get on his good side, but he was hard to get along with."

"Bitter?"

"Maybe. He never talked about himself very much. But that might have been why he drank." The young man's eyes narrowed suddenly and he eyed the brothers one by one. Then he zeroed in on Mike. "You guys really cops or something?"

Tate laughed. "No. We own a winery in the valley." He told him briefly about Jack and the death declaration now that he'd been gone for seven years. "There was a search conducted at the time," he added, "but nothing came of it. We just thought we'd give it one more try."

The clerk spread his arms in a gesture of finality. "That's all I know."

"Thanks. We appreciate your talking to us." Tate wrote their address and telephone number on the back of one of his old cards and handed it to the clerk. Then he searched the shelves for something to buy to thank the man for his patience.

He walked out with a couple of cans of pâté, three apples and, at Shea's insistence, six salsa bites.

"What are these anyway?" Mike asked as they all piled back into the car. He studied the deep-fried morsel in his hand.

"I don't know," Shea said, taking a bite and moving it to the corner of his mouth so he could reply. "That's why I thought we should try it. Mmm. It's hot."

Tate took a bite of what seemed to be a little bundle of rice wrapped in phyllo dough. It was spicy and somewhat dry from having been kept under heat lamps, but it was very tasty.

Shea popped a second one into his mouth. "This has potential. You guys like it?"

Tate nodded. "Yeah. Needs a little meat or something."

"Or a crunchy vegetable," Mike suggested. "Where to now, Mr. Holmes?"

Tate ignored the gibe and checked their map. He pointed north. "The next town looks a little bigger. Maybe we can find mochas. Even better, maybe there's a library with old business directories. We might be able to see who owned the grocery store before Tully and figure out if there's any connection to Jack's lady.''

"The Tully the clerk talked about,'' Shea said, reaching over the front seat to grab an apple out of the bag, "would have been too old to be the kid in the cowboy suit but too young to be Tess's husband. So that's probably not them.''

"Right. We have to find out who owned the store in the fifties.'' He peered out the window and jotted down the little market's address. Then he buckled his seat belt and gestured to Mike. "Forward, Mr. Andretti.''

CAPESIDE DID HAVE a coffee bar. Tate, Mike and Shea walked up and down the two-block main street from the highway to the ocean, looking for a familiar storefront.

They passed little gift boutiques, a stationery store, a bakery with wonderful aromas, a gallery and finally a tiny grocery store. Tate stood at the edge of the curb to compare it mentally with the storefront in the photo, but there was no resemblance at all.

He did notice that the man behind the counter was bald and paunchy and probably in his seventies. He might know who'd owned the Cave Beach store before Tully.

"I'm going to try in here,'' Tate said. "You guys can go ahead, if you like, and I'll catch up.'' He pushed open a squeaky old door.

The floor was bright-white tile, but everthing else in the store looked as if it had been there since the turn of the century. The refrigerated case was oak with brass pulls. The counter was also very old and had a vintage meat scale on it.

Canned goods were stacked on papered wooden shelves, there were potatoes and pickles in barrels, and a soft-drink cooler from the forties or fifties.

The storekeeper looked up from counting change into the till. "'Morning," he said.

"'Morning," Tate replied, and waited a moment until the man finished counting and closed the register. He introduced himself and realized he had to introduce Mike and Shea, too, because they'd followed him in.

"Al Bigby," the old guy said. "What can I do for you?"

"This your place?" Tate asked.

Bigby nodded. "Bought it forty-seven years ago. And I'm not selling, if that's what you're after."

Tate shook his head and explained about Jack and their search. "We have an old photo of a...friend of his that was taken in front of what might be the grocery store in Cave Beach. Looks like early fifties. I thought since you've been around awhile you might know who owned it in those days."

"Sure do. Charlie Purcell."

Startled by the instant and confident reply, Tate had to think about his next question. "Do you recall if he had a wife and a child?"

"Yep. Alaskan girl. Hair like midnight. And three little daughters."

Tate felt a rush of disappointment. But he considered another possibility. "I don't suppose you remember who worked for him in those days."

Bigby nodded with a big grin. "Turned seventy-eight five weeks ago, and not a trace of senility. Calista Iverson.'' His expression changed and he shuddered. ''Ugly and mean. Spinster lady before it was acceptable to be alone.''

Tate pulled the picture out of his pocket, sure they were now on a wild-goose chase. With a glance at his brothers, who appeared to share the same thought, he showed the photo to Bigby.

''You don't know who this is, do you?''

Bigby grinned again, that confident look in place. ''Yes, I do. Theresa Mullins and her boy, Danny. She and her husband and the boy lived in the apartment above the store.''

Tate was so astonished he didn't know what to say for a minute. He heard Shea's intake of breath and felt Mike shift his weight.

''Are they still around?''

Bigby frowned in concentration. ''Sad story. Mullins, the husband, was a wild kid and not much good for anything but smooth-talking the girls. And that pretty thing fell for it. I think she was just about deciding he wasn't worth her time—she even left him for a month—when he went blind. Diabetes, I think. Never took care of himself. Ate and drank. She went back to him, which I guess was a good thing because it turned out she was pregnant.

''Mullins got disability—the first real money he'd made since they were married. She kept her job at the dress shop and the boy went to college on a scholarship. But she never had more than that little place over the store.''

''Is she still there?'' Mike asked.

Bigby shook his head. "She died about eight or nine years ago."

Tate was surprised to feel a sense of loss. "What happened?"

"She and a friend were going to Seattle on the train to visit her son and there was a wreck. She was killed."

Tate absorbed that information with great sadness. He felt a curious kinship with the woman in the photo. "What about her son?"

Bigby shook his head. "That, I don't know. Could still be in Seattle. He worked for Boeing, I think. At least, he did when Tess set off to visit him."

Tate looked from Mike to Shea and saw the grimness on their faces.

Tate shook Bigby's hand. "Thank you," he said. "We appreciate your help."

"It was my pleasure," Bigby replied. "If you have any more questions, call me."

Tate was last in line as his brothers walked out the door. They formed a little circle on the sidewalk outside, expressions gloomy.

"That's a bummer," Shea said. "That would have been a year or two before Jack disappeared. I wonder if he just didn't care anymore. If he just drove off a cliff or something. That could be why the car never turned up."

Mike jammed his hands in the pockets of his jacket. The day was cold and the wind off the ocean bit deeply. "I've seen that happen a couple of times. Someone disappears without a trace, and you figure they must have wanted to because otherwise, there's usually some clue left behind."

"So, does it stop here?" Tate asked. "I mean, we might have been able to ask her about Jack, but if she's gone, then we can't ask her if her son ever knew Jack was his real father. And that's not the kind of news we have the right to impart even if we could find him."

"Well, we could look him up without telling him, couldn't we?" Shea asked, zipping up his coat.

"On what pretext?" Mike started back toward the car. "If we tell him we're searching for Jack, how would we ever explain to him how we discovered a connection between them without telling him about the picture? Or the letter?"

"Oh, yeah."

Mike unlocked the car with his remote and Tate pulled the door open.

"I hate to think this is it," Shea said. "That we found out so much so quickly, but that what we learned puts an end to the search."

Tate climbed into the Blazer. "Maybe we just suspend things while we think about it."

"I don't see that we have any other choice." Mike put the key in the ignition. "If you want, I've got friends who could run a search on Daniel Mullins for us. See if there's anything at all about him that would tell us if he knows about Jack."

Shea snapped his seat belt in place. "Like what?"

"I don't know. I'm grasping at straws."

"Is that legal?" Tate asked. "The search, I mean."

Mike turned the key in the ignition and grinned in Tate's direction. "Not if I'm not on duty. But cops have been known to do that for one another."

Tate had visions of launching a new business with a lot of publicity only to be revealed as guilty of fraud.

"We'll retain that as an option," he said. "Meanwhile, let's find someplace to have lunch. It looks as though the sky's about to open up on us."

"But..." Shea leaned forward between the front seats. "Do we have something that should really belong to someone else. I mean if Jack was his dad..."

"He's right," Mike said, turning sideways in his seat. "This is something we should consider. Legally, the winery's ours, but is it morally?"

Tate nodded. It was something he'd begun to think about, too. "I don't know. If we could find Daniel Mullins, would we be doing him a favor if we told him his real father left behind a winery, or if he doesn't know about his mother and Jack, would we do irreparable harm?"

"I guess it's a moot point," Mike said, "until we find him."

Shea leaned back in his seat.

"What if we just cut him in?" Tate asked. "You know. Make him an invisible fourth partner until we see if we can find him and/or figure out the situation."

Mike nodded. "Works for me."

"Yeah, me, too," Shea replied from the back. "If only there were a way to make him do his fourth of the work."

Mike punched Tate in the shoulder and started the car. "Way to go, Tate. We just save his share. It's a good thing we decided on the winery business."

Tate was puzzled. "Why?"

"Because piracy clearly isn't in you."

## CHAPTER ELEVEN

TATE, MIKE AND SHEA watched the cloudburst from the comfort of a fireside table in a second-story waterfront restaurant. The pewter sky and the angry ocean had merged into one color and one substance—water.

But in the restaurant with its large stone fireplace, wood-paneled walls and carpeted floors, the atmosphere was warm and protective.

After downing combination platters of fresh seafood, they sat back with their coffee and stared alternately at the fire and the rain.

"Remember the summer we spent with Jack?" Tate asked his brothers. Free of the pressures of the winery for a day, he felt relaxed, despite the dead end they'd hit. He was cheered by their mutual decision to cut Daniel Mullins in for 25 percent, and feeling unusually expansive. Colette didn't care what he thought, and he needed to tell someone. "I felt as though my life changed. Dad was about to be transferred for at least the fifth time, and Mom's business was doing really well and she loved our house and didn't want to go. You guys remember that?"

Mike nodded, picking up his cup with the tips of his fingers and giving it a complete turn. "Yeah, I do. I was scared to death." He gave Tate a puzzled look. "But they stayed together, so why did your life change?"

Tate stretched a leg toward the fire. "Because I learned that I could admit fear without it diminishing me. Until then, I had only the superhero concept of courage. You know, face down a comet with nothing but your bare hands and a smile on your face. I was sure there was something wrong with me because I was afraid."

"Afraid they were going to get a divorce?" Mike asked.

"Well, yes, but also that we'd have to go with Mom if they split up, and that meant I've have to do for the two of you all the things that Dad did for us. I'd have to be in charge."

Shea laughed. "But you *like* to be in charge."

Tate laughed with him. "Only when I know what I'm doing. And what in God's name would I have done with the two of you?"

"You put up a good front." Mike held up his cup as the waitress passed with the coffeepot. She topped up their cups, then moved on. "I remember leaning on you because I was terrified that if Dad left, no one else would understand me."

Tate heard that with surprise. "What do you mean? You got the best grades, were the best looking…"

"But you were the one who got everything done, the one Dad and Mom depended on. I knew I wasn't as together as you or as charming as Shea." He turned to their youngest brother with a look of teasing disdain. "You were such a little twerp, winning everybody over with your big smile and your friendly disposition.''

''The classic middle-child syndrome?'' Tate shook his head at Mike in disbelief. ''Mom and Dad always used to brag to everyone that you never experienced it because you were such an achiever.''

''I was just trying to keep up with you and stay ahead of Shea.''

''That's what I was most afraid of that summer,'' Shea admitted with a smile that seemed reluctant. ''I knew you both hated me, and I thought if the family came apart, that the two of you would finally leave me somewhere the way you were always threatening to, and I'd end up in an orphanage.''

Tate and Mike laughed, then sobered when Shea didn't.

''Oh, come on,'' Tate chided. ''You didn't *really* think we'd abandon you.''

''Well, you were always giving me a hard time. I thought if Dad was gone and Mom was busy, I could fall through a crack somewhere and never be found.''

Mike turned to Tate. ''Maybe it isn't too late to dump him. Now that we know he expected it, it wouldn't be so bad.''

Tate appeared to consider that, then finally shook his head. ''No. He hasn't run through the entire menu for his restaurant yet, and you wouldn't want to miss that.''

''Sorry,'' Shea replied. ''I know how to find my way home.'' Then he gave each of them a measuring look. ''I can't believe you guys were scared, too. The question is—are you scared now?''

''Of what?'' Tate asked.

Shea shrugged. "Of anything."

It was on the tip of Tate's tongue to deny that he was. After all, he'd made such a point of saying that he'd learned fear wasn't fatal.

But that knowledge didn't preclude *having* fear. And he did.

"Yes," he admitted finally. "I'm afraid that we'll get this place on its feet, and it'll be the success we all hope and I still won't have anything personal."

His brothers accepted that information in silence, then Shea asked quietly, "Because of Colette?"

Tate met his gaze. "Because maybe it isn't her, maybe it wasn't Sandy, maybe it's just me. Maybe I don't know how to hold a relationship together. I make the bluelines for it, but it never comes out according to the plan."

"It's not your fault," Mike said staunchly, firmly. "Sandy was into her own thing, and being without Susan and Sarah must be awful, but they *are* fine. As for Colette, she doesn't know what's going on with her life. You can see it in her eyes. She's still spinning. Just be there to catch her when the spinning stops."

Tate was buoyed and somewhat mollified by that assessment of his situation.

"I, however," Mike went on, pausing to take a sip of coffee, "am preaching without practicing. I haven't even had a date since the first hostage situation because I'm afraid of everything that can't stand up and defend itself—women, children, babies. I don't want to be responsible for them in any way. I can't risk losing them."

Tate opened his mouth, but Shea spoke the very

question he'd intended to ask. "How many people have to tell you that wasn't your fault before you believe it?"

Mike stared into his coffee. "The thing is it doesn't matter who was at fault, because you assume the blame anyway. But I thought I was past that, until I went back and walked into that second situation." He looked up into Shea's eyes, then Tate's. "I knew it was stupid but did it anyway. I can't trust myself anymore."

Tate had no idea how to reassure him about that, so he didn't try.

Shea apparently didn't, either. "I'm afraid," he said, "that I'm never going to have something that's mine ever again. And I'm not talking women and relationships, because I don't even want that until I have a savings account again, and I don't see that happening in the near future. I'm going to owe the two of you until I'm in my dotage."

Tate frowned at him. "You're as thick as Mike. I told you we're going to share equally in whatever comes out of this. Your investment isn't cash, but it's essential all the same."

"Well, it's not the same to me."

"I'm not having this argument again."

"Good. I'm getting tired of listening to you. About my plans for the restaurant…"

They talked about the restaurant all the way home.

Tate reconsidered his position. He had lost everything personal, but he still had his brothers.

It was interesting to him that when he'd been younger, he'd loved and respected them, of course, but he'd been so busy building his own life he'd forgotten how close they'd once been.

Now that they were reunited and working together, it was great to discover their ties were as strong as ever.

Maybe even stronger now that they'd shared their fears.

He listened to Mike and Shea argue over the merits of tables versus booths and let his mind drift to the vineyard.

And with thoughts of the grapes came an image of a woman, red hair flying behind her as she rode the tractor, and he felt his contentment dissolve.

Business would never be everything to him. He was a family man by nature. He loved sharing his life with a woman and looking after children.

So he had to figure out how to do that.

He had to figure out how to do that with Colette.

AS SHE'D PLANNED, Colette kept her distance from Tate. And happily, he kept his distance from her, but the loud noises coming from the compound on the Monday morning of the second week in February forced her into his territory to investigate after she'd dropped the girls off at the bus stop.

Scaffolding was being erected around the winery and the bunkhouse, and the hilltop was swarming with men in hard hats.

Her father was in the thick of things at the winery and Shea was in deep conversation with one of the workmen at the bunkhouse.

Rachel was rounding up her animals, which

roamed freely on sunny days, and drove them toward her pen with the help of her dogs.

Tate stood with Mike and another man on a bare spot of grass. Tate was gesturing while Mike and the workman held open a set of blueprints.

It was happening, she thought, trying to feel grim about it. The beginning of the end of her private little paradise.

But it was hard not to get caught up in the excitement. A dozen conversations overlapped, punctuated by the whine of a saw and the curious sounds of other power tools.

Even as she watched, the scaffolding that would surround the winery took shape. She stared, fascinated in spite of herself.

"If you're going to rubberneck," a male voice said from behind her, "you have to wear this."

She turned to see Tate standing with a hard hat in his hand.

She hadn't spoken to him at any length since the day Felicia had appeared. Even at the two weekly meetings that had taken place since, she'd let her father do all the talking.

When Tate had asked her specifically how she thought the vines looked, she'd answered pithily, "Fine."

Later her father had said Tate should have fired her for such a reply, but she still held her job. And she was doing it as well as she was able.

She diligently walked the vineyard every day. She watched the weather with fervor and often got up in the middle of the night to make sure the weatherman hadn't been wrong in his predictions.

She'd never been more conscious of all she *didn't* know, or that what she *did* know was from books and not from experience.

When he was able, her father walked with her, and when he didn't feel up to it, he listened carefully to her reports, but even he told her she was obsessing.

She wanted to do her absolute best for Tate Delanccy—but since their argument and then the Felicia incident—she would have died before letting him know that her dedication had to do with anything other than business.

"I'm not staying," she said, pushing the hat away as Tate tried to hand it to her.

"The entire compound's a construction site," he said, handing it back. "Put it on until you're off the hill or you could have us shut down for safety violations."

She snatched the hat from him and put it on. It fell to her nose.

He took it from her, adjusted the sizing cap, then replaced it on her head. It rested there comfortably.

"Want to see what we're up to since you're here?" he asked pleasantly, then added with a wry quirk to his lips, "Or have you already decided you hate it?"

"I don't—" she began.

"Good," he interrupted. "Come and look." He caught her hand and tugged her toward a table set up under a canopy in the middle of the compound. Pinned to it were several blueprints.

She did her best to focus on them instead of the tingling sensation on her hand where he was touching it.

He pointed to the largest blueprint on the table. It was a rendering of the completely remodeled compound.

She studied the drawing in astonishment. "You did all these blueprints over the past few days? By hand?"

"No. My stuff arrived from Boston. This was done on the computer, and I have a pencil plotter, which prints out the design as it appears on the screen. The fact that it's in pencil allows me to enhance it." He gestured at the designs. "Also we don't call them 'blueprints' anymore because this makes blue lines on white instead of white lines on blue. So we call them 'bluelines.'"

She nodded as she studied the drawings. The winery retained the barnlike northwestern flavor of the original now standing, but the shape had been refined and windows had been added on the second level to what was now a loft.

"We'll have offices up here," Tate explained, indicating the upper level, "and cameras for security. We'll also keep a small kitchen so Shea can store food for the tasting room."

He showed her a rendering of the winery's interior.

She pointed to the lowest level. "Is this the cellar?"

"Right. If we're going to be producing wine again, we have to restore it."

She nodded, her enthusiasm building despite her attempt to remain simply cool and observant.

He pointed to the main level again. "We decided to go with oak barrels for aging. Though lots of other wineries use stainless steel, your father decided to trust you on this. He says the best product is made by combining new technology with old experience, and that you've studied everything from every angle.''

She blinked at him. "I know he trusts me. I'm surprised you agreed. You don't believe in my ability to make wise decisions.''

"I trust your ability to make business decisions," he corrected quickly. "It's your heart decisions I question.''

She let that remark die uncontested, and he continued to explain the plans. "This is Shea's restaurant. Potentially, we can add rooms upstairs to support the B and B. We're still playing around with a name. We thought about something with a folksy flavor but with a little elegance. Or maybe something else entirely. I don't know. A million details are still up in the air.''

"This is the B and B?" Colette pointed to the drawing of an elegant Victorian house, then looked up at the spot where there was nothing but a view of the vineyards. "That's...beautiful.''

"Yes." He smiled as he studied the empty lot as though envisioning the house there. "I like it, too. I was a little surprised to discover I had it in me after all those years of high rises and made-to-order public buildings that had to maximize the use of space and allowed only slight ornamentation. Who knew that inside me there was a Victorian house?''

"What's this going to be?" She indicated the large barn on the other side of Rachel's cottage.

"Nothing yet. It's a pretty good size, so we thought about renting it as office space or artists' studios or something just to get a little money to help make the compound a paying proposition. We thought we'd put in a floor, buff it up inside and out and see what becomes of it.''

"Good idea.''

"And when this is all done, we'll landscape the middle here—'' he ran the tip of a long index finger over the central area ''—with—I don't know—a fountain, maybe. And flowers all around it. What do you think?''

"It sounds beautiful.''

"So you're not going to sit in the path of my 'dozers and protest the construction?''

He was teasing, and she had to admit to herself that she was happy they were on a slightly more normal footing again. The cool politeness and careful neutrality felt all wrong.

Not that it would be good to push their relationship any further. She simply wasn't ready to accommodate a lover, but she liked having him as a friend.

"No, of course not.'' She smiled amiably. "But I reserve the right to hate it if we're crawling with unruly tourists in the summer.''

"We're going to invite tourists to look around, nibble hors d'oeuvres and sweets and drink coffee at the wine festival in June,'' he said. "That way we can let everyone know that we're here and we're working, but I imagine the lack of wine will keep the tourist numbers down.''

"That's true.''

"And by the time we do have wine,'' he added, folding up a blueprint—blue*line*, she mentally corrected—"you might have decided you hated it after all and moved on."

The easy way he made that suggestion stung, but Colette was careful not to show it. She forced a smile. "Could be. Anything can happen in a couple of years. Well." She took a few steps backward. "I'd better get out of..."

He caught her arm and pulled her toward him, wrapping his arms around her and lowering his head to hers.

Excitement and relief burst inside her. He was going to apologize for that remark and assure her she would always be welcome here. In fact, she was sure he was about to tell her that he would always want more from her than this insipid friendship, that he wanted—

Her reverie was interrupted by a small clunk that sounded against his hard hat. There was a shouted oath, then a quick apology from a rough-voiced man. "Sorry, Tate. Didn't see you there."

Tate freed Colette and she saw the workman who was apologizing, and the four-by-four carefully balanced on his shoulder.

"Okay, Stretch," Tate said. "No harm done."

"Not on that brick you call a head."

Tate straightened away from Colette. "Thanks, Stretch," he said dryly.

"Anytime." Stretch touched the bill on his hard hat. "Sorry, ma'am."

"My fault," Colette said, embarrassed, disillusioned and depressed. She kept that to herself, too. Instead, she smiled up at Tate. He looked solicitous yet politely removed, and she was flustered from the close contact and horrified by how eagerly she'd hoped it was something more. "I guess you were right about staying out of the way." She reached up to remove the hat. "I'll just give this back to you—"

He stopped her, holding the hat to her head with the palm of his hand. "Leave it on until you're off the site."

"But won't you need it?"

"I'll walk you to the road."

He put a hand on the small of her back and ushered her across the compound to the road that led to her father's house. Rachel stood on her porch, watching the construction. She'd tied the dogs, and the cats sat on the porch railing, interested but prepared for flight.

Colette waved.

"Can you stop for tea?" Rachel asked.

Colette smiled but shook her head. "Thanks, but I have lots of errands today. Need anything from town?"

"Oh, yes!" Rachel reached behind her for the doorknob. "Flour and butter. I almost forgot pastries for the meeting tomorrow."

"Don't go in," Colette called. "You can pay me when I come back." And just to show Tate she didn't care that what she'd thought was going to be a kiss had simply been an attempt to protect her from a wayward four-by-four, she asked brightly, "Do you need anything?"

"No, thanks," he replied. "I have a list from Shea, but I'll pick it up later. I have a meeting with Felicia later this afternoon."

The bravado was getting more and more difficult

to hold on to. But she managed. "All right, then. Thanks for the look at the plan. I hope it all comes together the way you want it. Bye."

"Colette!" Tate shouted as she started away.

"Yes?" She turned back, that damnable eagerness in place again.

He did have a hand stretched toward her, but all he said was, "The hat."

The hat. God. She removed it, still smiling, and handed it back. "Sorry."

"No problem. Be sure to come back and check on the progress."

"Sure. Bye."

Once she was certain his back was turned, she strode home, ignoring all the bright-green mustard sprouts between the vines. She usually loved to see them come up.

But this year her love of the grape was compromised by her attraction to a man. And she didn't want to think about it, but it kept getting in her way. Tate Delancey was the only thing her children and her father talked about.

She picked up her pace. She knew what he was doing. He was only pretending he wasn't affected by her nearness.

And that *was* upsetting because it meant he knew she cared and was trying to force her into action.

Not that there was anything she could do about it. He'd told her her life was a circle, and he'd been right about that, too. She and Ben and Katie were inextricably connected and that could only change when and if Katie spoke again.

"Let someone else in," he'd said. And she was

beginning to believe that if she did do that, she might be able to put the past behind her. But what if that didn't free Katie? Her daughter would be forever tied to what she'd seen that ugly night. Alone. Speechless.

Colette couldn't let that happen.

## CHAPTER TWELVE

BRIGHT YELLOW mustard plants lined the rows of grapes at the Delancey Vineyards by the end of March. Tate loved gazing down on them from his office above the winery.

Finally the air was a little warmer, and it wasn't quite so long between sunny days.

The work on the winery and restaurant was almost finished, and they'd sunk a basement for the B and B. He couldn't believe it. He was so much more delighted by the small successes in the restorations going on here than he'd ever been by the big-money buildings he and his partners had put up in Boston.

This was his. Well, it was theirs; his, Mike's and Shea's. But their separate visions had become one entity, one dream.

Daily e-mail from his daughters revealed the ups and downs of settling in, but also an underlying happiness and excitement that eased his mind. And the daily insistence that they missed him soothed his soul.

Tate looked down on the vineyard and realized again that he would still never be satisfied by business success alone.

He wanted Colette. And Megan and Katie.

But who ever got everything he wanted?

He smiled at the thought of Colette's daughters. They reported in every afternoon after school to see if there was anything they could do.

He manufactured projects for them because if he didn't, they would be a serious danger to themselves, wanting to look at what had been done, watch what was being done and ask questions about what would be done.

The crew had grown very fond of them and had used scrap lumber and shingle to spruce up an old shed behind Armand's house.

Rachel had provided the curtains, and Tate had given them money to buy a small table-and-chair set they'd seen in the JC Penney catalog.

The girls followed Tate around in hard hats on which their names had been printed, doing his bidding like eager little slaves. Megan talked nonstop, but Katie simply held his hand and stared at him as though he were personally responsible for the risings of the sun and the moon.

He'd forgotten how empowering and how humbling a child's adoration was. Susan and Sarah had reached the stage where their hero worship was directed at movie stars and rock bands.

And then there was Colette.

She came by once in a while to see what progress had been made and to tell him with a smile he wanted to wipe off her mouth with a hot kiss that she was happy for him.

He'd hoped over the past month that casual references implying he no longer thought of them in permanent terms would force her to rethink her position.

But her father had warned him that no one forced her to do anything.

And she'd warned him that no one could force her to *feel* anything except Ben.

Tate couldn't help resenting him and couldn't help admiring him. Fine position to be in.

He'd felt that way about Dudley and look where it had gotten him. An ocean away from his daughters.

Well. That kind of thinking wasn't going to change anything. Tate loped down the still unbanistered stairs to the ground floor, then out into the compound. He kept telling Shea he didn't want him to think he had to cook for him and Mike, but Shea studiously ignored him.

And now Tate found himself looking forward to his brother's latest test for the restaurant menu.

Tate's cellular phone rang when he was halfway across the compound. He flipped it open, held a hand to his ear and shouted, "Hello!"

Despite the sound of the power tools, he recognized the distressed voice immediately.

"Tate! Are the girls there?"

He tensed. He knew the girls weren't here; if they were, they'd be right behind him. But he did a quick scan of the site anyway.

"No," he replied. "Why? Aren't they at the bus stop?"

"Well, I was supposed to meet them in town today for dental checkups. Dad and a couple of his poker cronies went to visit a friend in the hospital in Portland, and he called me just before I was ready to leave to tell me he wouldn't be home for dinner. I'd cut it kind of close already and was a few minutes late getting to town. Of course the school bus was a few minutes earlier than usual and we missed connections.''

Her voice was high-pitched and urgent, and he heard her swallow.

''I called the school, who got in touch with the bus driver, and she said she watched them go into the dentist's office, but the receptionist said they never came to the desk. I thought maybe they'd run into somebody from the compound and gotten a ride home or something. I know that's far-fetched...''

''Where are you?'' he asked.

''The phone booth in front of the drugstore.'' He heard a sound of anguish. ''Where could they be? I *know* they wouldn't purposely scare me like this!''

''I'm sure they're fine,'' he said calmly, deliberately dismissing from his mind all the horrors that arose when children were missing. ''Your dad left the Jeep in the compound. I'll take a minute to run by your house to make sure they didn't come home, then I'll head right there. You going to be okay?''

''No,'' she said, and she didn't sound as though she was kidding. ''Hurry. I'll wait at the bus stop.''

He took a moment to tell Mike what had happened and asked him to call him on the cell phone if the girls turned up. Then he leaped into the Jeep and got to Armand's house in three minutes flat. The girls weren't there.

He was in town ten minutes later and found Colette looking pale and tense, standing behind the bench at the bus stop. She grabbed his forearms, her eyes miserable.

''Still no sign of them,'' she said, her voice tight,

her grip painful. "I've been in every shop, up and down every street. Tate, what if...?" She couldn't form the words.

He shook his head, unwilling to hear it. "That didn't happen. When were you supposed to meet them?"

"Almost an hour ago," she said. "I checked the library 'cause Megan can get lost in a book, but they weren't there. I checked the bakery because every time we meet here I have to buy them cream horns, and I thought they might have gotten impatient waiting..."

Her eyes brimmed with tears and he knew she was very close to losing control.

"I should have been on time..."

"Don't do that to yourself," he said. "You didn't do anything wrong, and nothing's happened to them. They're here somewhere."

"Where?" she demanded. "I've looked everywhere! Town is only two blocks long."

"We'll look again," he said quietly, reasonably. "You take one side of the street and I'll take the other. You were probably walking into one store while they were walking out of another and missed them."

"But they *knew* they were supposed to meet me at the bus stop!"

"Colette, they're children. To them, an hour is like five minutes. They probably went to do something quickly since you weren't at the bus stop and have no idea a whole hour has passed. Now, come on. You take this side, I'll take the other, and we'll meet at the end of the second block."

She heaved a ragged sigh and swiped a hand over her eyes. "Okay," she said, drawing a breath. "Okay. I'm sorry."

He gave her a quick hug. "Don't be sorry. Get ready to be happy. We're going to find them."

Tate went into every little shop on Frenchville Street, up and down every aisle, asked the clerks to check dressing rooms and rest rooms.

At the end of the first block, he stopped to look across the street as Colette came out of the sporting goods store. She shook her head at him, the expression of fear back on her face.

He waved at her, trying to seem confident, and crossed the side street to the toy shop, praying that he would find Megan and Katie there, enraptured by a three-foot teddy bear.

He found the teddy bear in a corner, but no little girls around him. He gave the clerk a brief description of them and asked if he'd seen them.

He, too, looked worried and followed Tate back out the door. "I'll keep my eyes open, though," he promised.

Tate forced a smile of appreciation and went into the next shop. He got halfway in, discovered that it sold New Age products—crystals, candles, aromatic bath salts—and was about to dismiss it as nothing of interest to the girls, when he heard a voice behind a tall display say, "There you are, ladies. All wrapped up for you. Thanks very much."

"Thank you," a very young voice replied.

Tate remained where he stood, afraid to believe he'd found them, waiting for visual evidence to convince himself.

Then Megan and Katie walked out from behind the display in dark pants and bright-red coats, carrying colorful backpacks. Their hair was disheveled as it always was, their cheeks lively with color and excitement.

His heart resumed a steady rhythm for the first time since Colette had called.

Megan rolled down the top of a paper bag. "Hi, Tate!" she said, hurrying to him. "What are you doing here?"

Katie ran to grab his hand and smile up at him.

He had to take a moment to compose himself.

"I came to help your mother look for you," he said sternly, not at all surprised by his own paternal reaction. "Weren't you supposed to meet her at the bus stop?"

Megan's smile faded and her eyes widened. "What time is it?"

"It's almost five."

The color drained from Megan's face. That made Katie frown.

Megan said quietly, "We were supposed to meet her at quarter to four, but she wasn't there yet, so I thought we'd have a little time to…" She held up the paper bag.

Tate nodded in understanding. "Well, I hope you can explain that to your mom, because she's pretty frantic." He caught each girl by a hand and walked out of the store onto the sidewalk.

Across the street, Colette stepped out of the stationery store and saw them. She put a hand to her heart, and he could almost feel her relief as she tipped her head back for an instant and simply stood there.

Then, without looking left or right, she walked toward them.

"Watch the…!" he shouted, his heart rising into his throat as a courier truck bore down on her.

The truck screeched to a halt within inches of her. Everyone walking by stopped to look.

Colette danced a few steps away from the truck, waved a quick apology, then hurried toward Tate and her daughters. The others went on about their business.

This family, he thought, was going to make him old before his time.

Tate felt the girls lean into him as Colette approached.

She was even paler than she'd been earlier, and anger had replaced the misery in her eyes. She took each girl by an arm and pulled them in front of her, leaning over them with an expression that scared even him.

"Where have you been?" she demanded. "What happened?"

"You weren't there," Megan said, her voice small, "so I thought we had time—"

"What's the rule," Colette interrupted stiffly, "if we're supposed to meet and I'm not there?"

"We wait for you," Megan replied, "and we stay together and we don't talk to strangers and we don't take rides from anybody."

"Why didn't you *do* that?"

"Because it's…"

"Do you have any idea how worried I've been?"

"I…"

"Do you know how frightened I was? I've been

looking for you for over an hour! I thought someone had taken you! I thought…''

''Colette.'' Tate put a soothing hand to her back. Her lips were beginning to tremble and her voice was rising. Megan and Katie were starting to cry. ''Want to talk about this over cocoa and coffee?''

She straightened and met his gaze, angry at the interruption.

''No, I don't.'' He could see her struggling to maintain her composure in the midst of a relief that had to be debilitating and an anger she just couldn't shed. ''I think I'll take them home and they'll be lucky to get dinner, never mind cocoa! Megan, whatever made you *do* this?''

Megan, now sobbing, handed her the brown bag.

''You went shopping? I'm having cardiac arrest because I don't know where you are, and you're—'' While she lectured, Colette drew a brightly wrapped and beribboned package out of the bag and stared at it, adding absently ''—shopping.''

''Happy…birthday…Mommy.''

COLETTE WANTED TO DIE. And she wasn't kidding. She'd have happily given up the ghost at that moment and gone to rest with Ben, whom she'd understood so well, and who had understood her and their children. Certainly that would be preferable to being left to cope with things that were just too big to handle alone.

The tricky thing was that she kept thinking she'd reached a point where she could cope, then she'd come to realize that she couldn't.

The girls would do something that reminded her

how much they needed a father in their lives. Or she would meet a man who reminded her that she didn't want to be alone.

She hated her loneliness, but she didn't have the guts to move herself and her girls into another man's life.

So. The upshot of all this was that she'd been railing at her children for the past five minutes because they'd taken the opportunity of a few moments' freedom to buy her a birthday present.

If she couldn't die willingly, she should be shot.

She pulled them both to her and wept with them.

"Okay." Tate wrapped his arms around the three Palmers. "I think we'll just overrule you and have a birthday celebration. Come on."

Paradise Pizza was a dark and quiet haven. Three men in baseball caps sat in a corner over beer and an enormous pizza while they watched the news on a big screen TV.

The girls chose a table near the window that looked out onto a rock garden and a fishpond.

Tate brought a pitcher of cola and menus to the table.

"Katie doesn't like anything but cheese on hers," Colette said, her composure restored, if a little uncertain. "And Megan likes only meat, no veggies."

"What do you like?" Tate asked, scanning the combinations.

"Anything but anchovies or pineapple. I don't think pineapple belongs on a pizza, and I don't think anchovies belong on anything."

"Well, I agree with you on the pineapple, but

there's no point in getting the pizza with everything if you're going to leave off something.''

Colette disagreed. "Why not? It's just discretion.''

"I think it's cowardice,'' he taunted, hoping her usual delight in arguing with him would banish the remnants of her fear. He closed his menu and gathered up the others. "Okay, so two large pizzas, both done in halves. One cheese only, one meat only, one with everything and one with everything but anchovies and pineapple.''

"And can we have those breadsticks you dip in sauce?'' Megan asked hopefully.

"Coming up. I'll be right back. I'm going to take a minute to call home and tell them the girls are all right.''

While Tate placed their order and made the call, Colette tried to reestablish a rapport with her daughters, yet also impress upon them the seriousness of what they'd done.

She tapped the still-wrapped box in front of her with the tip of her index finger. "I think it's very thoughtful that you remembered my birthday. But I want you to understand how worried I was when I got to the bus stop and you weren't there. It would have been a better idea to meet me, then after your appointment, ask me if you could have a little time to go shopping.''

"But we wanted it to be a surprise,'' Megan explained, her eyes grim with penitence. Katie nodded.

"Well, sweetie, this way I had a really bad surprise.''

Megan sighed and slumped in her chair. "I'm sorry,'' she said. Katie nodded vigorously. "I didn't mean for that to happen. The shop had all this neat stuff and I sort of forgot about the time.''

''I understand how that can happen.'' Colette leaned toward her earnestly. ''But when I couldn't find you, I called Tate away from his work to help me because I was so worried, and we missed our dentist appointment.''

Megan tried a frail smile. ''That's kind of a good thing.''

Colette bit back a smile and shook her head. ''Not for the dentist who didn't have anyone to work on for that hour and didn't get paid. Usually if you miss an appointment, you have to pay for it anyway, but Dr. Stewart says he isn't going to charge me for it because he was worried about you, too. But he could have.''

Megan's eyes brimmed guiltily. Colette reached across the table to cover her hand. ''I just want you to remember the next time you decide to do something we haven't planned together that lots of people are affected when you don't let somebody know.''

''I'm sorry.''

Again, Katie added her nod to Megan's apology.

''Okay. You're both forgiven. But if you scare me like that again, there'll be dire consequences.''

Two little frowns greeted that warning. ''What's 'dire'?'' Megan asked.

''Very serious.''

''And what's 'consequences'?''

''It's what happens to you as a result of what you did.''

''Oh.'' Megan made a face. ''It wouldn't be a good thing.''

"I'm glad you understand."

Tate arrived with a steaming, aromatic plate of breadsticks and a container of sauce. He also had a fistful of napkins, and tucked under his arm was a shaker of chili peppers, and one of Parmesan cheese.

He placed everything in the middle of the table, then sat down beside Colette. "You know," he said, handing her a napkin, "there's a little trick to having a birthday called 'advertising.' If you let people know, you get presents."

Megan immediately employed the principle. "Mine's December 12."

Katie elbowed her, then pointed to herself. "And Katie's is June 16," Megan added.

"Okay. Pizzas on your birthdays, too." Then he returned his attention to Colette. "Are you reluctant to reveal which birthday this is?"

"Not at all," Colette replied, pulling the empty glasses toward her and pouring cola. "It's my thirtieth."

Tate groaned, helping himself to a breadstick. "Just a kid. No wonder you're not anxious to get involved with anyone again. When the girls are young women, you'll still be young yourself and the three of you can travel together like bachelor girls, hitting all the high spots and celebrating life."

"What's a 'bachelor girl'?" Megan wanted to know.

"A woman who isn't married," Colette answered, passing her a glass. She poured another cola and gave it to Katie. "And who doesn't have any responsibilities."

"But you'd always have us." Megan looked up

from peeling the paper off a straw. "So you couldn't be one of those."

"Tate meant I'd be one of those when you were grown because I wouldn't be responsible for you anymore. You'd be responsible for yourselves."

"But you'd still be worried if we were supposed to meet at the bus stop and we weren't there."

"Yes, I would."

"Then I don't get what's different. Except maybe if we were bigger, there wouldn't be those...those dire things."

Colette laughed. "Dire consequences. Right."

Tate frowned in puzzlement as he accepted his glass from her and passed her the breadsticks. "Dire consequences? Did I miss something?"

She told him about her conversation with the girls.

Megan leaned toward him conversationally, half a breadstick in each hand. "Did your daughters ever have dire consequences?"

"A couple of times," he said, pushing the sauce toward her. "But you don't have to worry, because you're not going to do that again, right?"

"Right."

"Then let's see what you got your mom for her birthday."

Feeling absurdly lighthearted considering the anguish she'd just endured, Colette pulled the glittery curling ribbon off the rainbow-colored paper.

Inside the paper was a simple cardboard box, a light floral scent emanating from it. Colette opened it to discover a lilac-scented soap, a votive candle of the same fragrance and a decorative bag filled with lilac bath salts.

"How wonderful!" she said with genuine pleasure. "I love it—all of it!" She put the soap to her nose and inhaled the fresh fragrance.

"Mom *loves* to take baths," Megan told Tate. "But mostly she has to take showers 'cause we're so busy. But sometimes on Sunday afternoons, or when it rains and she can't work outside, she takes a bath for a long, long time."

Tate enjoyed imagining Colette, naked and languid, scented water lapping at her curves, dipping into the hollows. He saw her read that in his eyes and braced himself for a vicious elbow in his ribs or at least a silent protest. But she did neither.

She simply returned his look, not approving but not condemning, as if she hadn't a clue what they'd come to mean to each other.

He, on the other hand, knew what they meant to each other. Love. Marriage. She'd felt desperate and she'd turned to him. And that was all the proof he needed.

Whatever contemporary courtesies dictated, he would always be a man who opened doors for women, who paid the check, who stepped between them and danger, who offered marriage and who never even considered walking away an option.

He grinned when he realized he was probably the same kind of man Ben had been. He just had to find a way to put the man to rest.

Colette held the soap under his nose. "Want to smell?"

Obligingly, he sniffed. It was more floral than her usual fragrance, but he liked it.

A score of playful remarks with which to taunt her

came to mind, but two pairs of bright eyes watched him from across the table, so he kept them to himself.

"Very nice," he replied, instead. "But I feel cheated that I didn't get to buy you anything."

"You're buying us pizza."

He scolded her with a look. "That's not the same thing. First chance we get, I'll take you shopping."

"For what?"

"For whatever you want."

She opened her mouth, probably to protest, but a young man in jeans and a red T-shirt with the Paradise Pizza logo on the pocket, arrived with their pizzas.

For an hour their conversations were sporadic, held between bites of the succulent meal. When the girls had finished, he gave them quarters for the video game, then went to the counter to refill the pitcher of pop.

He returned to find Colette daintily pulling an anchovy off the last piece of his half of the pizza.

"Are you stealing from me, Mrs. Palmer?" he asked, pretending severity.

She smiled up at him, clearly unimpressed. "I'm trying to disprove the suggestion that I'm a coward because I didn't have these on mine." Then she studied the limp length of fish, closed her eyes and popped it into her mouth.

She chewed once, then made a face that brought Tate to uproarious laughter.

He held out a napkin in which to dispose of it.

But she shook her head, pushing his hand away, and finally swallowed. Her eyes watered.

He handed her a glass of pop. She took a long sip,

then put down the glass. ''There!'' she said, clearly pleased with herself. ''No one calls Colette Palmer a sissy.''

He leaned toward her and lowered his voice. ''Well done. Now, if we could only transfer that courage away from pizza and into a relationship, we'd have something worth being brave about.''

## CHAPTER THIRTEEN

THE GIRLS PLEADED to ride home with Tate, but Colette insisted they ride with her, that they'd put him out enough for one day.

He let her know with a look that it was a poor excuse and that she was using the girls to try to keep her distance, when she no longer really wanted to.

But she climbed into the old truck, thanked him politely for the fourth time for the pizza and turned the key in the ignition to silence any reply he might make.

He got into the Jeep and followed her home, thinking it was a good thing he'd been born stubborn and that nothing had happened since to change him. He watched her taillights while guiding the steering wheel with one hand and wondered if this was the way he was going to spend the rest of his life—following her through it in a separate vehicle.

No, he told himself firmly. It wasn't. And he was going to make sure of that when the moment was right.

He just couldn't predict when.

He followed her up the road and stayed at the fork while she turned into Armand's driveway.

Once they were out of the truck the girls shouted goodbyes to Tate and Colette waved. He tapped the horn and drove up to the road to the compound, then to the house.

The site was eerily quiet, the scaffolding on the winery, the bunkhouse and the B and B making weird patterns against a moonlit sky. Every roof had been covered with plastic against the rain that wasn't forecast for the next few days but might appear anyway.

He'd come to love this place, sunny or wet. And now that the old buildings were getting fresh faces and a new companion in the Victorian B and B, he liked it even more.

And he loved working with his brothers, learning from Armand and the weekly staff meetings with everyone presenting ideas, haggling over details, then implementing the final decision.

He loved being followed around by two eager little girls, loved discovering what they were thinking, what they were feeling and being the focus of their affection.

More than anything, he loved Colette Palmer. But he was no closer to figuring out what to do about her than he'd been the morning he'd left for Boston and she'd reached to touch him.

She did that in some subtle little way every time he saw her, but she didn't seem to realize it.

He parked the Jeep around the side of the house and walked up the steps, thinking about his uncle's romantic problems since he didn't know what to do about his own.

Had Jack been heading off to find Daniel Mullins the day he disappeared? Had he been thinking about Tess and feeling the same ache Tate experienced because he couldn't have the woman he loved? At least, Tate thought with some comfort, Colette was alive, so he still had hope.

However thin it was.

The house was silent. A note hung at eye level from the brass loop on the living room's chandelier: "Gone to McMinnville for dinner," it read. "Trying out a new B and B-restaurant to make sure we're going to be better. Glad girls are okay. Kittens have been fed and are asleep on the heating vent in the dining room. Don't wait up. Mike and Shea."

Tate shook his head over the note. His brothers certainly were taking their work seriously.

He wandered into the dining room as he pulled off his jacket. All three kittens were draped in a pile on a simple square grate on the floor.

He loved that, too, he decided.

His computer, plotter and worktable filled up the room, pushing the table and chairs into one small corner. But he liked seeing it there even more than he'd liked it in his plush Boston office.

He tossed his jacket at a chair and went into the kitchen, where half a pot of coffee still stood on the warmer. He poured a cup, added a splash of cream and headed for the living room, intent on putting his feet up and thinking about nothing.

COLETTE DID LAUNDRY and straightened the living room to keep herself busy while the girls did their homework at the kitchen table. An edgy tension had taken control of her sometime during dinner, and though she'd labeled it leftover fear, she was beginning to understand it was something else entirely.

As the girls watched an hour of television, then got ready for bed, Colette scrubbed the kitchen floor. She was unable to sit still, unable to relax, unable to concentrate on anything but mindless tasks.

When she tucked the girls into bed, she remembered her terror of a brief few hours ago, and was finally forced to confront the source of this disquiet.

Katie's and Megan's sleepy, pink-cheeked faces reminded her of how frantic she'd been when she couldn't find her daughters, how urgently she'd wanted Tate with her. And the moment he'd appeared, big and competent, she'd felt a little steadier, a little more hopeful.

What she felt was need. She needed Tate.

It was probably lucky, she thought, rummaging under the sink for floor wax, that she was alone with the children, or she'd climb right back into the truck and…

The sound of a motor on the road sent her to the window, where she saw her father climb carefully out of a station wagon and wave at the two men still inside. He carried a grocery-store bouquet of flowers.

She opened the door for him.

He wrapped her in a hug. "I am so sorry," he said, stepping back to hand her the flowers. "Stretch and Lou called me about visiting Wally and I forgot about your birthday. What kind of father would do that, I ask you?"

She felt a smile on her lips she couldn't control. She put the flowers in a teapot with a broken spout. "It's all right, Dad. I had quite a birthday anyway." She told him about missing Megan and Katie at the bus stop, her call to Tate and the pizza party that had resulted when he'd found the girls.

Her father looked pleased with the scenario.

"I'm not sure I remembered to thank him, though," she said, struggling desperately to school her features into some semblance of conscientious gratitude. "Since you're home, would you mind if I ran to the house? I'd hate to just phone him."

"Of course not." He seemed uncharacteristically serious himself as he cleared his throat. "Take all the time you need. The girls are asleep?"

"Both of them." She had her jacket, had snatched up her gift from the girls and was running for the door. She stopped to blow him a kiss. "I love you."

His grin was rich with paternal intuition. "I love you, too."

TATE HEARD THE SOUND of a motor in the compound and knew by the faintly emphysemic sound of it that it wasn't Mike's Blazer. It sounded like Colette's truck, but it couldn't be.

It was. He pulled the drapes aside just in time to see her leap out of it and run toward the porch.

His heartbeat accelerated with an adrenaline rush as he ran to the door. He yanked it open and stepped outside.

"What?" he demanded.

She was pale, but her cheeks were flushed and her eyes bright. Panic? he wondered. Fear? Had something happened to the girls after she'd gotten them home?

She studied him wordlessly for a moment, opened

her mouth as though to speak, then flew into his arms, instead.

"Nothing," she said, her voice muffled against his chest. "Nothing's wrong. I just had to be here."

He looked around the decrepit front porch, missing the point. "Here?" he asked skeptically.

She tightened her grip on him. "No, *here*. In your arms."

Suddenly, his world shifted. He was reminded of the expression "the earth shook." It was true. He had to brace his feet apart to withstand the impact of her words.

He struggled to steady his brain. Yes. There *was* a bundle of fragrant femininity in his arms. She *was* holding him as if he were a life jacket and she was drowning. She *had* said she wanted to be here.

His mind groped blindly for some clue that would put this all together for him.

Then Colette made the search unnecessary.

"I don't understand," she said in a voice that seemed strained, yet curiously strong, "I don't know what to do about it. I don't know if it's right, and I can't see how it can possibly resolve itself, but…" She made a sound like a little gasp for breath, and her brow furrowed as if she were confused. "I'm in love with you."

That time the world took him by his feet, held him upside down, then shook.

"You ran to my rescue without hesitation," she said, moving her arms from around his waist to around his neck. "It wasn't until I got the girls settled in bed that I realized how often you're there for me. And you never even imply I'm in your debt."

She smiled, almost unwillingly. "How do you do that, anyway?"

He had no idea, but he didn't want to lose the moment. "Genius, probably," he replied, lowering his head to kiss her. She responded eagerly and he felt passion ignite inside him, crowding out everything else. "I'm magnanimous..." he went on a little drunkenly as she planted kisses along his jaw. "Unselfish...insightful and...understanding... And I love you, too."

He took several steps into the house and pulled her with him. He closed the door behind her, pushed her gently back against it, then kissed her with all the fervor built up over long weeks of wanting her.

COLETTE TOOK his kisses hungrily, responding with all the feeling she'd struggled to suppress since the evening she'd walked across the compound, feeling alone and aimless, and caught sight of Tate for the first time.

She remembered thinking how out of place he'd looked in his cashmere coat, but also how handsome and vital he'd been.

She couldn't fight the attraction any longer. She felt abysmally lonely when she didn't see him, and she loved the way her daughters lit up when he was near.

She would never forget walking out of the stationery store and seeing him between Megan and Katie, holding their hands. Her relief at their safety had been paramount, the picture they made together, so right.

She was suddenly aware of being lifted off her feet

and into his arms. She tried to stop thinking, to give herself over to sensation, but there was so much more to what she felt for him than simple passion.

He gave her one punctuating kiss, then raised his head, his eyes suddenly very serious. "Do you know what you're doing?"

She smiled and rested her head on his shoulder. "Of course. I'm seducing you."

He shifted his weight and bounced her once in his arms to get a firmer grip on her. "Yes. I got that right away. I just keep wondering…why?"

She lifted her head again to look into his eyes. She could see gold shards in the dark brown of his irises. Her reply was absolutely genuine. "Because I love you."

TATE SAW NO REASON to question her further. He carried her up the stairs and into the cool darkness of his room.

"Where are your brothers?" she asked as he set her on her feet beside his bed.

"Gone to McMinnville for dinner," he replied, framing her face in his hands and kissing her. "The girls okay?"

She ran her hands up his arms. "Yes. I told my father I had to talk to you." She turned her face into his palm and kissed it. "He told me to take as long as I needed."

All he could think was that they would need—at minimum—an eternity for what he had in mind.

He swept a hand down her back, rested it in the hollow below her waist and felt her move into him with a little sigh. He caressed her hip, shaped it in the palm of his hand and pulled her closer.

"Tate," she whispered, the quiet sound somehow loud with longing. He felt her fingertips slip under his sweatshirt and up his back over his cotton T-shirt.

He tugged off both shirts, the need to have her hand against his flesh urgent and desperate.

The sensation was so sharp, so detailed, he could feel every fine line of her fingerprints against his back as her hands stroked up to his shoulders. What he hadn't been prepared for was the exquisite touch of her lips against his collarbone.

He found the ribbed hem of her sweater and pushed it up, then took a step back for an instant to relieve her of it. He tossed it aside and pulled her back to him again, only to encounter lace against his ribs.

He felt for hooks, undid them easily and removed her bra.

"You did that skillfully," she said with a laugh.

"Every architect is at heart an engin-eer." The word took on two separate syllables as the beaded tips of her breasts pressed into his ribs and scrambled his senses.

"Tate!" she whispered urgently.

"I'm here," he replied, tightening his embrace.

"I guess…that's what I can't believe."

"Believe it," he insisted. "Believe it." He put a hand to the back of her head and guided her gently backward onto the bed, slipping a hand under her knees and easing her up against the pillows.

Her hands were at his belt, his went to the waistband of her cords. Within moments, she freed the buckle and he unfastened her button and zipper.

He tilted her legs toward him, caught his fingers in the elastic waist of her panties and pulled them off with her slacks.

After getting rid of the rest of his clothes, he worked the blankets out from under her, then climbed in beside her. The sheets were cool and she came into his arms trembling.

"You need flannel sheets," she teased, snuggling into him with her hands between them. "Brrr."

He tucked her into his arm, his other hand rubbing her bottom so that he could provide maximum warmth, causing her to make a little sound of pleasure.

Then Tate's seeking hands were everywhere and Colette hitched a knee over him to allow his gentle exploration.

For so long her life had been about caring for her children, looking after her father and nurturing the vines that her needs were ignored and finally forgotten.

But all those needs returned, clamoring, demanding.

He met them all.

And she abandoned her last vestige of control and gave herself to him.

"Did I tell you I love you?" she whispered, kissing his throat.

"Yes." He crushed her closer. "But I'd like to hear it again. And again."

"I love you. I love you. I love you."

THIS WAS HOW he wanted to live his life, he thought. With this woman in his arms, telling him over and over again that she loved him.

Her artful hands roved his chest down to his stomach, their calluses creating a delicious friction as they moved even lower.

She took him in her hand and he instantly lost all ability to reason or analyze. He wanted to be inside her, to fill her, to make her part of him.

He caught her hand and forced himself to concentrate, at least for the minute it took, on providing protection. Then he rose over her and entered her, feeling her contented breath against his cheek, the smile on her lips when she kissed him.

She wrapped her legs around him and he remembered nothing after that except the impression of mounting pressure, a more fine-tuned pleasure than he remembered experiencing in a long, long time.

COLETTE CLUNG TO HIM as they lay still holding each other.

She slipped a hand between them to her stomach. She felt brightness there. Warmth. Hope. Expectation that now life would be different. *She* would be different.

Tate eased away from her, his frown just barely visible. ''Something hurt?''

She kissed his jaw. ''No. I was just thinking that I feel different.''

''God. Me, too.'' He tucked her against his shoulder and kissed the top of her head. ''Do you realize that today you ate an anchovy *and* came here? I retract my suggestion that you're in any way cowardly.''

"Thank you." She laughed wickedly. "And I apologize for ever having called you 'a boy.'''

"And well you should."

They lay quietly for several moments, then she stirred against him and sighed.

"Please don't tell me you have to go home," he said, tightening his grip on her. "I'm not letting you go.''

"I don't want to go. But I *have* to. I'm not one of those bachelor girls we talked about yet."

He was comforted by the fact that she sounded as reluctant to leave as he was to free her.

He wanted to tell her what he intended to do about tonight, that this was something destined to last forever and as soon as she could explain it to the girls, he wanted to marry her. But the moment remained fragile and he didn't want to do anything to shatter it. She'd come a long way today.

"I hate to leave this warm bed," she groaned. "I'd like to keep you and the blankets wrapped around me while I drive home."

He had a sudden inspiration. "I've got an idea," he said, and pushed back the blankets on his side.

"No!" She caught his arm, her voice plaintive. "Where are you going?"

"To run you a hot bath." He pried her fingers from his arm, then kissed them. "Then you *will* have me wrapped around you while you drive home."

"Then how will you get home?"

"I'll walk."

"In the dark?"

"Fearlessly."

He went to the closet, felt for the robe hanging on the inside hook and took it back to the bed. "Get into this when I call you," he instructed.

In the bathroom he shared with his brothers, he flipped on the light, blinked against the glare, then proceeded to fill the old ball and claw-footed tub with hot water. When it was two-thirds full, he called her name.

"Colette!"

"Coming!" she replied, then appeared at a run, her small body enveloped in the dark-blue robe she hitched up with one hand.

They'd done their lovemaking in the dark, and they stood together for a moment in the middle of the bright bathroom and simply stared at each other.

Her cheeks were pink from his stubble, her hair a wild red mass against the shoulder of his robe.

Her eyes went over his face, feature by feature, and he felt an instant's panic at the frown he saw there, the look that said he seemed somehow to be a stranger.

Then she gave him a smile that made a noodle of his spine, and he realized he'd misread her. The circumstances may have been strange to her, but the smile said she loved him.

He put his index finger in the loose knot of the robe and undid it. Then he slipped it off her shoulders. She had something clutched in one hand and gave it to him so that she could slip her arm out of the robe.

It was the bath beads, soap and candle from her daughters.

He looked up at her to comment on them as the robe puddled at her feet. But the sight of her porcelain skin prevented him from thinking or forming words.

She shifted and crossed her arms over her breasts. "Can you edit out the stretch marks?" she asked.

"Stop that," he scolded. He uncrossed her arms and allowed himself the pleasure of a slow perusal of small but beautiful breasts, a flat stomach that made her question ridiculous, the neat flare of hips and the long, shapely legs that he'd have insisted she wrap around him again right this minute if he didn't know her children were waiting for her at home.

Gooseflesh had risen on her skin while he studied her, and he silently berated himself as he dipped a hand into the water to test its warmth.

He handed her the bath beads. "Put this in and see if the water's too hot." He held one of her hands to steady her as she complied.

"Hot," she said, dipping in a toe, "but great." She sprinkled in some of the beads. The light floral scent rose up with the steam that permeated the air.

She grinned at him over her shoulder. "Care to join me? You can scrub my back."

"Deal." He left the candle on the sink and placed the soap in the metal dish hanging over the side of the old tub. He climbed in, then helped her, easing her down between his knees.

She took the soap and made a lather in her hands. "Is this going to be too feminine for you?"

"I'll risk it," he said, taking the bar from her and soaping her back. He worked his hands in a circular motion over her delicate shoulders, down the scalloped ridge of her spine, then wrapped his arms around her to lean her against his chest.

He soaped her stomach, her ribs, her breasts—then nipped her soapy shoulder when his tender ministrations started to tax his resolve to do nothing more than warm her so that she could go home.

She tried to turn in the tub to return the favor, but he wrested the soap from her and put it in the dish. "That would not be a good idea," he warned, rinsing her off with his hands. "You'd better put on the robe and get out of here. I won't be talked into letting you go a second time."

She stood, and Tate breathed a sigh that combined relief and regret. But before he could seriously feel either, she placed her feet carefully on either side of his hips and lowered herself, this time facing him.

He sensed trouble. "What are you doing?" he asked as she moved a few inches backward and encouraged him to follow.

"Oh, I'm sorry," she said with exaggerated sweetness, batting her eyelashes at him in an innocent gesture that was also exaggerated. "Did you think you always had the final word?" She tucked her legs around him so that they were very, very close.

His body immediately went to work to prove what it could do in such circumstances.

"Colette." He huffed out a breath, knowing he was lost but realizing the defeat was a victory. "You said you—Jeez!—had to get home."

She'd taken him inside her with the smallest movement of her hips.

"I do," she said, reaching for the soap and working it over his shoulders and his chest. "But from now on... Ah!"

He wrapped his arms around her and cupped her bottom in his hands, pushing himself even deeper inside her. She tipped her head backward, eyes closed, soap forgotten in her hands.

He watched with great satisfaction while she was racked with little shudders.

"From now on," she finally whispered breathlessly, her eyes on his again, just a little glazed, "I'll have two homes. With my children and...in your arms."

He exploded inside her, the words as much a catalyst as the contractions of her body around his.

The instant he could think again, he buried his face in her hair. "I love you, Colette," he said. "I think for efficiency's sake, you should downsize to *one* home."

She kissed his shoulder, then began the complicated process of untangling herself. "I really have to go," she said, shifting backward, then crossing her legs in front of her and getting gracefully to her feet.

He was alone in the tub before he knew what had happened. And he didn't like the fact that she'd ignored his suggestion.

He leaned an elbow on the back of the tub and watched her pull on the robe and belt it.

"You're not thinking," he asked mildly, "that you're going to just evade the issue, are you?"

She leaned over the tub to kiss his forehead. "Don't make it an issue, Tate." And she walked out of the bathroom.

Temper began to dilute the evening's delicious euphoria.

Tate stood, yanked a towel off the rack and wrapped it around his hips. Then he stepped out of the tub and headed for the bedroom, leaving a trail of wet footsteps.

He found her sitting on the bed in her undies, pulling on her cords.

He stopped in the doorway and watched. She glanced up at him, her expression friendly but defensive. "Please, Tate," she cautioned.

"If what results from this," he asked quietly, "is not an issue, then you're suggesting the whole thing didn't matter."

Her look became impatient. "Of course I'm not."

"Than you admit it's important."

"Yes."

"But not worthy of discussion."

She stood to push her arms into her sweater. "Not at the moment."

"Why not?"

Arms halfway in, she drew the whole thing over her head, the turtleneck hanging limply as she struggled. "Because I don't know what to do about it now!" There was a trace of irritation in her voice, and a definite problem with the sweater. One hand protruded through the neck and the watch on her other hand was caught. She didn't seem to be able to get into the sweater or out of it.

He smiled to himself and considered leaving her like that, midriff bare, arms stuck out, making her look like some surreal little tree.

"If you're staring at me," she warned from inside

her oatmeal-colored trap, "instead of helping me, you're going to be really sorry."

He went toward her, steps unhurried. The fragrance of lavender wafted around them. "More of your 'dire consequences'? You're going to ground me or withhold my dessert?"

She reached a foot out and lightly kicked his bare shin with it. "No. But I would no longer consider you the gentleman I thought you to be."

"I just took advantage of you in the bathtub. I think I lose the badge of gentleman anyway."

"*I* took advantage of *you*," she corrected, shifting her weight, her arms drooping a little.

"All right." He found the empty sleeve and tried to slip his arm into it to retrieve hers, but the opening was too small. He simply put a few fingers in, then tapped her hand that protruded through the neck hole. "Pull this hand in and find my fingers in the armhole. Okay, let's blame you for the bathtub incident. That means you lose your badge of lady."

She made a sound of indignation, and her arm pushed through the sleeve to his fingers like a battering ram. "Because *I* made love to *you?*"

"No." He proceeded to start to extricate her watch from the sweater. "Because you did it just for fun."

She punched at him blindly with her sleeved arm. He dodged.

"I did not do it for fun! I did it because I had to. Because I needed you! Because I couldn't stand another minute without connecting with you."

"Connecting with me." He repeated her words as he carefully untangled a loop of yarn from the stem of her watch. "Interesting choice of words."

"Don't be arbitrary," she said through clenched teeth. "Connected, made love, had sex. I have no problem knowing what we did. I just don't know what to do about it now!"

Her watch finally free of the yarn, he released her arm and held out the empty sleeve so that she could find it.

"Well, if you knew that was going to be a problem, why did you come? If you don't want to make something permanent out of it, then you did it just for fun."

With both her arms now in the sleeves, she yanked the sweater down and he could finally see her face. Her eyes were filled with anger.

"If you say that one more time…"

He rolled his eyes. "I know. Dire consequences. Well, so far, with your threats just as with your *connecting*…" he gave her word special emphasis "—you're all smoke and no fire. Great sex, but nothing adult to back it up."

Still annoyed, she reached under her hair to free it from the neck of her sweater and it flew around her like some wild veil.

She squared her shoulders and, taking her hair at her nape, began to wind it into a coil. "It is also not adult to fling accusations at someone for whom you've just declared your love when you have no idea what they're feeling."

"Oh, I know what you're feeling," he said, reaching to the floor for his sweatshirt and yanking it on over his head. "Fear. You were heroic with the anchovy, but with this—there's definitely something lacking in the aftermath."

She reached into a pocket of her cords and produced a long brown comb, which she pressed into her hair with a vicious jab. "Ow!" she complained, her eyes telling him that was his fault. "You know I have to go home to the girls."

He dropped the towel without ceremony and stepped into his briefs and jeans. "And you know that's not what I'm talking about. The time after lovemaking is reserved for sharing dreams and plans, not running off without even a suggestion of what happens next."

She spread both arms out in exasperation. "What is *wrong* with this picture? That isn't what's happening here, but aren't guys supposed to like that? I don't want to tie you up because I'm not free to just move into someone else's life and you're *unhappy* about it?"

"That's a generalization that doesn't apply everywhere." He zipped and buttoned his jeans and yanked an old pair of tennis shoes out from under the bed. He sat down to put them on. "I've never notched my bedpost, and I've never believed in sex for the hell of it. Call me 'crazy.'" One shoe on, he stopped to frown at her. "You're not free to move into my life because you can't let Ben go. That's all it is, so don't try to complicate it."

"If I let Ben go," she said, her voice thickening, "I doom Katie to a life of silence."

He slipped on the other shoe and pulled the laces with a vicious yank. "No, you don't. When she feels secure again, she'll open up. And she's never going to feel secure while her mother's committed to someone who's no longer here."

"How do you *know* that?" she demanded, her voice rising. "Trained psychologists haven't been able to tell me how Katie's problem will play out!"

He got to his feet. "No, I'm not a trained psychologist," he replied, deliberately lowering his voice because he knew she hated to be the one out of control. "But I am a father. Every time she holds my hand, she's giving me her trust. She's comfortable with me. She feels safe with me. If she had me around all the time, she'd talk again."

He realized what an arrogant claim that was as he made it. Professionals with long experience hadn't been able to predict Katie's future. But he couldn't help the belief that fear had closed her throat and a sense of security would open it again.

Colette shook her head at him. "You just want what you want, Delancey. Your family's gone and you want to reestablish your little kingdom with me and my girls. You want subjects you can lord it over with great benevolence the way you do everyone in the compound."

That cut as deeply as she intended. That she could have shared what they just had and still think that he somehow wanted to rule her—benevolently or not— made him realize how wrong he'd been to think they were connecting.

"I'll follow you home," he said, reaching for his keys on the bedside table, thinking how far the situation had deteriorated from the moment when he'd promised her he'd be wrapped around her on the way home.

His gut ached again, more than it ever had before.

"There's no reason for you..." she began with a reasonableness that pushed him close to the edge.

He yanked the door open. "You want to talk dire consequences?" he asked with a cold anger. He'd never act on it, but he didn't mind that for a second she couldn't be sure of it.

She stormed out ahead of him and down the stairs.

## CHAPTER FOURTEEN

HE SLAMMED BACK into the house ten minutes later, enraged enough to rivet the B and B with his teeth. He strode into the kitchen, intent on finding something alcoholic.

Mike and Shea sat opposite each other in the nook. The kittens ate hungrily in a neat little row on the floor. He remembered that he'd noticed the Blazer beside his truck when he'd climbed in to follow Colette home. He didn't really care how much they'd heard.

"You guys have a good dinner?" he asked, opening one cupboard door after another.

"Yeah," Mike replied. There was silence while Tate rummaged through an upper shelf.

"What are you looking for?" Shea asked.

"Something to drink," he replied stiffly. "And Kahlúa's not going to do it."

"There's brandy in the corner cupboard near the window."

Tate went to it and found a bottle of Courvoisier. He took it down and poured a couple of inches into a waterglass. He started to walk off with it, then Shea called, "Hey! Come and join us."

He turned, spoiling for a fight, but Mike beckoned

him to join them, and he and Shea looked sympathetic.

"I was in love with a woman just like that." Shea sat as Tate slipped into the booth beside him. "When they don't hear you, there's nothing you can do, so give it up."

He didn't want to give it up, but he wasn't admitting that to anyone, particularly himself. Not that Colette had left him much choice.

Another silence hung heavily in the room for a moment, then Mike said without preamble, "Actually, I think she had a point."

"What?" Shea asked in disbelief.

Tate just looked at him, certain his need to do damage was visible in his eyes.

If it was, Mike wasn't impressed. Of course. He'd dealt with people who had actually acted on such an impulse.

"How much did you hear?" Tate asked.

Shea leaned into the corner. "We came in before it started to get loud. We heard you talking and were trying to decide whether or not we should leave again, when she screamed something about you being arbitrary because you couldn't decide what to call what you'd done, but it seemed to be a bigger problem to decide *what* to do now that you'd done it."

Mike sipped at a cup of coffee. "And then we decided it was just too interesting to leave."

"And when did you think she had a point?" Tate asked.

"When she said you were trying to reestablish your kingdom. I know, I know." He forestalled Tate's and Shea's protests with a raised hand. "You mean well and you do it only because you have this need to be a big brother to the whole world.''

''I assure you my feelings for her are not remotely fraternal,'' Tate said, swigging brandy. It was burning his throat, but it wasn't warming him yet.

''We detected that.'' Mike leaned toward him on folded arms. ''Your big problem is that you're a man who takes charge, and you're dealing with a woman who's *had* to take charge, and that's all complicated by the fact that she loves you, but she's afraid of you.''

''What?'' Tate and Shea again spoke simultaneously.

''Pain is a weirdly comfortable place,'' he said. ''And when the world's done something vicious to you, pain is the only part of it that's familiar, so it's easier to hide in it than to take the chance that you'll get creamed again.''

Tate thought that through. ''That's illogical,'' he said finally.

Mike nodded. Then Sterling leaped up onto the table, and Shea placed him on his lap. The other two kittens wrestled under the table. ''We aren't all architects put together with perfectly straight lines. Some of us are a lot sloppier inside, and there's no point in your trying to tell us what to do because we couldn't if we wanted to.''

Tate drank more brandy, mostly because he didn't want Mike's words to make sense. But they were starting to.

''You're a caretaker,'' Mike went on with a slight smile. ''It's all so clear to you. You know how to help Katie talk again and brighten Colette's life and you want to do that right now. But people who are grieving move slowly because grief is like thick honey and it spreads out to fill every corner. She can't move as fast as you want her to. You have to give her time."

Tate absorbed that, and to a point even felt he understood it. But something still confused him. "But *she* came to *me*."

Mike nodded again. "It was a brave step. But I imagine your…evening…" he said carefully, "was vital and exciting to her.…" He smiled and winced at the same time. "I'm basing this, you understand, on your general level of skill at everything else. I hope I'm justified."

Tate winced himself. "Go on."

"She caught a glimpse of what life could be like if she could just shed all the old stuff. But she apparently doesn't know how to do that yet. Just like me. I thought I knew what I was doing, but I didn't. And rather than hurt anyone else, I had to back off."

Tate was beginning to grow calmer—no happier, but calmer. He resented Mike's analysis of what to him had been a very delicious, then a very demoralizing, evening. But he had to appreciate the experience that went into the insight.

"You seem to have it together," he praised Mike grudgingly.

Mike made a scornful sound before downing the rest of his coffee. "Knowing how it works," he said, "and living with how it works are two different things." Then he grew serious and met Tate's eyes. "I'm the last one to preach patience. It just doesn't come naturally to a Delancey. But I think that's what this is going to require.''

"God." Tate let his head drop back against the wall. "Are there no uncomplicated women in this entire world?''

Shea laughed. "Felicia Ferryman's pretty straightforward. She had dinner with Mike and me tonight.''

Tate raised an eyebrow. "You didn't mention that in your note.''

"We didn't know we'd have the pleasure of her company. She was in the lounge when we walked into the restaurant. She spotted us and invited herself to our table. Supposedly to make sure we're going to be involved in the tasting tours in June.''

"Really.''

"Yes. And she asked about you." Mike grinned devilishly.

"We told her you had a date with Colette. She did not seem pleased. Apparently, Colette once dunked Felicia's head in the john.''

"What?" Tate expelled a laugh along with the exclamation. That was something he couldn't quite picture.

Shea laughed, too. "Seems Colette pushed her headfirst into the toilet at last year's winery association dinner. She insists it was deliberate and malicious. Now that Colette's not speaking to you, you can't even ask her for the skinny.''

Tate downed the last of his brandy and was just beginning to feel the warm glow in the pit of his stomach that meant the alcohol was doing its work. And, strangely, rather than muddling his mind, it seemed to be clearing it.

He began to formulate a plan.

"I will ask her about it," he said, leaning back again. "As if we haven't just ripped each other's hearts out." He raised a hand as Mike opened his mouth, probably to protest the plan.

"Relax. I'm not going to push her in any way, but I'm not going to give her an escape route, either. If she's ever going to trust me and believe I'm what she needs, then I've got to be there when she finally decides that and turns to me."

He saw Mike and Shea exchange a worried look.

Expecting more of an argument, he was surprised when Mike reached into his shirt pocket and asked, "What to see my sketch for the label?"

"Yeah." Tate and Shea leaned across the table as Mike spread out the paper.

In the middle of the white square was a shield decorated with a bunch of grapes complete with leaves and tendrils. In a spray behind the shield were three lances at an angle. In the background were the hills around French River.

The Delancey Vineyards name was in the upper left corner, with Delancey in a large bold script.

"I like it," Shea said, obviously surprised. "The lances are a good idea."

Tate nodded his approval. "A great idea. It's us— ready for battle. Good work."

"Thank you. I think it's attention getting. A label's such a small amount of space in which to sell something until people know the wine. We don't get to use it for a couple of years, but we can have a sign painted for the tasting room. And we'll need another sign for the road and the entrance to the compound.''

A flicker of excitement edged aside Tate's depression. "Can you see about signs, or do you want me to?''

"No, I'll handle it.''

Shea elbowed Tate. "Don't worry about Colette. You still have us.''

Tate looked mournfully into his empty glass. "Please, Shea,'' he said. "I was just beginning to feel better.''

COLETTE AND THE GIRLS delivered groceries to Rachel the following Saturday. As they arrived, Katie spotted Tate wandering over the B and B site abandoned by the crew for the weekend and bolted from Colette's side to run toward him.

Megan followed, shouting his name.

Colette groaned as Tate turned to them, a genuine smile of delight on his face. He opened his arms to welcome them. Megan talked excitedly and Katie nodded.

Then Megan pointed toward Colette.

*Oh, no, no, no,* Colette thought, trying to stiffen her spine as they came toward her. The night she'd gone to him had been entirely her fault, and though she hadn't admitted it to him yet, she did accept that.

She knew what had sent her to him. He was everything she missed in Ben, and something else besides. She'd needed to be in his arms.

But that had been selfish and unreasonable, because she'd known she couldn't just walk off into the sunset with him.

Still, she was hard-pressed to regret it. Even after their argument, the warm, tender moments of that night returned to her a hundred times in a day, and she prayed for the courage to resolve the dilemma.

She'd kept close to the house the past few days, hoping she wouldn't run into him. Now he was striding toward her, holding her daughters' hands, and she had no idea what to say to him.

The girls hopped along beside him.

Energy still crackled in him, but it was a smooth adult thing that emanated from him like something he'd learned to harness and use.

Ben, on the other hand, had never harnessed anything. His energy had been unfettered and...

She was stunned to realize she couldn't finish. The picture of Tate coming toward her with Katie and Megan in tow crowded out her thought about Ben, and though she tried to recapture it, it wouldn't come.

Tate filled her frame of vision, filled her mind, filled every part of her body.

And then he was a foot away from her.

"Hi!" he said cheerfully, his eyes going over her dark blue leggings and long blue sweater. She'd caught her hair back in a ponytail because the dry air had made it unmanageable. His eyes lingered on it a moment, then dropped to her eyes.

She looked for awareness in him, for the sexual attraction she felt at his nearness, but it didn't seem to be there. She was acutely disappointed.

She handed Megan the bag of groceries she held. "Would you two carry this in to Aunt Rachel, please, so I can talk to Tate?"

Megan took the bag with mild belligerence. "We like to talk to him, too, you know."

Colette bit back a smile. "I know. But you see him every day after school."

"Well, Grandpa said you should come down to the site and see what's happening, but you—"

"Thank you." Colette interrupted her before she could inadvertently reveal that Colette had been deliberately keeping her distance from Tate. A fact she was sure he'd figured out for himself. "Please do as I ask and I'll be along in a minute."

Rachel opened the door to admit the girls, waved at Tate and Colette, then closed the door again with a speculative little smile.

"I want to apologize for the other night," Colette said quickly before she could lose her nerve. She tried to look him in the eye, but he was watching her with such careful distance that she found it difficult—and painful. "I should never have done that. It was all my fault."

"Which part?" he asked.

She wasn't sure why she found that simple question so annoying. "What do you mean, which part? The whole thing. I'm accepting responsibility for the whole thing!"

He lost his neutrality enough to appear to be thinking about that night, then he leaned a hand on the corner post of the picket fence. "I'd like *some* credit for the excellent lovemaking," he said finally. "But the embarrassing retreat that followed is all yours."

Her temper ignited instantly, but she held on to it with great determination. "Fine. I said I accept full responsibility. I just didn't want you to think—"

Colette stopped, but Tate could easily read what she didn't seem able to say. He didn't want to feel sympathy for her, but he knew Mike had been right in his assessment of her position. And though it made his life miserable, he was almost able to understand. Not quite, but almost.

"That you were using me for comfort in a frightening moment?"

He expected her to deny his words. She even parted her lips to probably do just that. Then she closed them again, shook her head and put a hand to her forehead.

"I did do that," she admitted finally, dropping her hand and looking him in the eye. "I'm really pretty tough, but there are times when I just don't know what to do or how to go on. And you always seem so confident. So assured. I wanted to absorb that."

He considered the reply that came to mind, hesitated for a moment, then decided however she chose to interpret it, he couldn't lose.

"Well," he said, arms outspread, "it's yours anytime. You know where to find me."

He saw the confusion in her eyes, followed by anger, followed by longing, coming full circle with renewed confusion.

Was he offering her simple, uncomplicated sex any time she thought she needed his arms around her? Did he mean he would always be there, and she could make their relationship permanent at any time?

He wasn't sure which of those choices brought the anger to her eyes, then decided he meant it either way. He felt confident that given enough time with her, he could ultimately offer her whatever she needed.

He suspected that thought was in direct conflict with Mike's suggestion for his behavior, but his brain didn't seem to have a coasting mode. He had to think in terms of solutions.

"My brothers had dinner with Felicia Ferryman the night you and I spent together," he said, changing the subject. "And they learned something from her I hadn't heard before."

She rolled her eyes and folded her arms over the bulky sweater. He made himself look away from her nicely defined breasts. "I hate to ask, but what was that?"

"She says you knocked her headfirst into the john at last year's winery association banquet."

She studied him. He wondered what she was thinking. "Would that upset you?" she asked.

He had to smile. "Not necessarily. But it would definitely strip you of your lady badge. So you did do it?"

She nodded, a quick but satisfied grin coming to, then going from, her lips. "Yes, but not deliberately. She'd done far too much tasting and had run into the rest room—I guess to toss her cookies—and unfortunately decided to stand behind a stall door that was closed but not locked."

"Ah. I see it coming."

"Right. I hurried in for quite another reason, pushed my way into what seemed to be an unoccupied stall just as she was leaning toward the bowl."

"And sent her all the way in?"

She giggled despite herself. "No. I sent her into the tile wall behind it and knocked her unconscious."

"Ouch."

"She was understandably upset when she came to, but said some rude things to me and to Rachel and my girls, who'd come to try to help, and has hated me ever since. I'm afraid it's pretty mutual."

"Then you probably don't want to represent Delancey Vineyards on the tasting tours committee? I believe she's on it."

Colette looked surprised, then pointed to most of the compound's buildings still being remodeled. "You're sure we'll be ready? It's the first week in June. That's only two months."

"I'm sure. Everything will be ready but the B and B. That'll probably take us until the fall. Mike's going to make sure to get the word out to the news media that it's our first year and we'll have food but no wine until this year's harvest is ready. We think it's important for us to get on the tour list right away so we're taken seriously. And since you and your father are the ones who know everything—and your dad's not really up to it—it seemed logical that you should represent us at meetings. But if that'll be a burden for you because of Felicia…"

"I can deal with Felicia," she assured him. "But you might want to be careful around her. And warn your brothers. I think she's out to land a handsome young thing."

"Why, Mrs. Palmer," he teased, "are you calling me young and handsome?"

She gave him a dry smile. "I saw you react to her

when Victoria frightened her. I'm calling you 'vulnerable.'"

"Now, that's where you're wrong."

"Why?"

"Because I'd never be tempted to follow her into a bathtub. Tell Rachel I said hello."

He liked the flustered look in her eyes just before he walked away.

## CHAPTER FIFTEEN

SPRING BROUGHT TATE a host of new discoveries. The only unfortunate thing was that they all related to the winery. Colette remained as much an enigma to him as ever.

But he began to learn the cycle of the grape.

The first sign of life did occur in late March as Colette had predicted, and it did look as though the vines were pussy willows. First the soft, fuzzy buds were pale pink, then green flower clusters appeared.

Tate mistook them for the grapes.

Colette, walking him through the vineyard to show him the early progress, shook her head. "It'll be a few more weeks before we even see grapes. These buds will produce the blooms that will eventually bring the grapes."

In the middle of April, Tate helped Colette plant rootstock for a new vineyard on a couple of acres that were lying fallow. When they were finished, he thought it looked as though they'd planted sticks, but Colette said the tendrils would be visible in a month. It would be two years before they grew up the stakes, and four before they would yield a crop. They wouldn't be considered mature for ten years.

In May they trained the vines, pulling off super-fluous shoots, leaves and flower clusters. The leaves were a bright green-gold, and he could think of no more beautiful sight than the shoulder-to-shoulder armies of vines.

The weather was bright and beautiful now, the rain far less frequent.

"We thank the Fates for this," Colette told him, "because heavy rain would mean that the grapes would be nothing more than little green berries by October."

He split his days between the site and the vineyard, and seemed to have very little time for his life.

Mikc had taken to his role as public relations person seriously and had almost everyone in the state of Oregon talking about the Delancey Vineyards. He got interviews with several newspapers and on radio shows. A female reporter referred to them as the "Beautiful Bachelor Brothers" from French River. They enjoyed that enormously.

The restaurant was finished, though the appliances hadn't arrived yet, and Shea was fine-tuning the menu. He'd chosen a dozen dinner entrées, and he kept making another six for dinner so that Tate and Mike could help him decide whether or not to include them.

Tate considered it a very good thing that he had so much physical work to do, as well as a very high metabolism.

The kittens were growing, now almost four months old. They were plump and playful and always a source of entertainment. Joe slept on Tate's stomach at night and woke him early every morning by standing on his face.

The subject of Jack's disappearance and the photo

had been set aside until they could figure out how to proceed without hurting anyone involved.

Romance was the only part of Tate's life that showed no progress. And considering the amount of time he spent with Colette, he couldn't understand it.

Mike kept insisting that it was because love couldn't be managed, and Tate was finally beginning to believe he was right.

Colette was hardworking, smart, conscientious and always studying. Her approach to wine making was that of a scholar with built-in savvy.

When they weren't in the vineyard, however, she was cool, quick-tempered and contrary with him. He had trouble deciding if that was good or bad.

On one hand, he couldn't believe she'd be so difficult if she didn't care. On the other, he didn't know how much longer he could put up with her growly behavior.

The situation came to a head one sunny afternoon in the last week in May when he stood on the roof of her father's house, looking for the source of a leak in Armand's bedroom.

Armand and Tate had deliberately chosen a time when Colette was absent because although she'd repaired it the previous spring, the problem had reappeared and Armand didn't want her to know.

Unfortunately she returned home early from a tasting tours committee meeting. Armand was at the winery, supervising the arrival of one hundred Limousin oak barrels.

"What are you doing?" she asked from the front lawn.

He tried to think fast to protect Armand's confidence, but he'd been working day and night and his synapses were slow. "I'm trying to find the source of a leak," he said, concentrating on the tiles. "I'll be out of your hair in a minute."

"If only that were true," he heard her mumble.

"Pardon me?"

"What leak?" she demanded. "I fixed the one in Dad's bedroom."

He was suddenly tired of dancing around her bad moods. "Well, apparently not very well," he replied, "because he says it's still leaking."

"I put nine new shingles up."

He'd just discovered the patched area. Two of the shingles came right up in his hand. "That's apparently the problem. You didn't use galvanized nails. A couple of them are already gone, and two just came off when I touched them."

There was a moment's angry silence and he half expected her to accuse him of having ripped them off deliberately.

"Well, get down," she ordered, "and I'll change my clothes and fix it."

"I'll fix it tomorrow now that I know what I need. It's going to be dry tonight."

"No! I'll take care of it. I wouldn't want you to put yourself out for someone you consider so difficult."

"Then stop *being* difficult!"

"Fine," she said, taking the ladder and dropping it onto the lawn. "Stay there." He heard her slam into the house.

COLETTE WAS READY to admit that her actions had been juvenile, but he always seemed to have the last word in their arguments, and stranding him on the roof had been such a satisfying way to have the final say.

She couldn't leave him up there for very long, of course. Maybe only as long as it took her to fill the kettle, put it on the burner and change her clothes.

Or maybe not.

She did fill the kettle and place it on the burner, but when she turned to head to the bedroom to change, she was facing him. And he did not look pleased. There was a sprig of cedar on his shoulder and fire in his eye.

She resisted the impulse to take a step back, but her voice wasn't as strong as she'd have wished when she asked, "How did you get down?"

She did have to take a step backward when he advanced on her. "The tree against the back of the house." He now had her trapped in a corner and held her there with a hand to each side. The line of his jaw was very square, his voice ominously quiet. "If you think a little thing like a ladder is going to allow you to hide from me much longer, you're mistaken. I can get up, down, in, out—anywhere you go. And I can deal with your surliness for as long as it takes you to realize you want to spend your life with me."

She trembled, but it wasn't from fear. He was so close she felt as though every part of her body was reaching for him and she had to get a grip on the counter to prevent her arms from wrapping around him.

"Why would I want you," she asked, her voice

surprisingly steady, "when I know you think of me as a coward?"

"Because you know I'm right."

"Hah!" It was a stupid sound, but it seemed to relay the indignation she felt. "Well, you're wrong. I *don't* want you."

He shook his head slowly, his eyes telling her he was aware that was a lie. "I know how to get the truth out of you."

It was a threat. She realized instantly what he intended and realized, too, she'd never withstand it.

And didn't want to. She began a paltry protest.

"Don't you touch…!"

But he already had her in his arms, one hand wound in her hair, the other cupping her bottom and pressing her to him as he kissed her with a familiarity she resented—for two seconds. Then she leaned into him, driven to remind him that this need was not at all one-sided, that he longed for her every bit as much as she longed for him.

Some part of her heard the front door open and close, but the fact that they were no longer alone didn't register until she heard giggles.

She wedged a space between her and Tate just in time for her daughters to force themselves between them.

"You were *kissing!*" Megan exclaimed, clearly delighted by her discovery. Katie puckered her lips and mimed the gesture.

Tate laughed and wrapped an arm around each of the girls. "Yep, you caught us."

"Then you're her boyfriend!"

Tate pinched Colette's chin and stepped out from

between the girls. "Hear that?" Then he pointed a finger at her. "Do *not* get up on that roof. I'm coming back tomorrow to fix it."

"I don't—"

"Ah!" he interrupted, then threatened, "Dire consequences."

"What?" she asked skeptically, "Another kiss?"

"Maybe *never* another kiss. How would you feel about that?"

She guessed he had his answer, because the instant desperation she felt at that thought was probably reflected in her eyes.

He studied her change of expression and suddenly seemed penitent. He leaned toward her to give her a quick, apologetic kiss. "Never mind. It was an idle threat. See you tomorrow."

"Are you gonna get married?" Megan wanted to know, standing beside the chair as Colette sat down at the table, afraid her legs might not hold her. "Can we be bridesmaids? Are you gonna have a white dress with a veil?"

Colette opened her mouth to deny anything like that was imminent, when Katie brought the photo magnet of Colette and the girls with Ben to the table. Katie held it in front of Colette's face and pointed to Ben, a questioning look in her eyes.

"Have I forgotten Daddy?" Colette asked.

Katie shook her head and rubbed her hand in the air to erase Colette's question. She gestured to the photograph again.

"Would it be okay with Daddy?" Colette guessed.

Katie shook her head and repeated the erasing action.

"She wants to know if he's going to *be* our dad," Megan explained.

Katie nodded vigorously, waiting expectantly for the answer.

Colette looked into the child's always watchful eyes. "Would you like that?" She turned to Megan. "Do you want another dad?"

Megan seemed surprised by the question. "Yeah. I mean, Daddy—this one—" She pointed to the photograph. "We can't be with him. And Tate's kind of like I remember Daddy. He knows different stuff, but he feels the same. He doesn't push you off his lap, and he holds on to you when you cross the street, and he says 'Hey!'" she mimicked his voice in an authoritative tone many notes lower than her own, "when you get too close to the men with the tools or you don't do what he says, and he looks angry like dads do when they yell at you, but he's not. You know what I mean?"

Colette knew precisely what she meant. That explanation had been a little convoluted but was surprisingly clear. He'd be a good father.

And a wonderful husband. She wanted him. She wanted him desperately. But she looked at the man in the photograph and thought about putting him forever aside, and felt a swell of painful emotion clog her throat.

Maybe the pain didn't mean she wasn't ready, she told herself. Maybe she would always feel it.

But would that be fair to Tate?

Her brain muddled, she pulled the girls to her and told them honestly, "I don't know, girls. I love Tate a lot, but we have too much to do around here to think about weddings and daddies, so we'll make that decision later, okay?''

Both girls stared at her with puzzled frowns. They looked at each other, then Megan said, "Okay, but we already made the daddy decision. We want him."

Colette hugged them. "Okay. I'll bear that in mind."

IT WAS APPARENT that Rachel thought Colette was insane. Colette leaned against the animal pen, watching her raccoon wash a handful of food in his bowl of water.

"I don't think you're keeping Tate at bay because you're afraid of letting Ben go," Rachel said, putting her hands into the pockets of an old purple all-weather jacket. "I think you're keeping Ben close because you're afraid of going to Tate."

Colette thought that ridiculous in view of the night she *had* gone to him.

Then she remembered she had left—and not just because she had to get home to the girls. She'd run right back into her comfortable, sticky grief.

"Why," she asked of Rachel, "would I be afraid of Tate?"

Rachel shrugged. "Because you remember that marriage, while wonderful, is a lot of work and you're not sure you want to work that hard again? Or maybe because he has a strong personality, and you know you'll have to rein yours in a little to get along. Maybe because you'll have to share your girls and your father with him." Rachel touched her cheek affectionately. "Right now, you're everything to them—a little like a deity. You might not want to move aside and give him equal space.''

Rachel smiled and started toward the cottage's back door. "It's hard to say why you find it so difficult. If I was younger, I'd snatch him out from under your nose."

Colette, walking beside her, put an arm around her shoulders and squeezed. "I think he'd enjoy that."

TATE STOOD on the porch at 2:00 a.m. and inhaled the wildflower fragrance of the valley. It was warmer now, the threat of frost gone, and he leaned against the porch post in nothing but the old sweatsuit he wore to bed.

Joe Boxer had opened an eye when Tate had moved him off his stomach and onto the blankets but apparently had decided his devotion did not extend to getting up at that hour.

Tate wasn't quite warm enough, but he thought the slight chill was probably good for him. It kept him from slipping into comfort and relaxing. He had to be sharp and alert now.

The day after tomorrow, the newly remodeled, newly formed Delancey Vineyards would open its doors to the tasting tour. The first impression would help seal his and his brothers' futures.

He prayed desperately that he hadn't given them bad advice when he'd encouraged them to join him in this venture. He prayed that his decisions had been sound, his choices wise. Mike and Shea had been through so much. He wanted Delancey Vineyards to guide their lives in a positive direction.

The front door opened and Mike wandered out,

two coffee cups in hand. He still had on the jeans
and sweater he'd worn at dinner.

"You haven't been to bed yet?" Tate asked, then
accepted the cup Mike handed him. "Thanks."

"No. I was folding flyers to put in the tasting
room. Looks good, by the way. And our label looks
dynamite on the wall, don't you think?"

"Yeah, I do. I'd have helped you with the flyers
if you'd asked."

"No need." Mike leaned against the opposite
post. "You worried about the tour?"

Tate sipped at his coffee. It was the strong and
robust French roast that had helped them work four-
teen-hour days during the past month. The odds for
sleeping at all tonight didn't look good.

"Yeah, a little. A lot depends on our making a
good impression."

"We've done our best. And you've been heroic.
Now whatever happens happens."

Tate frowned at him. "Casual talk for a man who
kicked in forty thousand bucks and may never see it
again."

"Thirty-nine," Mike corrected. "One thousand
was Shea's."

The front door opened again and Shea wandered
out in a T-shirt and pajama bottoms. He turned
around immediately, then returned wearing a hooded
sweatshirt, his hands bunched in the front pocket.

He looked at the coffee in their hands. Went back
inside and came back again with a cup. He stood
between them in the middle of the porch. "What are
we doing up at this hour?" he asked, his voice thick
with sleep. "I hear Mike messing around in my

kitchen, then I hear Tate go downstairs. Did dinner give everybody indigestion or something? Maybe paprika hazelnut chicken isn't a good idea?''

"The chicken was great.'' Mike sat down on the top step. "I was folding flyers.''

Tate sat a step below him. "My brain just won't relax. The chicken was good. I think it's a keeper.''

Shea sat at the top, his legs stretched out on the porch rather than on the steps. "I'm not worried,'' he said. "I can't believe how well all your plans for this place came together. There's no reason to believe the rest of it won't come together, too.''

"And if for some reason it doesn't,'' Mike added, "we've had a great time, and all we're out is money. There's so much more in life you don't want to lose.'' Then he grinned at Tate. "That's kind of shaky for you right now, too, isn't it? Colette's not coming around?''

Tate sighed. "I think she loves me, but she's not convinced it's the right thing to do.''

"I can understand that,'' Shea said, looking up at the stars. "Love's important, but if you don't have other parts of your life in order, you can't give love what it needs.''

Tate frowned up at him. "Love helps you cope with everything else. Not the other way around.''

"Then why isn't it working for you?''

"Because she won't give in to it. You have to surrender to it to receive its strength.''

"Yeah, well.'' Shea shrugged. "I don't surrender to anything.''

Mike turned to Shea. "You want to tell us about her?''

"No," Shea replied simply.

"It might help."

"Nothing helps."

He sounded so genuinely distressed that even Mike seemed willing to let it go.

"I like the fountain," Mike said, pointing toward the middle of the compound. "Aunt Rachel says she and Colette are putting primroses all around it tomorrow."

Tate nodded. "I've rented tables and chairs to put in the compound so people can sit outside if they want to, and also a couple of tents on the chance the weather's bad. The forecast yesterday was a little iffy."

"You've thought of everything."

"Let's hope so."

"You know..." Shea brought a fist down lightly on Tate's shoulder, "you're not responsible for the world turning. Or the weather. We've prepared as best we can, and if things don't work out, as Mike says, we've had a great time. And we've learned something important." He grinned suddenly. "We can still do whatever the hell we put our minds to. Whoever chooses to stay behind is missing a great ride." He sighed and stretched, then looked at each of his brothers in turn. "I personally think we're destined for big things."

Mike raised his cup in a toast. "Hear, hear."

After that, Shea went back to bed, Mike went back to his flyers and Tate remained on the porch, staring into the darkness.

Mike didn't have a woman in his life, and Shea

had clearly been at odds with one when he left San Francisco.

But Tate was in love with one and couldn't quite accept the philosophical dismissal of women from their lives. He wished he could take Colette upstairs with him now. He wished the girls were asleep in the next room, Armand smoking his pipe by the fire.

Why, he wondered pessimistically, was happiness always just beyond his reach?

COLETTE WORKED her iron carefully between the pearl buttons on her silky flowered dress. She hadn't worn it in four years and hoped the forecast for tomorrow—sunny skies and temperatures in the low seventies—was accurate.

Megan and Katie hung over the ironing board, munching cookies. "I don't remember that dress, Mom," Megan said.

"That's because I haven't had anywhere to wear it in ages." Colette brushed crumbs off the skirt. "Girls, move back a little, okay? You're getting crumbs all over. Megan, aren't you going to take those flowers to Aunt Rachel?" She pointed to the double bouquet on the kitchen table.

"What are they for, anyway?"

"For an arrangement on the counter in the tasting room. I got them when I went to town to buy shoes just before I picked you up."

Megan, all girl, waggled her eyebrows. "New shoes, too! You're going to look beautiful."

Megan and Katie exchanged a smile. Colette ignored it, preferring not to think about what was going on in their conniving little minds.

A knock on the door sent both girls running to answer it. Megan yanked the door open and Katie flew into Tate's arms.

"Hi, ladies!" he said cheerfully, ruffling their hair.

"I'm taking these to Aunt Rachel." Megan held up the flowers. "Want to come?"

He shook his head apologetically. "I came to fix the roof. Tell her I said Shea has a couple of vases for those, okay?"

"Okay." Megan gave him a quick hug and skipped off.

Tate looked at Colette, the rich energy in him turning to simple courtesy, as if someone had flipped a switch. "Hi," he said. "I just wanted you to know I'll be on the roof."

She set the iron on its edge. "Why don't you let it go for now. With the tour tomorrow, you must have a hundred details…"

"I made time," he insisted.

"Then would you like some coffee first?"

He shook his head and backed out of the doorway. "No, thanks."

The door closed, Katie on his side of it, Colette alone in the house. The significance wasn't lost on her.

TATE BALANCED HIMSELF on the slope of the roof and pulled up the rest of the loose shingles. Out of the corner of his eye, he caught a glimpse of Katie watching him from the grass below. He blew her a kiss. She giggled and blew one back.

He was applying the second new shingle when he heard a cry from somewhere below him. He turned instinctively, remembering Megan on the road to the compound, wondering if he could see her and if she was all right.

The movement shifted his weight from his right leg, which was leaning higher on the roof's slope, to his left leg.

And that was all it took to pitch him backward into thin air.

## CHAPTER SIXTEEN

COLETTE FITTED a hanger into the neckline of her dress, then hung it on the hook on the back of her bedroom door. She held the skirt out and smiled, liking the way the flowered fabric felt.

Then something collided with her hip, and she turned to find Katie tugging on her, her face pale, her eyes alight with horror.

Cold dread rushed through Colette's body with a horrible sense of déjà vu.

Katie's breath was coming in gasps, and her small fingers dug into Colette's arms as she tried to pull her mother along.

*Oh, God, oh, God!* she prayed, as they hurried to the front door. The look in Katie's eyes was so torturously familiar. Something horrible had happened. She'd seen…death? Again?

Tate! Tate had been on the roof!

Katie dragged her around the house to the side—and she truly was dragging now because Colette didn't want to see whatever it was Katie had seen. She didn't want to know what the horror was. They'd barely survived the last time. *Please,* she prayed. *Please!*

Her worst fears were realized when she found Tate

on his back on the lawn. He lay very still, his face ashen.

"Oh, my God!" she heard herself say as she knelt beside him, feeling his throat for a pulse. It wasn't there! Or was it? She moved her hand slightly higher, pressed a little harder.

Was that it? Or was it her own?

Something small and black was shoved in front of her face. His cellular phone! Katie waved her hands in front of Colette's face, holding up nine fingers, then one small index finger twice.

911! Right. Colette stabbed out the number and gave the somewhat complicated directions to the dispatcher. Then she called Tate's house and got Shea. She had no idea what she told him.

She threw the phone down and leaned over Tate again. Then she heard him gasp, an ugly labored sound.

"Tate!" she shouted. "Tate, can you hear me?"

He made the sound again.

The air was suddenly filled by a high shrill sound. ``*Daddy! Daddy!*'' Katie put her hands on his shoulder and tried to pull him up, tears streaming down her face. ``*Daddy! Daddy! Daddy!*''

Colette stared at her screaming daughter in stupefaction for a full ten seconds before she realized she had too many traumas to deal with to do nothing.

Who to help first? Her child, who had finally reconnected with the worst night of her life and was dealing with it—unless this set her back irrevocably? Or the man she loved, who'd just fallen two stories and sounded as though he was dying?

He made that gasping noise again and raised a hand, as if looking for support.

Katie wrapped herself around his chest and tried to help him, still screaming.

"Katie, baby." Colette tried to peel her off him, while pushing Tate back to the ground as he struggled to sit up, but both resisted her efforts.

"Tate, you *have* to stay down!" Colette said firmly, taking Katie around her waist and lifting her off of him. "Honey, you have to let Daddy breathe!" She realized belatedly what she'd said, but she had bigger problems at the moment than editing herself.

Katie struggled against her, arms reaching for Tate.

Not only was he not lying down, but he was trying to stand. "Wind…knocked out…" he said feebly, gasping for air. He rose to one knee and winced, pressing a hand to his side. The little finger on that hand stuck out at an odd angle.

Realizing how determined he was, Colette put a shoulder under his good side to help him. Katie threw herself at him again.

"Did I—" he focused his attention on Katie, his eyes filled with pain, yet surprisingly clear "—hear you speak?"

She nodded, leaning over the hand he braced to his side to wrap her arms around him as far as she could reach.

"That's a nod," he said, leaning heavily on Colette. "Can you say yes?"

She looked up at him, her little mouth contorted, and nodded again.

"I can't hear that," he said.

"Yes," she whispered.

Tate took his arm from around Colette to embrace Katie. "Good girl," he praised, his disbelieving gaze finding Colette's. "Good girl."

Then Mike's Blazer screeched to a halt in the driveway and Mike and Shea rushed out of it, running to lend support.

"God!" Mike exclaimed. "What are you doing on your feet? Colette said you fell off the roof!"

"I think...I'm okay," he said, pain in his voice. "Broken rib, maybe. And finger." He held up his hand.

"Oh, that's cute," Shea said, wincing. "But I think having your little finger in the air works better for tea parties than for wine tastings. Shouldn't you be lying down? Did you call an ambulance, Colette?"

"It's on its way," she replied, "but maybe it'd be quicker if you took him to the hospital."

A crowd of people appeared; the workmen on the site were followed by Armand between Rachel and Megan.

Mike and Shea were helping Tate to the Blazer when they heard a siren. Almost immediately after that they saw the white truck, red lights rotating.

"I want to come!" Katie said loudly, clearly.

A paramedic was already beside them, holding a gurney in position while another helped Tate onto it. The first winked at Katie. "You'll have to ride with your mom, sweetie. But he looks pretty good to me. You'll probably have him back in no time."

Tate held a hand out for her. "I'd like her to come," he told the paramedic.

"But, it's not…"

"Come on," he cajoled. "I'm not going to croak. Let her ride in the front where she can see us. My family will be right behind us. Right, guys?"

"Right," Mike promised, his voice faint as he stared at Katie.

Everyone was staring in disbelief.

"I guess it's all right," the second paramedic said. "He's stable."

In a moment the ambulance was gone. Armand volunteered to stay with Megan while Colette went to the hospital with Mike and Shea.

"I want to go," Megan protested, her bottom lip trembling.

Mike held a hand out to her. "Then come on."

Rachel patted Colette on the shoulder. "Armand and I will take care of things here. You take your time. Just let us know how he's doing when you can."

THE WAIT FELT interminable. Mike supplied Colette with vending machine coffee, while Shea distracted Megan and Katie with a board game they'd found among the magazines.

Shea had tried to coax Katie to speak for the past two hours. He'd earned several smiles, a hearty giggle but no words.

Mike had called home to tell Armand and Rachel that Tate was still undergoing tests but seemed fine except for the rib and the finger.

Colette watched her daughter and prayed that talking hadn't been just a momentary thing, that the sight of Tate injured hadn't given her only the words she'd wanted to speak when she'd found her father dead but had also restored the words for happy, childish things.

Colette wondered if she herself had been robbed of speech when she'd seen Tate lying on the ground, pale and still. She wanted to talk to Mike now; she wanted to ask questions, to learn about Tate's childhood, to know about his daughters, but her throat was too tight to permit sound.

She wondered if that was what had happened to Katie.

Certainly the "Daddy! Daddy!" she'd screamed over and over had burst out of her like something long suppressed and under pressure.

Then something struck Colette with all the power of a sledgehammer on the top of her head. She jumped to her feet with the impact of it.

Mike turned to her in concern, putting a soothing hand on her arm. "What?" he asked.

She shook her head, her brain still processing the thought. It wasn't only Katie who'd been robbed of speech that night—but Colette, as well.

She'd had the use of most words, all right, but those that would admit love and need and promise had been lost to her when Katie was silenced.

That was why she couldn't promise Tate anything. Not because she didn't love him and not because she couldn't say goodbye to Ben. But because a mother followed her children everywhere so they would never be alone, even into the realms of silence.

It was all so clear now. And words of love were on the tip of her tongue. Ben had been a hero who'd risked his life for her. But Tate was willing to live for her, and that, too, was heroic.

"I'm fine," she whispered, sitting back down. Then she handed Mike her empty cup. "Do you think I could have one more?"

"Right away." He was on his feet and on his way to the vending machine at the end of the hall.

Katie, rubbing her eyes sleepily, left the game and came to climb into Colette's lap.

"Hi, sweetie," Colette said, brushing the hair out of her face. "How are you doing?"

Katie nodded.

"What does that mean?" Colette prodded.

Katie smiled, kissed her cheek and rested her head on her shoulder.

So. She had words only for "Daddy."

When the nurse brought Tate out in a wheelchair half an hour later, he felt amazingly well for a man in excruciating pain. God. Nothing hurt like a broken rib. It was far less serious than the scores of other injuries he might have sustained, but it made every breath painful.

But all he had to do was see the look in Katie's eyes and remember the sound of her voice to make the world seem like a place where things were good.

She came to him now and took his hand. "Hi," she said, her voice quiet and gravelly.

"Hi," he replied. "You want a ride?"

She came around the front of the wheelchair so that he could lift her onto his lap. Mike reached down to help.

"Well, you're a spoiled little daddy's girl, aren't

you?'' the nurse said cheerfully. "Okay, here we go.''

He wasn't in too much pain to look up into Colette's eyes and give her a silent "I told you so" as the nurse wheeled him out to Mike's Blazer.

At Colette's house, Tate insisted on going in with them for a few minutes.

Mike studied him worriedly. "You're out on your feet, Tate.''

"I promise I won't be too long. I have to talk to Katie.''

"Okay. We'll wait out here.''

"Why don't you go home," Colette suggested to Mike and Shea. "I can drive Tate back.''

Mike shook his head. "We'll wait.''

In the house, Tate was hugged carefully by Rachel and had his good hand crushed by Armand.

"You are a lucky man," Armand told him, his eyes moist. "Very lucky. And we are lucky to have you back.''

"Thank you, Armand." Tate indicated the living-room sofa. "Would you mind if I stayed and talked to Colette and the girls for a few minutes?''

Armand shook his head. "I will take Rachel home. It will be time for us to be up for the tour before we know it.''

Rachel pointed toward the kitchen as Armand helped her into her jacket. "Cold chicken and rice in the refrigerator if anybody's hungry.''

The door closed behind them and Tate settled on the sofa, Colette beside him. He pulled Katie into his lap, and Megan sat on the edge of the coffee table facing them.

He drew a breath and immediately regretted it. Pain shot up his side and vibrated there for a long moment.

"You're taking one of those pills right now," Colette said, going to the kitchen for a glass of water.

"We have to talk first!" he said, raising his voice to be heard as she disappeared into the kitchen. Shouting, he discovered, had the same effect on his rib as a deep breath.

"I won't talk," she said, coming back with a glass half-filled with water, "if you don't take the pill." The nurse had given her the bottle, and she shook one out, then dropped it into his palm.

He downed it with the water. "Happy now?" he asked.

She smiled exaggeratedly, taking the glass back and placing it on the far end of the coffee table. "Very. Go on."

"Okay." He looked from Colette to Megan to Katie, thinking it unfair that he would be somewhat sedated for this, when they were the ones who needed insulation from the pain. "This is going to be hard, but I think we have to do it." He gave Katie a comforting squeeze. "We have to talk about the night you found your dad, Katie."

She leaned into him, tracing the pattern on the front of his sweatshirt as though she was far removed from the conversation.

"You have to talk to us, Katie," he said. "We weren't there, so you have to tell us what happened."

Katie cast a pleading glance at Colette.

Colette put a hand on Katie's knee. "It's okay,

sweetie. We all know it was scary, but you were the first one there. You know what happened.''

''She just found Daddy,'' Megan said helpfully. ''Remember? She—''

''Honey.'' Colette silenced her with a look. ''I know you want to help, but Katie has to tell what she saw, okay?''

Megan subsided.

''Your mom told me that you got up to go the bathroom,'' Tate encouraged. ''Is that right?''

Katie nodded.

He held her a little closer. ''Katie, you have to talk to me, okay? You have to say the words so I can understand them. You went to the bathroom?''

''Yes,'' she said, her voice just above a whisper.

He rubbed her arm gently. ''And what did you see?''

She blinked rapidly as if trying to dismiss the image. He kissed her temple. ''What did you see?''

''Daddy.''

''Where was he?''

''On the floor.''

''Was he moving?''

''No.''

''Did he say anything?''

''No.''

''Your mom thinks he was already...'' He hesitated only a fraction of a second, wondering how someone said the word *dead* to a child. Then he realized that the only honest way was to say it straight out. ''Dead.''

She shook her head, her brow furrowing.

Tate turned in surprise to Colette. Then he asked Katie, "You didn't think he was dead?"

She shook her head again.

"Why not?"

"Because…" Her voice was high and strained and she'd made a little fist that had a handful of his shirt. "Mommy said."

Colette covered the clutching little hand with her own. "Sweetie, I never said that Daddy was alive. Remember, when you brought me into the bathroom he didn't move. I called his name and he didn't answer me."

"You told Grandpa," Katie said, big tears falling.

Colette seemed completely at a loss, then Megan spoke. "On the phone, Mommy. When you called Grandpa to tell him when the funeral was. Me and Katie could hear you from our room. You said the doctor said they might have saved him if they'd gotten to him sooner. I bet that's what she means."

"Oh, Katie." Colette stroked her hair. "I didn't mean that *you* should have found him sooner. I meant—"

"I tried to call you at first," Katie said, "but it wouldn't come." She put a little hand to her throat. "So I ran to get you, but it still wouldn't come. If I'd made you come right away…"

"No. No." Colette, crying herself, leaned over Tate to reach her child, and he found himself holding both of them. "Katie, that's not what I meant. The doctor thought Daddy had probably had a headache all day, and if he'd told us, we'd have known something was wrong and we could have taken him back to the hospital. He was dead when you found him, sweetie. Even if you'd been able to call me right that first minute, it wouldn't have made any difference. He was gone.''

Katie sobbed uncontrollably and Colette joined her. Megan, alone on the coffee table, fought valiantly to withhold tears.

Tate beckoned her with the hand that held Katie to him. ''Come here, Megan. It's all right. Everything's going to be all right.''

She came to him, kneeling beside him on the sofa and wrapping her arms around his neck.

''You saved Tate, remember?'' Colette continued. ''You gave me his cell phone and you told me to call 911.''

Katie nodded and gulped between sobs. ''You heard me call…you,'' she said to Tate, her voice strained as though her throat ached from two years of silence. ''And you came back. My other daddy couldn't come back.''

''I'm sure he wanted to,'' he told her, holding her close despite his throbbing rib.

''I'm glad you did.''

Tate let himself absorb the moment and knew whatever happened, despite the pain, this was golden. A child relieved of unnecessary guilt, her mother's burden lifted, another child simply knowing where to go for comfort.

Seeing buildings rise was good. This was even better.

And he figured he had another two minutes to enjoy it before he was out for the count. The pill was beginning to take effect. A lethargy he'd begun to notice a few moments ago was now moving to his limbs—to his eyelids.

Time seemed to be stretching out, slowing down.

Which was fine. He'd like to make this last forever.

Then he felt a pair of lips against his cheek. "I love you," Colette whispered. "I love you. I love you."

The words rode over him like a tender touch. He wanted to reply, but either the connection between his brain and his lips had gone to sleep or the feeling was just too big for words.

Then Colette moved away to look at him and went to the door to shout for Mike and Shea.

He was vaguely aware of being supported to the car, then helped inside. And that was all.

TATE AWOKE EARLY the following morning, reached up to stretch and gasped at the resulting pain. Ah, yes. He remembered his test of the laws of physics. The gravity principle remained undisputed.

He took another moment to identify the source of the strange bundle of emotions in his chest.

Satisfaction.

Katie had spoken, explained her silencing guilt and purged it. She would be fine.

Excitement. The winery was open to the public today.

Under the excitement, he was surprised to discover a curious peace. They'd worked hard and done absolutely everything to make the winery as presentable and as impressive as possible.

Whatever happened now was in the hands of providence.

At the bottom of everything he felt was a strange uncertainty. Now, why was that?

He tried to recall more of what had happened the previous night. He remembered Colette and her children weeping in his arms and how grateful he'd felt that he was there to hold them. Then he had another recollection.

"I love you. I love you. I love you," spoken in Colette's voice.

He concentrated on it, trying for more detail, but failing.

No wonder he was uncertain. She'd said that once before and had walked away anyway.

Had she meant it this time? Or had she meant "I love you for helping me with my child."

He hadn't a clue. And he wouldn't even have a moment to ask her until late tonight.

He closed his eyes and wondered if there was another man in the world who was forced to prove so much by falling on his head.

He would have rolled onto his side, intent on getting up, but Joe had walked up to put his forepaws on Tate's face.

"Hey." Tate stroked the kitten's head and a sweet purr grew in volume.

A sudden knock on his bedroom door forced him to move the cat.

"Yeah?" he asked.

"Breakfast!" Mike's voice replied. "You decent?"

"Yeah." The door burst open and Rachel appeared carrying a tray. Tate smelled sausage and coffee.

"Good morning!" Rachel greeted cheerfully. "I understand you've been quite the miracle worker."

He opened his mouth to deny her claim, but she was still talking. "Colette and the girls are already in the tasting room with Shea because a lot of people didn't seem to notice the hours and are already wanting tours and treats. Katie's talking up a storm, just like Megan."

Rachel set down the tray on the chair beside his bed and leaned over him to kiss his forehead. "Bless you," she said.

Joe ran over to inspect the contents of the tray.

"I forgot your fruit," Rachel said, scooping up the kitten. "I'll be right back. And I'll feed him and his buddies. Shea left too early to take care of that."

As she headed back toward the stairs, Mike offered him an arm. "Bathroom first?"

"Yeah." Tate leaned on him to get to his feet.

"You should take a pill with breakfast," Mike said, helping him to the door. "Colette gave them to me last night and I put them on the tray. You going to make it?"

"Yeah. I seem to be okay once I'm upright. Did Aunt Rachel say people are here already?"

"Yeah, but don't worry about it. Everyone's on duty. Armand's giving tours and Aunt Rachel's going out to help him. The tasting room's manned, and I'll be mingling in a minute. You need help with anything else?"

"Ah…no."

"Okay. Take your time with breakfast. I'll be back in a while to help you get dressed."

Tate rolled his eyes at him. "I can get dressed. Go."

Mike looked unconvinced. "You sure? You don't look as if you could pass a sobriety test. We don't want you showing up in plaids and stripes or anything."

"I'll be fine." Tate waved him off and went into the bathroom.

Forty-five minutes later Tate walked out into the compound, his pain eased by medication, his heart fueled by the sight of forty or more visitors wandering about. A few were already sitting at tables, eating Shea's madeleines and drinking coffee. Several stalwart souls carried bags that suggested they'd already made purchases at the gift shop.

They'd done it, he thought, stopped in his tracks by the realization. Granted, they had yet to produce a wine, but everything else was ready.

This was a warm and welcoming place in a beautiful spot where a road-weary traveler could stop for a while and be pampered with thoughtful service and good food.

And the air. Tate took a big breath. There was sunshine in it this morning, along with the fragrance that was uniquely the vineyard. The pain that bit into his side with the draft of air did not dilute his pleasure at all.

He was home.

Now, if only Colette would come home to him.

But there was too much to do today to fit in self-indulgence. So he stepped into the crowd, determined to make himself useful.

## CHAPTER SEVENTEEN

IN THE MIDDLE of the afternoon, Colette made a cup of tea and left the tasting room in search of a little quiet and solitude. The day had been crazy.

The tasting room was just starting to slow down, though the compound was still packed with people, all of whom appeared disgustingly happy.

She seemed to be the only one in the place with a problem. Specifically, Tate. Of course, he had a million details to see to on a day that was all-important to everyone who lived on the compound, particularly the Delancey brothers.

But a man couldn't just make a miracle happen, listen to her declaration of love, then fail to respond.

Last night the medication had knocked him out, but today he looked strong and vital and had smiles for everyone. Still, he hadn't found a moment for her, and it was now three o'clock in the afternoon.

Avoiding the crowds, Colette headed for the back lawn behind the now roofed-and-walled B and B, certain she would find the peace she craved there.

But a young woman already sat cross-legged in the grass. She was dark eyed and slender, with glossy brown hair cut very short. It made her eyes enormous and her neck appear long like a ballerina's. That im-

pression was intensified by a silky white blouse and
a gauzy dark skirt.

Presuming she'd come here, also looking for quiet,
Colette turned, intending to leave her to her haven.

"Please don't go," the young woman said, getting
to her feet. "I saw you behind the counter in the
tasting room, didn't I? So you need this more than I
do. I'll leave you to a little peace and quiet."

"I'm willing to share it," Colette said, coming
forward to offer her hand. "I'm Colette Palmer. Welcome to Delancey Vineyards."

"Thank you." The woman took her hand, her
smile warm. "Veronica Callahan. I'm here with the
bus tour from Portland."

"The valley's a great place to spend a quiet day."

They walked together to the edge of the slope and
looked down on the long rows of vines.

"I've just moved to Oregon from Los Angeles,"
Veronica said, eyes closed, face tilted to the sky,
"and I can't believe this air. I know most of the job
opportunities are in the big cities, but I'd happily
trade a smaller income to live out here." She spread
her arms, a small leather purse caught in one hand.
"In fact, given my choice, I think I'd settle right
here." She opened her eyes and grinned at Colette.
"If only a winery had a need for a primary-school
teacher."

Colette laughed with her but thought she spotted
a kindred spirit—someone just a little lost, adrift.

"Are you widowed?" she asked gently.

Veronica smiled and sighed. "No. Well. Maybe,
in a way."

Colette had no idea what to make of that reply.

Veronica laughed. "It's complicated. But if you're detecting in me a woman at loose ends, you're right. But I'll find my place."

Colette was surprised by Veronica's quick, spontaneous hug. "Thanks for letting me share your spot. And thanks for being part of such a welcoming place. Bye."

Veronica started to walk away, but Colette caught her arm, suddenly realizing all she had, unwilling to let this woman disappear without trying to share some of it.

"Do you have a business card?" she asked. "My father has a few connections in town. And I can send you the classifieds on the chance there's a job that appeals to you."

Veronica delved into her purse, pulling out an envelope and a pen. "No card," she said, writing, "but here's my address and phone number." She handed over the note, her eyes filled with gratitude. "Thank you. I'd love to hear from you."

"All right." Colette hugged her in return. "Good luck Veronica."

"To you, too."

Colette waved as Veronica walked away, then turned to look out on the vineyard. And she felt her life slip into place like a rose in a vase—smoothly, comfortably.

Everything she'd prayed for in the past two years had happened—the return of Katie's voice and her own release from the past, a sense of security and belonging for both her children, an easier time for her father, work she cherished for herself.

Love.

Tate Delancey had fought beside her to make it all happen. And he'd sometimes fought valiantly all by himself to earn her love and to help her give it back.

Thanks to him, she didn't have to have that look in her eye Veronica Callahan had—that look of having lost her way.

Colette *knew* the way, and it led straight to Tate.

She set off to find him, determined to prove to him that even if he'd come to consider her impossible, she wasn't. She finally—finally—saw the light.

Colette rounded the corner of the B and B and spotted Felicia Ferryman in the middle of the compound, the bright early-summer sun highlighting the length of leg visible below her yellow skirt and short jacket.

She was posing as she talked, the toe of one yellow shoe angled on the ground to glamorize her stance, her arms held out daintily, her hair tossed and flung as she spoke with great animation.

Her audience was Tate.

Colette squared her shoulders and strode purposefully toward them.

Tate turned her way as she approached. She wedged herself between him and Felicia and wrapped her arms around his neck.

"I *adore* you!" she said with a conviction she felt to the very tips of her toes. She saw something flare in the depths of his eyes and knew he believed her.

He braced himself to balance both of them as she rose on tiptoe and kissed him. She gave and took and shared and gave even more. Then she drew her head back to look into his eyes and saw everything there she hoped for. Love as intense as hers, understanding, desire, amusement.

She laughed because it was funny that she'd figured it all out. Then a thought occurred to her and her sense of amusement instantly lost its edge. "It isn't too late, is it? You do realize that I was just stupid and confused and worried about Katie and felt as if I couldn't have anything for myself until she—"

He put a hand over her mouth. When she stopped talking, he removed his hand and maintained her silence by kissing her.

She felt it down to her toes. Love that would be forever. Affection that would survive difficulties. Warmth that would protect her from the night. A sense of humor that would protect her from herself.

"Would you two, please…!" Felicia said in a horrified whisper. "This is a community occasion! Everyone is staring!"

Tate watched Colette turn in his arms, her eyes stormy gray. "Would you like to go headfirst into the fountain?" Colette asked in a voice heavy with purpose. "Last year *was* an accident, but this wouldn't be." She stabbed Tate's chest with the tip of her index finger. "This man is mine. Is that clear?"

There were no other words, Tate decided, that could have made him happier than those four did. He experienced the delicious joy he'd known he'd feel when she eventually declared herself to be his.

Actually, she'd declared him to be hers, but he wasn't about to split hairs.

Felicia's cheeks went crimson.

"Why don't you come with me, Felicia." Mike

appeared and gently but firmly took Felicia's arm. "I don't think we're needed here." He added with a wink at Colette. "Way to go. Only way to deal with him is to be more difficult than he is."

Felicia, chin in the air, allowed herself to be led away.

Colette looked at Tate. "Did I mention that I'm very possessive?"

"Did I mention," he asked, relishing the passion in her eyes, "that I've spent most of the past five months dreaming of possessing you?"

She leaned into him and dropped her head to his shoulder. "Stop dreaming. You do. Are we alone at last?"

He laughed lightly. "Not quite."

Megan and Katie flung themselves at them. He and Colette opened their arms to allow the girls into their tight little knot.

Across the compound, Mike and Shea watched from the front of the winery building.

"I think," Mike said, "that the three beautiful bachelor brothers are down to two."

*Watch for SECOND TO NONE—
the next book in Muriel Jensen's*
DELANCEY BROTHERS *trilogy.
Coming in June 1999.*

Don't miss your chance to read
award-winning author

# PATRICIA POTTER

### First Scottish historical romance

# THE ABDUCTION

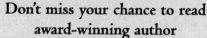

An eye for an eye. Clan leader Elsbeth Ker longed
for peace, but her stubborn English
neighbors would have none
of it—especially since the
mysterious Alexander had
returned to lead the
Carey clan. Now the
crofters had been
burned out, and the
outraged Kers demanded
revenge. But when Elsbeth faced her enemy,
what she saw in his steel gray eyes gave her pause....

Look for *THE ABDUCTION* this March 1999,
available at your favorite retail outlet!

**HARLEQUIN**®
*Makes any time special* ™

Look us up on-line at: http://www.romance.net          PHABDUCT

# Looking For More Romance?

Visit Romance.net

Look us up on-line at: http://www.romance.net

## Check in daily for these and other exciting features:

**Hot off the press**

View all current titles, and purchase them on-line.

What do the stars have in store for you?

**Horoscope**

**Hot deals**

Exclusive offers available only at Romance.net

Plus, don't miss our interactive quizzes, contests and bonus gifts.

PWEB

# IN UNIFORM

There's something special about a man in
uniform. Maybe because he's a man who takes
charge, a man you can count on, and yes,
maybe even love....

Superromance presents *In Uniform*, an occasional series that
features men who live up to your every fantasy—and then some!

Look for:
## *Mad About the Major*
### by Roz Denny Fox
Superromance #821
Coming in January 1999

## *An Officer and a Gentleman*
### by Elizabeth Ashtree
Superromance #828
Coming in March 1999

## *SEAL It with a Kiss*
### by Rogenna Brewer
Superromance #833
Coming in April 1999

Available wherever Harlequin books are sold.

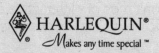

HARLEQUIN®
*Makes any time special* ™

HSRIU